THE FIRE TREE
Book 3
FLAMES

by **Ken Kirk**

Dedicated to the memory of Pamela Lang,
Cydara Verrier, Margaret Beatrice Kirk & Cecilia Reynolds.

Copyright © 2025 Ken Kirk - All rights reserved.

All non-historical characters and events portrayed in this book are fictitious. Any similarity to real people, living or dead, is coincidental and not intended by the author.

No part of this book may be reproduced, or stored in a retrieval system, or transmitted in any form or by any means, electronic, mechanical, photocopying, recording, or otherwise, without express written permission of the publisher.

CHAPTER 1

Janine needed to make a decision. Was she going to live or was she going to die? She was in mortal danger. The moment had come when she must fight or flee. She knew herself to be nothing like a fighter, but she knew that she could run like the wind. This being the case, she concluded, her decision was already made for her.

She said a little prayer, asking every power above and below the sky that the butcher's boy, who had run away from the manor house with her, would have the sense to stay hidden. Then, without looking away from the three men who were about to attack her, and without betraying her resolve in her eyes, she spun on her heels and ran with a fury she did not know she possessed.

She was able to clear a deep ditch and scramble over the lower rocks of the incline that faced her before they had collected their wits and given chase. Her lightness and agility had allowed her to pull herself up onto an overhanging ledge with relative ease. The three men had all been forced to go the long way around it, but had felt compelled — in a show of manly prowess — to make several attempts to scale the ledge before admitting defeat.

Janine stumbled and fell, cursing her clumsiness under her breath. She quickly looked back over her shoulder to see if the men were within sight. They weren't. She could, nonetheless, still hear them crashing through the undergrowth, far too close for comfort.

She had not trusted the men from the first moment she had seen them on the road. Their mock friendliness had put her on her guard, straight away, and the way the two younger men kept looking her up and down had made her flesh crawl. She could not believe her own recklessness. The rutted muddy tracks that were the roads of Scotland in 1622 were no place for a woman to be travelling as good as alone, having no more escort than a seven-year-old child.

The ground had become even more treacherous as the trees and bushes had given way to thick, coarse grass, strewn with ferns and nettles. Sharp outcrops of rock made the going even worse, rearing up at intervals, each with an apron of gravel at their base. As the terrain grew steeper, the ferns became darker and sharper and more reluctant to let her fight her way through them. They tugged at her dress, snared her shawl and scratched her legs until they stung and bled.

Suddenly, Janine's legs shot from under her and she fell. She hurriedly regained her feet and set off again, ignoring the pain in her leg. She was usually nimble and speedy, she reprimanded herself, and nothing like this clumsy. Her heart was pounding in her chest, like a hammer on an anvil, and she could feel her pulse in her neck.

As she reached the top of the rise, she heard a shout from behind her. One of the men had spotted her. Her heart almost broke with dismay and she felt like she was going to cry. She had promised herself that she wouldn't do that, but was unable to stop herself from misting up.

Janine crossed the top of the ridge and began to run down the slope on the opposite side. The incline stretched below her, its vegetation sparser, but still cluttered with swathes of ferns and nettles. No matter what she did, her feet refused to keep connected with the ground, which lay hidden beneath the greenery. At times, she sank into unseen gullies, causing her to stagger wildly. She swayed and lurched but was grateful to keep her feet.

The two younger men had soon overtaken the older man on the long climb, both eager to get their hands on her and vividly imagining what they would do to her when they caught her.

Two thirds the way to the top, the older man began to catch up, his superior stamina and army training finally making itself count. The younger men were both dismayed. If he got to her first, then he would have rights to her. They would have to wait their turn. Those were the rules.

As they crossed a shallow gully, the older man shouted for one of the younger ones to follow it as a shortcut up to the ridge. By that route, he observed, there was the possibility of getting down the other side ahead of her and cutting her off. Perceiving this as an opportunity to become the victor, the one with the longest legs, followed his suggestion.

Janine felt the ground fall away beneath her and reached out to grab the drooping branches of a tree. She managed to secure a grip of it just in time to stop herself from plunging into a ravine. Hot tears began to stream down her face. She whimpered and sobbed in frustration. Hearing the sound of her own distress, she growled with annoyance. All at once, she was filled with embarrassment. Embarrassment that she would be letting her mother down by behaving this way.

'Feeling fear will harm your chances,' her mother used to say, *'But showing fear will damn them.'*

Janine flinched at the thought and shook herself back to reality. She needed to keep her wits about her. She needed to think clearly. She needed to survive. If they caught her, the men who were chasing her would almost certainly beat her savagely before they raped her. They would also likely kill her to stop her talking.

Greatly relieved, she managed to pick up a sheep trail. At least this would lead somewhere, she told herself. The footing, however, was dangerous and the undergrowth snagged and brushed against her from both sides. She clambered over some fallen logs a little too hastily and almost slipped, again. She had only just recovered her balance when she tripped over the roots of a nearby tree. She succeeded in staying upright and, much to her relief, she saw that the path ahead became a little more distinct. This spurred her to put on a burst of speed.

She heard a noise to her left, through the bushes, and desperately hoped that it came from an animal – a boar or a deer she had disturbed – and not a person. She ran faster, but the noise kept pace with her.

"Callum!" Janine called, her voice hoarse from exertion.

"My lady!" Replied a young voice.

"Stop! Hide! Wait for me!" She cried, her breath searing her lungs, and was grateful to hear the butcher's boy obey.

After another minute of running, Janine reached a clearing where the path widened out. Breathless and panting, she stopped for a moment by the gnarled, moss-covered trunk of an old tree. She looked all around her. There was nobody there. She knew that it was dangerous to tarry, but it was so very tempting to rest for a moment. Still breathing hard, she straightened up and brushed down her clothes, in readiness to set off, again. A second later, one of her younger pursuers – a man with mean, narrow lips – jumped out into her path. Her heart leapt into her mouth.

"If you had not run," he said, gasping for breath, to tell his lie, "We might not have ended up having to hurt you," he leered at her, then added: "But now…," he let his words hang in the air, menacingly, and shook his head, sadly, in an evil parody of regret.

"Please!" She begged, "I have not done anything!"

This appeared to amuse him.

"No?" He asked, still panting heavily from his exertions.

"I have done nothing to you at all!" She insisted.

The man's mean, narrow lips contorted into a mocking smile.

"Then you have nothing to worry about. Do you?" He said and laughed a disgusting laugh.

Behind her, Janine could hear the approach of the man's companions in the distance. Her heart sank. The man started to approach her, stepping slowly and with exaggerated care, as if he were trying to avoid frightening a horse he wanted to harness.

"We are going to do things with your body that you can hardly imagine," he told her, "Then, as a kindness, we are going to kill you."

Somewhere in her head, clearly and distinctly, Janine heard the sound of bells. They were tiny bells that tinkled softly. Their sound was peculiarly comforting.

Janine took a step backwards, away from her enemy. Her foot shifted on a stone and she fell to the side. Instinctively, she reached out to steady herself and her hand came to rest against a nearby tree. As it did, something sharply spiked sank deep into her palm. She winced and cried out in pain. The man hesitated in his advance for a moment.

Janine suddenly felt a rush of overwhelming calm. She stood to her full height and clenched her jaw. The sensation in her hand was completely gone in an instant. She looked at it, confused. Then, slowly and deliberately, she turned her gaze to meet the man's eyes.

He froze and stared at her as if he had not seen her before. His eyes widened in alarm. Whatever he saw unquestionably made him afraid. His eyes shot over her shoulder, scanning the distant foliage, vainly seeking the reassurance of his friends' approach.

With a fluid movement, Janine dropped into a stoop and picked up a thick length of strong, stout wood with a vicious looking jagged point at the end. She slipped nimbly into what the man immediately recognised as a fighting stance.

He stared in open-mouthed disbelief, a question writ unmistakably across his face: *'How had this weak and defenceless girl suddenly become so dangerous?'*

In a single second, she lunged and struck. The man's expression turned from fear to terror. The wood came up at lightning speed, striking him under his chin. Janine moved her weight onto her forward foot and the end of the wood pierced up through his jaw and into his mouth. Blood gushed from his lips in a torrent and he made a gargled sound of surprise.

Janine firmly arranged her grip on the wooden shaft. Then, quickly repositioning her feet, like a dancer, she crouched to bear the force of her next move. Leaning powerfully forward into the motion, she lifted the end of the makeshift weapon upwards, raising the man off his feet and suspending him in the air.

The man – impaled and writhing – gave a shrill, ear-splitting cry of agony that rose higher and higher. As the spiked end of the pole penetrated the roof of his mouth and plunged into his brain, his cry peaked and then trailed mournfully away, echoing through the forest.

Behind her, the two men making their way through the bushes in her direction instantly halted. The older man exchanged wide-eyed looks of horror with the younger, the blood-curdling scream still ringing in their ears. Fear, like fingers of ice, climbed up their spines. They shuddered.

After a fleeting moment of hesitation, without exchanging a word, the two men set off as fast as their legs would carry them. They sped away with a frantic desperation. As they ran, they knocked Callum completely off his feet and into the air, sending him sprawling in the mud. They were running for all they were worth and paid him no heed. Primitive instinct told them to get as far away from the unseen danger as quickly as possible.

CHAPTER 2

Alex Brennan cried out in his sleep. His head thrashed first to one side, then to the other, as he gasped and choked to say the words his sleeping body would not permit. After a few moments, he seemed to calm.

Over the past few days, his nocturnal noises had become routine to the other residents of the inn. For most of them, their reaction was to pull the covers over their ears and go back to sleep.

On the nightstand by Alex' bed, stood a candle in its holder, its flame not long extinguished. The pool of hot wax around its wick bulged precariously around the brim of the candle, threatening to spill over. Like a bird on a cliff, unsure about taking to flight, it hung there, seemingly undecided. The wax quickly cooled and began to solidify, its escape to join the rolling waves and ripples of its predecessors, now thwarted.

Next to the candle lay a silver cloak clasp in the shape of a bird's claw, an antler-hilted knife in a leather cover, almost black with age, a brass uniform button and a miniature tinder box, the size of an adult thumb.

The owner of these objects stirred, again, his body momentarily tensing in the action of a person straining against something, before slowly relaxing and resuming sleep. Presently, however, he began to moan and murmur. Not long after, he cried out, again. The words, all incoherent, tumbled from his lips with urgency and desperation.

He arched his back and clenched his teeth, as if trying to stifle sudden pain. His hand rose to his neck, clawing at the sweat soaked collar of his nightshirt. He had already kicked his blankets down to his knees and now he flailed his legs, as if hurriedly walking on the spot. The blanket eventually tumbled to the floor in a heap on top of his kilt.

All at once, he became placid and his body relaxed, as a smile played around his lips. He could hear a distant roaring sound. The noise of a waterfall? In his dream, he strained to hear it. No, it was not the sound of a waterfall. It was the sound of flames. Something was burning, but he could not tell what was on fire. Whatever it was, it was close by, not far from the window.

Alex Brennan became vaguely aware that he was asleep. He tried to open his eyes and wake up, but his lids were simply too heavy. Hanging midway between sleep and wakefulness, his smile widened. In his dream, he could see the glow of the flames dancing on the wall. In the real world, his brow creased as he studied the flames. They were friendly flames. They were good flames. He sighed a long, heartfelt sigh and returned to a deep, tranquil sleep.

In the hallway, beyond the door to his room, the innkeeper, Hamish Pottle, stopped mid stride. His candle, which had been flickering and swaying precariously, suddenly began to burn steadily again, its flame once more rising straight up.

The innkeeper, a strong and muscular old man of kindly temperament with the weathered, salt-scarred face of a sailor, listened intently for a few moments, cocking his head this way and that. Satisfied that his guest was no longer in any kind of distress, he slowly turned around and crept back to his room. With the practised stealth of a former smuggler, he silently lifted the latch. A few soundless steps later, the door was closed and he was carefully and gently climbing back into bed.

His wife, alerted only by her inexplicable awareness of his presence, opened her eyes and peered out at him from under the blankets. As the candle flame wafted and swayed, throwing its crazy lengthening and shortening shadows across the walls and ceiling, he spied a questioning look on her face. He shrugged his shoulders, pursed his lips and rocked his head from side to side in a gesture of cluelessness. His wife smiled a weak, wistful smile and shook her head.

"He's a good man," she said, before yawning and falling back to sleep.

The innkeeper laid awake for a while, listening to the wind and rain outside. An owl hooted, bad temperedly, somewhere in the bright moonlit night. Further up the valley a fox barked, softly, as if in reply. Straining his ears, he could hear the gurgling of the little waterfall at the foot of the valley wall, to the West. Across the yard, the handle of the winch, atop the well, began to squeak as the wind gusted and caught its dangling rope.

The innkeeper raised himself up on his elbow and blew out the candle on the bedside stand. It extinguished with a little flutter and he watched the glowing red tip of the wick appear to hover in the air for a few moments, before it winked out.

Leaning back into the pillows, he looked up at the wall, studying the constantly changing patterns thrown by the moonlight shining through the rivulets of rain on the windowpane. The light was, at one moment, pale yellow, and then, the next, a ghostly white.

As he yielded to sleep, his eyelids flickered and reopened a couple of times, before finally closing. His lips began to form a smile as he began to hear the soft, oddly comforting crackling of a fire. Now, in his sleep, he could see the reflection of the fire on the wall. A friendly patchwork of yellow, orange and red flames danced and shimmered from floor to ceiling.

The stranger, across the hall, had brought a warmth to the inn since his arrival a few nights ago. A feeling of peace and tranquillity. A feeling of calm.

Next to the innkeeper, his sleeping wife shared her husband's smile, and gave a little sigh at the beauty of the flames.

CHAPTER 3

"Dear God," said the blonde girl, crouching among the rocks at the edge of the stream, "I cast into the water this fragment of material that I have worn and which may have absorbed my spirit or the essence of my being and I ask that you allow it to convey my prayer to the ocean, into the darkness of its oblivion, and, from there, into the light of your glorious eternity. Please bless my mother, Cydara, taken from us before her time, and let her dwell with You in paradise."

She let the small square of cloth from her old cloak fall into the water. She watched as it turned around in a little spiral for a few moments, before being swept down the stream and away, twisting around rocks and boulders, cavorting with the flows and eddies.

Taking a deep, ragged breath and beginning to cry, she added her own, personal prayer: "My dearest mother, let me be worthy of you and of my ancestors. Let me hold high the torch that you and they have carried. Let me guard its flame so that the love of God may shine across the world."

Annis stared, forlornly, after the little piece of cloth, until it was completely out of sight. Then she sighed. She came to the water at least once a week, wherever she might be, to perform this ritual of reverence and celebration. Marking her mother's life always made her sad and she could never complete it without tears. She had learned the ritual from her mother, who had offered it as a prayer for her own mother and for all the generations before her.

Annis had an old cloak, too tattered and worn to be given to the poor, which she kept in a wooden box. She cut the cloak into small fragments and always carried some of them in her pocket. She committed a single piece of it to the water wherever she might be on her travels. She didn't know whether clothing truly did soak up a person's aura or if it could convey a prayer, but it soothed her, at least a little, to think that it did.

The Vikings, she knew, had performed grand ceremonies where they burned their kings and queens in boats and set them out to sea. She thought that, by some peculiar convolution, this tradition might somehow be related to that.

Wearily, she stood and put her sandals back onto her feet. Carefully, she made her way up the bank and into the woods, passing the guard who had faithfully stood watch over her. The guard followed her, at a respectful distance, as she made her way back to their encampment.

She could see the very early light of this late Summer morning beginning to show through the trees. There was just enough illumination for her to find the path and follow it.

Once she was safely past the boundary line, the guard stood tall, saluted her, and pressed his fist over his heart. She lowered her head in acknowledgement, for she might be a queen, but she still liked to avoid making anybody in her service feel insignificant.

As quietly as she could, and with great care, she found her way to her bed and slipped into its welcoming warmth. Within a very short while, she was soundly asleep.

CHAPTER 4

Annis stretched and yawned, several times. She sighed heavily and stared at the taut canvas above her head. She was not looking forward to today.

The wind was not particularly strong, outside the tent, but the occasional bluster would cause the material to flap. A certain strength of wind would make the ropes holding the canvas hum for a few moments. She liked to hear it. The wind thrumming the tent ropes reminded her of being a child. When she was little she used to call it "listening to the wind talk". Her mother would always smile when she heard her say that.

Annis allowed her gaze to follow the iron pipe, which was the chimney of the fire, up to where it disappeared through the roof of her tent. She stretched a foot to rest her big toe, tentatively, against it. It was still warm. She placed both her feet onto the pipe to absorb its welcome heat. The fire in the hearth beneath it had been kept alight, through the night, by at least four visits by her attendant, Morag. Morag now lay, gently snoring, beyond the curtain at the far side of the tent.

Annis kept as quiet as she could. If she were to stir too noisily, at this time of the morning, Morag would inevitably awaken and would propel her to her trunk to get dressed.

Dressing, today, would be something of an ordeal. Today, as Queen of the West, she must walk the far bank of the River Spey to assert her royal authority and mark the boundary of her lands.

As if able to read her mind, even from within her sleep, Morag snuffled and snorted awake, and Annis could hear her push open the outside flap of the tent.

"Och!" Exclaimed Morag, "The sun is rising and the birds are singing!"

Annis had not failed to hear the birds. They were the reason she was awake, again! They had been loudly celebrating the new day, calling from here to there across the forest, for almost half an hour.

"My Queen," Morag said, quietly but insistently from behind the curtain, "I'll prepare you for the ceremony, if I may?"

Annis considered the merits of pretending to be still asleep but decided that there was little likelihood of success in such a deception.

"Aye," Annis replied, reluctantly standing up, "If things are to be done, then we had best do them quickly."

Morag bustled into the main chamber of the tent and promptly pushed the queen into a low, woven chair. Drawing her lower lip over her bottom row of teeth, Morag pressed her tongue behind her top front teeth and emitted a sharp whistle. A commotion could immediately be heard from within the tent pitched just behind them and, within a few moments, Jet and Jade, two young girls of around 10 years old, padded across the grass and sprang in through the tent flap.

"Hair," said Morag.

Without a word, the two new arrivals began to industriously brush and comb the queen's long, blonde hair. They relished this task, for hair of such a hue was quite unusual in the Highlands of Scotland and clearly declared, with absolute clarity, her very particular ancestry.

Morag, meanwhile, had lifted the lid of Annis' trunk and was closely examining its contents.

"Clothing," she said, mostly to herself.

She began clucking and tutting to herself as she busily set about pairing and assembling various items of attire. As she progressed, she hung each item onto hooks and placed them on a wooden rod fixed along the eye level seam of the tent's canvas wall.

Annis watched Morag from the corner of her eye and allowed a faint smile to flicker on her lips. Annis knew that Morag was careful to plan and organise everything a long while in advance and that she would have taken extreme care to choose each item of clothing with great diligence.

After her painful and earnest deliberations were concluded, Morag presented the selected attire to the queen for appraisal. Queen Annis, in turn, made a pretence of assessing the suitability of the clothing. She pursed her lips and screwed up her nose in mock contemplation, before solemnly affirming that the choice was absolutely perfect.

Morag supervised while Annis was undressed and then dressed, again, by the girls. She fussed endlessly, carefully smoothing and aligning each of the garments and insisting on positioning them to perfection before allowing her royal charge to look at herself in the mirror.

"Now," she said, "You may see."

Annis knew, from long experience, that she must not compliment the choice of clothing too quickly nor declare them to be suitable too soon. Doing so would catastrophically undermine any opinion she expressed. Instead, she turned this way and that, judging herself from different angles, before finally announcing her satisfaction.

"I am very happy with all your hard work."

Morag glowed with pride. The two juniors, who had been standing quietly and pensively, now both visibly relaxed. Morag gave them an almost imperceptible nod and they scooted out of the tent.

Annis returned to considering herself in the mirror. She reached up and touched her hair, adjusted her collar and studied her own face. She wondered – as she often did – what her ancestor, Kiffan, had looked like. It was Kiffan who had stood against the ones who would, many years after their time, become known as the Vikings. It was Kiffan who had fled to the mountains from her fortified stronghouse to resume her people's nomadic lifestyle. One that had been passed down to this day.

Annis sensed Morag watching her quizzically and gave a weak smile.

"I was thinking about my ancestor, Queen Kiffan," she confided.

"She was a mighty queen," Morag replied.

"What must it have been like to have been her?"

"More wonderful than we could ever imagine, I should think."

"Tell me about her, the way you used to do when I was little."

"They called her 'Kiffan the Defiant'. She appeared, history tells us, as if from nowhere. It was the year 793 and the Vikings had begun an invasion of Scotland. They came ashore in their longboats, plundering, murdering and burning their way down the settlements on the East Coast. Once they established a foothold, they pressed inland."

Annis had heard these words, or closely similar, over and over again, but she never tired of them.

"Kiffan and her people, the Picts, battled the Vikings ferociously, often pushing them back and inflicting heavy losses on them. The Vikings, though, were unrelenting. Their warriors were not only unafraid of dying, but were delighted by the idea. For them, to fall gloriously in battle was something to aspire to rather than avoid."

Annis nodded, savouring every word.

"Under the weight of this onslaught, some of the Pictish kings and queens began to make treaties with the enemy but Kiffan and her followers refused to yield to the Vikings in any way. She harried and attacked them without mercy. She would hit them, then flee, then return to hit them, again. She seemed to be everywhere! She circled all around them, appearing out of nowhere, like a ghost. Whenever her enemy moved their forces, Kiffan would patrol their rear, hunting down stragglers, intercepting supply wagons and burning what she could not steal."

Morag paused, allowing Annis, whose gaze was one of rapture, the time to relish her words.

"In recognition of her relentless campaign, the Vikings referred to Kiffan's people as 'Brydda'. This, as you know, translates from the Old Viking tongue to the word 'Duilich' in Gaelic or 'Annoy' in English. Their grudging admiration gave her great pride."

"Tell me about the cruelty of the Vikings, Morag."

"In retribution for her unrelenting stubbornness, the Vikings would maim, mutilate and flog anybody they suspected of having even the remotest connection with Queen Kiffan. They would flatten villages, burn crops and pollute wells with dead animals."

At this, Annis contorted her lips into a snarl.

"The Vikings," Morag continued, "Whenever they suspected people of helping the Brydda, would often impale them on the end of angled poles. These, they dug into the ground and propped up at a slant, using boulders and logs to support them. The locals called these victims 'Cunnartan' which, of course, is Gaelic for 'Danglers'.

Annis crinkled her nose in disgust.

"The Vikings' favourite form of execution, for its spectacle, was the 'Blood Eagle'," Morag announced, knowing Annis to be very well aware of the fact, "To perform that method of killing, they would use an axe to hack through their victim's ribs, either side of their spine, all the way down their back. Once they had finished, they would splay them apart, from top to bottom, like the open wings of a bird."

Annis gave a pained expression, but waved for her maid not to stop.

"Speak more of those times. I like them not to be forgotten."

"We know that the invaders would subdue the local folk savagely. They killed on a whim, made slaves of many and brutally bent them to their will. Resistance was crushed with maximum bloodshed in order to discourage others, but it could not crush their spirit. The Brydda still doggedly continued to resist them. Despite the best efforts of the Vikings, they always fell short of fully destroying them. The Vikings would mount massive offensives against the Brydda, forcing them back, killing as many as they could and driving them into the mountains, only for them to reappear again, a few months later. Kiffan and her 'strike and flee' army of fierce warriors were simply unstoppable. With a grim weariness, the Vikings slowly began to develop a grudging admiration for them."

"I believe that you said just exactly that, word for word, when I reached no taller than your elbow."

Morag smiled, "You have a good memory."

"I hope that Jet and Jade are learning these things."

"What? Them? Poor folk of common stock?"

Annis snapped her head around to confront her maid and gave her a frosty look, but this became a broad smile as she realised that she was being teased.

"We," Annis declared, "Are all just ants in the dust in the sight of the gods."

"You, Your Majesty, have a bloodline that stretches straight back to Kiffan. You are her direct and undisputed descendent."

"An ant with a crown," Annis quipped.

"I believe that you and your crown are eagerly awaited, outside," said Morag, gesturing through the canvas.

Annis took a deep breath and, urging her maid ahead of her, followed her out of the tent. She emerged into the bright sunlight of a day that was rapidly warming, but which still had a chill in the air. The encampment was awash with the busy noises of a dozen different activities as people bustled about their tasks and labours.

On catching sight of Annis, all of the camp's inhabitants immediately lowered their heads and stopped what they were doing to show their respect. Those who had not noticed her straight away quickly became aware of the stillness around them and turned to look in the direction of everybody's gaze. The men, on seeing the queen, all bowed. The women all curtsied. The children all dropped to crouch on their haunches for a moment before bobbing up again.

Annis raised her arms in front of her and then quickly crossed them, fingertips resting on opposite shoulders. Holding that pose for a few seconds, she then held her arms wide, in a symbolic embrace of all those gathered there.

In the background, a group of seven McRory clansmen – her armed personal escort for this journey – exchanged glances for several seconds, almost uncertainly, before they bowed. There was no reluctance, but Annis noted their lack of spontaneity.

In the background, Morag drew her assistants close and whispered to them.

"The loyalty of Clan McRory has been pledged to the Laird and Clan Chief of the MacDonalds for generations," she told them, "They are always rewarded with a seat at the top table at clan gatherings. These McRory warriors have been assigned to guard and protect our queen and they will do so with their lives if needed."

The army that Annis had of her own was only a small force of around twenty men. The Laird of the MacDonalds – or, simply, "The MacDonald" as his people tended to call him – had a heritage with its roots in the islands off the West Coast of Scotland, where loyalty to The Queen of the West was still fiercely observed.

The McRory horsemen began mounting their steeds, in preparation for riding ahead to scout the road for possible ambushes. Her encampment was not far from the bank of the River Spey and, in the region beyond it, the Queen of the West could not rely upon the general goodwill of the local population for her safety.

"We are close to the River Spey," Morag told the girls, "The Spey marks the edge of the Queen of the West's lands of the East. There is a tradition that, every three years, she must cross to the other side of it and ride a distance along its bank to show everybody that it belongs to her."

All around them, people were in the final phases of loading horses and piling things onto carts. Behind them, in a flurry of activity, the queen's tent was being dismantled and packed away ready to move off. The cooks were emptying out the embers from the stove into a metal tub and covering them with damp moss and a thin layer of soil. The heat from the embers would then be used to keep food warm on their journey.

Queen Annis, as she walked around, knew full well that everybody across the camp had been poised and ready, just waiting for her to wake up, but – just as she had been taught – she had carefully feigned a lack of concern. Her mother had often told her: *"When you are a queen, you must act like a queen. People will have expectations of you. You must not become aloof, but – nonetheless – you must never disappoint them by throwing their care, their dedication and their wish to serve you – well and selflessly – in their faces."*

As Annis moved from group to group, she smiled, acted graciously and spoke kind words. It felt like such a short a time ago that she, herself, had trailed behind her mother as she did the exact same thing. Annis still grieved as keenly for her mother, dead these past seven years, as she ever had.

Annis noticed people who were coming up from the nearby villages and hamlets to pay their respects, so she went to greet them. She reached to shake their hands, but most merely grasped her fingers, instead, and kissed them. The majority felt most comfortable in just lowering their heads and muttering words of respect and subservience.

At the rear of their encampment, Annis heard the distinctive sound of her armed escort noisily donning armour both on themselves and on their horses. The McRorys were clearly not intending their final preparations to be discreet or bashful. Annis felt the slightest flutter of vexation, sensing – at the back of her mind – that she was being hurried.

The huddles and clusters of locals began to disperse and Annis noticed that they had begun to look distinctly ill at ease, glancing nervously across to the McRorys with increasing worry on their faces. Annis clenched her teeth. She was Queen of the West. These were her people. She would take as much time as she wanted. She would not be rushed.

Annis whirled around and began to stride purposefully towards her armoured escort, her hands bunched into fists. Suddenly, she stopped dead in her tracks. She stared at the vision ahead of her. Her eyes widened. Her surprise could not be masked.

The McRory Captain, a handsome man by the name of Balgair, stood quickly to attention. His Second-in-Command sprang to attention, too, a second later. Within moments – operating on some kind of sixth sense – their entire close retinue had also abruptly straightened and stood their tallest.

Annis had to fight to stop her jaw from dropping open as complete and utter silence fell across the encampment.

Her eyes flicked from the soldiers' highly polished helmets, down to the gleaming copper-bronze of their body armour, down to their magnificent metal gloves, to the dazzling blades of their huge claymores and to the big circular battle shields they carried, each quartered in dark blue and gold with prominent burnished metal hubs at their centre.

Unlike the other fifty soldiers in their contingent, these seven wore kilts of the light green, formal tartan of the McRorys. This was the more splendid tartan used for ceremonies and special events.

The Queen of the West quickly regained her poise. Her gaze moved from each soldier to the next in their line. They must, she realised, be the very best McRory warriors. This, therefore, meant that The MacDonald was making a clear and unmistakable tribute to her and one that he wished to be noted and understood by all those they might encounter on this expedition.

These men, she recalled, had faltered before bowing when they had seen her. At the time, she had felt a fleeting pang of vague offence, one that she had quickly dismissed and scarcely allowed herself to acknowledge. Now, she understood. These men had been sent to accompany her as a formal Honour Guard. This was a highly symbolic, very significant and highly public expression of esteem by The MacDonald. The tradition of the old times was that an Honour Guard was not required to bow to her. These fighting men were regarded as being at one with their monarch and their loyalty deemed to be complete and absolute. As a result, they were above such gestures.

With a force that physically shook her, she swept her right fist upward, in an arc, to strike herself on the chest over her heart. She paused for a moment – a moment that seemed to hang in the air – then repeated the motion, this time drawing her fingers into a claw. She held the pose for several seconds before thrusting her arm towards the seven soldiers, her fingers gripping the air as an eagle might grip its prey.

"Aon chridhe!" She cried, this being the Gaelic for "One heart".

Her escort shouted back the same, at the top of their voices.

"Aon adhbhar!" She cried, using the Gaelic for "One purpose".

Her escort shouted it back, loud and clear.

"Aon anam!" She cried, the words meaning "One soul".

Her escort returned the words at an almost deafening volume.

Their voices echoed through the trees, sending birds to flight. Their voices rebounded from the hills, startling sheep and deer. Their voices reverberated across the river surprising cattle that stood drinking.

A group of troops from a neighbouring clan, camped at the far side of the river, heard their voices, too. They felt a chill run through them, as if someone had just walked over their grave.

CHAPTER 5

Janine felt herself gradually waking. With a huge effort, she kept her eyes firmly shut and tried to control her breathing. She took a deep breath and slowly opened her eyes. Everything was deserted. There were no people. There were no animals. There were no birds. The forest was unnervingly silent.

She shook her head, as if to dislodge the remnants of confusion, and wondered if she had been knocked out. She felt her head but could find no tender spot that might indicate a blow. Struggling to bring her thoughts into focus, she vaguely recalled a man about to attack her. She had survived the confrontation, but her memory of anything that had happened was completely blank. The only explanation that made any sense to her was that somebody had heard the commotion and had intervened.

"I'm so grateful!" She said in a hoarse whisper, in case they were listening.

Janine cautiously stepped forward and searched for any signs of a struggle or conflict that might have occurred. The ground was heavy with mouldy fragments of bark, rotting mulch and leaf litter, so finding any trace of footprints proved difficult.

After a little searching, she found an area where the brush had been disturbed. A little way on from it, she found a pair of feet sticking out from under the vegetation. She shivered, involuntarily.

Terrified of what she might find, but – even still – overwhelmed by curiosity, she approached the motionless feet and gingerly kicked them. There was no response. Cautiously, she swung her foot back and kicked a little harder. There was still no response. She pushed at the lower branches of the dense greenery surrounding the spot and, in reply, the thick stems of the bush swayed back and forth. As they moved, they alternately hid and revealed the horrifically wounded and bloodied head of a lifeless corpse. The eyes were wide open and stared vacantly upwards. They wore an expression of shock and terror permanently frozen into them. Janine shuddered, again, and backed away.

After struggling with a wave of nausea and a feeling of giddiness, Janine was able to calm herself enough to think straight. It was unlikely, she decided, that the body would be found any time soon and, having done no more than discover it, she could not be linked to the man's fate. She made up her mind that the wisest thing to do was to simply walk away. If a man who intended to assault her had somehow met a gruesome end, she was blameless.

She froze as she heard a noise ahead of her. It was a rustling in the vegetation. The sound became louder and, presently, a young boy sprang out into the open. On seeing Janine, he gave a squeal of joy and ran towards her. Janine stepped away from the dead body and held up her hand, urgently signalling him to stop.

"You are covered in mud!", she cried, glad for an excuse to curtail his advance.

Callum came to a halt and looked offended.

"They knocked me down," he declared, then – his face betraying a sudden inspiration – he added: "There was a struggle. I fought them. I could not hold them off. They all came at me at once."

"If you had struggled with **those** men, you'd have neither your ears nor your nose left intact. They would have sliced them off, just for devilment!"

The boy looked crestfallen.

"But," she added, "I'm sure you would have given them a good thrashing if they had dared to tangle with you."

Callum looked pleased.

"I once fought a bear with nothing but my fists," he declared.

Janine suppressed a smirk and, instead, managed to look impressed.

"I'm so happy you escaped the men!" He blurted, "There was an animal too, I think. Did you hear the terrible screeching?"

"No, I heard nothing."

"You heard nothing? Surely not! It was so loud!"

"I don't know. I cannot explain it."

"Did you fall and hit your head when they chased you? Did you lose your senses from the blow?"

"It is too strange to tell you, but I am lucky to be alive."

She froze at the thought. Lucky to be alive? This was not the first time that she had entertained that notion! There had been other times. She was certain of it. Yes! That's right! How could she have forgotten something like that? She had been in peril on previous occasions and had fainted or passed out. In just the same way that had happened now, she had come round to find herself disorientated but unharmed.

"I think somebody may have saved me," Janine announced.

She felt dismayed at being unable to express her gratitude to whoever the timely rescuer might be. She hoped that, one day, she would be able to catch them and give them her thanks. In her head, she referred to them as 'him'. She was sure that it **was** a 'him' because — judging by how they were able to overpower such an able opponent — they must be as strong as an ox.

"I didn't see anybody," said the boy, evidently puzzled, "Shall I search around?"

"No, don't search," she insisted, grabbing his arm to restrain him, "Don't do that. You don't know what you might find."

The boy looked at her quizzically. Janine looked around in all directions. She needed to ensure that they weren't being watched. Once she was satisfied, she led the way back onto the forest trail and they hurriedly set off along it. She scanned this way and that for any sign of her benefactor, but she knew that he would always be gone by the time she recovered her waking mind.

"What are you looking to see?" Asked Callum.

"I think somebody might have followed us."

"One of the men?"

"No, somebody who protects me."

"Somebody like a soldier, you mean?"

"I'm not sure."

"Or somebody from the other place?"

"The other place?"

"Past the dark curtain. The world outside of our world."

"A spirit? I don't know. I don't think so. I cannot be sure."

She wondered if her guardian continued to track her, for a time, to make sure that she remained safe. She wondered, too, if he had followed her on a regular basis, since he had a habit of turning up at the most opportune moments.

As she walked, she said a little prayer. A few words of gratitude to God and to fate for her salvation and a formal *thank you* to whoever had intervened for her. The boy began to pray, too, but his prayer was to the goblins, elves and demons of the forest, asking them not to kill them and eat their hearts.

Suddenly, Janine became aware of a pain in the palm of her hand. Looking down at it, she found a wound at its centre. It was slowly welling blood. Ripping some fabric from the length of rough spun cotton she wore over her shoulders as an improvised shawl, she wrapped it around her hand to stem the blood.

Her pace immediately slowed as her face contorted in thought. She had hurt her hand. When had she done this? She dimly recalled something about it, but it was like trying to grasp a wisp of smoke in the air and the memory slipped away from her.

"You are hurt!" Callum yelped, noticing her hand.

"Yes, I injured it. I don't recall how…."

The boy looked warily at her. It was clear that her uncertainty about things had begun to worry him.

As they walked through the dense, rugged forest, they started to hear birds, again. They began to sing and call, timidly at first, but then resumed their normal busy vigour. A wave of desperation overtook her as, without meaning to, her mind began to assess her situation.

"Earlier this morning," she pointed out, "We ran away, thinking we were escaping danger and misery, and now…."

The boy shrugged. He seemed happy just to be away from the brutality of the butcher.

"Where are your things?", he asked.

She had run away from her employer, taking with her a pillowcase stuffed with her meagre possessions. A pillowcase that she had hung in a bush, by the roadside, while she had used a nearby dip in the ground as a crude toilet. It was when she had been making her way back to the road that she had been accosted by the three men. Her heart lurched and her pulse raced at the recollection of the event.

"I left my pillowcase hung up in the greenery. Nobody would be able to see it from the road. If I am lucky, it might still be there."

The thought of going back there filled her with dread, but – having no other option – she took a deep breath and led them off to the right, along a path she hoped would intercept the road.

They had set off on their journey that morning, in the back of a hay wagon, having bribed the driver with some coins. Once they had gone a fair distance, he had invited her to sit up front with him. The driver, as it turned out, had wandering hands and he found it difficult to keep them to himself. After rejecting his advances one too many times, she had been thrown off the wagon and left to walk. Callum had jumped out after her.

"Maybe we should have turned back this morning, when we ended up on foot?"

The boy shook his head vigorously.

The moment they had set off walking, Janine had realised the peril of them being alone on the road. The likelihood of being discovered while sneaking back into the house, however, had horrified her. Both she and the boy had been beaten often enough for no real reason, so she hardly dared to imagine what might befall them if they gave them a reason to do it!

"What is the ring you wear, My Lady?"

Janine realised that he had noticed the ring because of the habit she had of subconsciously twiddling with it on her finger whenever she was nervous.

"It was my mother's ring."

The ring was all she had from her mother, whom she had not seen since she was small.

"It is a fine thing, My Lady. You must come from an important family."

"You have me wrong," Janine huffed, "I was born of poverty-stricken crofters."

The look he gave her conveyed his doubts.

"It is a fine thing, My Lady," he repeated.

Janine knew just what he meant, for her parents had spent their lives constantly breaking their backs just to make ends meet. The ring, which was strangely intricate and meticulously worked, was an odd possession for people of such humble means.

"My mother and father always struggled," she told him, "Money was always either very short or there was none of it at all."

"I grew up the same."

"My mother behaved differently to all the other women living around us. The other children's mothers were not like her. She was more graceful and more..." Janine scratched her head, trying to find the word that was on the tip of her tongue, "Refined. She was more refined. She did her best to hide it but, sometimes, it was really obvious."

The boy nodded, thoughtfully, before offering his verdict.

"She sounds out of place."

"Yes!" Janine agreed, "She was! She used to do strange things. She had some odd habits. They were little things, but I could not help noticing them."

Her mother, Janine realised, had passed on some of those peculiar customs to her. While some of them did not seem too inappropriate for their station in life, others were wholly uncommon, even quirky.

"My uncle said, once or twice, that there had been some talk about my mother. He said that, 'back in the day', as he called it, there had been witches in our family."

Callum looked distinctly worried.

"I think my uncle might have been joking," she reassured him, though – in truth – she was not entirely convinced, "My father once overheard my uncle saying those kind of things and he was really angry. He jumped at him and pushed him to the ground."

Janine had seen them struggle and scuffle, before, but – even though she had been only small – she knew that it was not the normal kind of "play fighting" they sometimes did.

"My father acted really strangely for a long while, after that. Eventually, he told me that he and my uncle had argued about a debt. He said that things had got out of hand, but I knew, deep inside, that what he was telling me was not the truth."

A while later, her uncle had told her that her mother's family had once been well placed in society but that they had fallen on hard times. He said that her father had supported another landowner in a long running dispute about who owned some fields. He said that there had been a lot of trouble about it and that the local laird had seized their property and holdings and had given them to a neighbour whom the laird felt was more loyal to him. Even then, Janine did not think that this was the whole truth of it.

Callum was content to quiz her no further and, with shared trepidation, they made their way along the rough, uneven road back to the bush, in silence. After twenty minutes – and after mistaking the location, once or twice – she found her precious pillowcase. She was grateful that it was exactly as she had left it.

"I'm glad it didn't rain," she said, clapping a hand to her chest.

"You are lucky the ants didn't find it!" Quipped Callum.

After her possessions were recovered, they resumed their journey with a renewed haste and a more pressing awareness of their vulnerability.

"If we hear anybody approaching," Janine announced, "However they are travelling – be it on foot, on horseback or in a cart – we need to get off the road and hide until they are gone."

The boy nodded, but then added, slyly: "Even if they are Rangers?"

Janine glared at him and he laughed.

"Tell me," she asked, "Did your family have many dealings with the Rangers?"

"I don't remember my family," he replied, "I was given away when I was too young to know much. They could not afford to feed me."

"I'm sorry for that," she told him and, instinctively, reached out to put an arm around him.

He shuddered and recoiled from her. There was no mistaking that he had little experience of affection. After a moment, he bowed his head and took a step towards her, without looking up. She reached out slowly for him, drew him against her and, very gently, wrapped her arms around him. At first, he stiffened, but then he gradually relaxed.

"My Lady, I'd never let anyone harm you."

"Thank you," she said and held him a little longer.

"I would die to protect you, My Lady."

She knew he meant it. He sniffed and she suspected that he was on the brink of crying. She felt a tear fall onto her hand and she was sure. She tried to reposition him – to avoid the worst of the mud on her own clothing – but he resisted her, fearful that she might see his face. Pulling out a piece of cotton from her pocket, one she intended as a handkerchief, she shook it harder than was necessary to unfurl it.

"Oh! I'm sorry!" She said, "I have shaken all this dust in your face and in your eyes!"

Unaware of her deliberate ruse, he automatically rubbed his eyes and then wiped them on the back of a grimy sleeve.

"It's no matter, My Lady," he assured her.

She decided that she needed to change the subject quickly.

"Many around these parts refer to the Rangers as the 'Watch'."

"Aye, they do. I knew who you meant. You could have used either word."

"They are widely disliked."

"I know that the butcher had no love for them."

Despite being charged with keeping some sort of rudimentary law and order, the Rangers were as much a threat to public safety as they were protectors of it. With her fingers trembling, she took off her mother's ring and slipped it into a hidden pocket in the band of her skirt.

They had been walking for almost thirty minutes when their feet began to tire. Janine's had started to ache and Callum announced that he was developing a blister on his heel.

"It hurts with every stride," he complained.

"My feet feel like I have been walking for a week," replied Janine.

They suddenly became aware of the distant sound of a wheeled vehicle heading in their direction on the road behind. Quick as a flash, they scrambled into the undergrowth, seeking safety among the trees and bushes.

Before long, a coach came into view, pulled by not one but two horses, both of which looked to be in far better condition than most of the ones found in these parts. The driver and his companion were well dressed and wore something approaching a uniform. Each was armed with both a musket and a pistol. All four of these weapons were set prominently on display. In addition, a pair of tall pike staffs were attached, like flag poles, to either side of the coach body at the front. Rippling from their tops, below the blades, were long purple banners bearing a white cross.

Janine breathed a sigh of relief at the sight of these banners. This, she recognised, was the conveyance of a bishop or a very highly placed member of the church.

"It's somebody important in the church," she told Callum, "It's as safe a vehicle as we are ever likely to encounter."

The two moved out from the cover of the greenery and stood at the roadside as the carriage came closer. One of the coachmen leaned to the side, turning his head, and clearly called something to the occupants. A head appeared, briefly, from a window and – after a shouted exchange – it popped back in again. She could hear neither the question, nor the answer, but the tone of both parties sounded amiable.

At ten paces from her, the driver called to the horses: "Whoa!" And they obligingly came to a halt, stopping no more than an arm's length from where she was standing. Having travelled to Edinburgh, several times, with her mistress – which was one of the privileges of being a personal maid to a lady – Janine knew that these horses were well trained and that they were used to town work, where distances and positioning were essential for safe and comfortable travel.

"A bheil feum agad air cuideachadh?" Asked the driver, in a mediocre Gaelic approximation of "Do you need help?"

"I would be most grateful for your help, Sir," Janine replied in perfectly enunciated English, "We have been set upon by thieves and narrowly escaped with our lives."

"Where are you heading?" Asked the driver.

"Anywhere that isn't here, if you please!" She replied.

At this, there was a snort of laughter from inside the coach.

"That is the story of my life!" A man's voice called to her, followed by the noise of him slapping his leg in merriment.

Callum reached out to the horse. The horse studiously ignored him, remaining completely aloof.

"You don't exist until I tell him it's okay," the driver told him.

After a slight pause, the driver spoke to the horse.

"Stand easy."

The horse gave a soft neigh and seemed to visibly relax. It turned to the pair with big, intelligent eyes that studied and appraised them. After a few moments, its soft, warm muzzle gently snuffled them both and, then, nudged them approvingly. It was not long before the horse was sniffing the neck of Janine's pillowcase. It, then, looked directly into her eyes, with an unmistakable twinkle in them. Janine smiled and reached into her makeshift sack and withdrew an apple which she gave to Callum.

"Here, you can feed him if you want."

The boy placed the apple on the palm of his hand and offered it to the horse. With slow and infinite care, the creature took the apple in its mouth, but stood without chewing. The other horse looked across at Janine, quizzically, and then – after a few moments – nudged the first horse lightly on the nose. The first horse began to chew, but it was with evident reluctance. Janine quickly produced a second apple from her bag and, leaning across, gave it to the far horse. The horse took it gratefully and both began to eat, contentedly, happy that the feast was shared. The driver gave a little chortle.

"They are almost welded, one to the other," he said, "They cannot abide that one might have what the other does not. You are lucky that he didn't spit that apple onto the ground and stomp it into two pieces so that the other could share it!"

"They like you," said the man from within the carriage, hanging his head out of the window, "And horses are a good judge of people."

"I'm glad we meet their approval," Janine chuckled.

There was a click and the door to the carriage opened slightly allowing one of the occupants to lean out.

"Is there somewhere we could take you?" He enquired, arching an eyebrow.

"I believe that there is an inn, a few miles ahead," she said, "I was making my way there, with my helper, before…," she shrugged her shoulders, almost apologetically, and left the sentence unfinished.

The man nodded, solemnly.

"Before your incident," he offered.

Janine nodded, her bottom lip beginning to tremble. The man jumped down, landing with unexpected grace for someone she guessed to be closer to forty than thirty. Janine opened her mouth to speak, but no words came out. The man held up his hand, happy to do without an explanation in light of her clear distress.

His eyes took in the rips in her dress, the mud on it and the blood still caked on her leg. On seeing the tears smudged on her cheeks, he immediately looked sad. His hair, neatly tied behind his head with a leather thong, was dark brown with highlights of copper and red and a few random strands of grey.

Seeing his fine, shiny boots, elegant white shirt, neatly tailored waistcoat and silk handkerchief protruding from his breast pocket, Janine quickly dropped into a curtsy and Callum bent into an enthusiastic bow. Janine's eyes then found the stiff purple collar of his shirt, hung open and loose around his neck.

"Your Holiness," she said.

The man smiled a smile that hovered on the brink of a grin.

"That's a little formal, for me, young lady," he complained, "I am to be consecrated Bishop in Brechin, in a few weeks, but – for now – I am a humble priest!"

"Humble, indeed?" A voice rang out from inside the coach, "Humble but only too happy to ride in a fine carriage to keep your humbleness under strict control!"

"Pay no attention to my brother," the priest told her, "He is jealous that I inherited the lion's share of good looks in our family!"

This reply was met with roars of laughter from within.

With a deft nudge of his toe, the man dropped the folding steps of the vehicle and then, flailing his arm with an absurd exaggeration of manners, bowed deeply to her.

"Our transport is at your disposal" he declared.

Janine took the hand he offered and allowed him to help her up into the carriage. Callum hesitated, unsure whether he should follow her, but was quickly reprimanded for the idea by the loud voice of the driver.

"You can keep your muddy hide on the outside of my carriage!" He boomed, "You can travel on top at the rear!"

CHAPTER 6

Alex Brennan went to the window of his room. Drawing aside the curtain, he peered up at the sun. Performing a quick mental calculation, he decided that the time was around Nine O' clock. His brows furrowed and he pursed his lips. He had not intended to sleep so late.

He scanned down the road, along the short level section that swept past the inn and around the long curve to the point where it disappeared into the forest. Then he scanned the opposite way, up the shallow rise and then up the long climb, into the far distance, to the top of the hill. The road was deserted in both directions.

The only sign of life was the stable boy, who was sitting on a tree stump carving at a piece of wood with a little knife. Alex lifted a metal lever at the base of the window and pushed it ajar on its hinge.

"Hey!", he called, loud enough to be heard but quiet enough to be discrete.

The boy, taken by surprise by his voice, sprang to his feet and stood tall.

"Yes, Sir?", he asked, lifting a hand to shade his eyes from the sun.

"Has there been anybody on the road this morning?"

"No, Sir, no-one."

"You are sure of that?"

"Yes, Sir, I'd swear my life on it."

Alex tipped the youngster a little salute and closed the window.

He knew, for sure, that anybody on their way to Inverness would have to pass this way. There were only six routes in Scotland that were more than just mud tracks and this was one of them. He shrugged his shoulders and resigned himself to wait. *'There was no hurry,'* he told himself, *'And no problem with biding my time.'*

Alex dressed quickly and strode to the door. Gently lifting the latch, he took great care to make no noise as he slowly opened the door. There was no sound from the hall, outside. He waited for several seconds and then poked his head out. He looked left and right. There was nobody there. He paused, listening intently. All he could hear was the clanking of a spoon against a metal pan, downstairs in the kitchen. He sniffed the air. Somebody was making porridge. It smelled delicious. As he caught the vague whiff of honey and nutmeg, his mouth began to water and his stomach began to rumble.

"Quieten down, you, and be patient!" He whispered to it.

Straightening his kilt and adjusting his shirt, he ran his fingers through his hair. Feeling reasonably presentable, he crossed the hall and descended the stairs. As he came around the narrow turn, halfway down, he could hear the innkeeper, Hamish Pottle, in the public bar. He was sweeping with a coarse brush. Alex turned left at the bottom of the stairs and took the few paces to the door of the bar. He stood, hesitating, on the threshold, unsure if he should intrude. Hamish saw him and, nodding cheerfully, he tipped an invisible cap and called out a greeting.

"A fine morning to you."

"And the same to you."

Alex stepped in and glanced around the bar. His eyes took in the many decorative objects placed on shelves and in alcoves. They had an unmistakably maritime theme to them. He knew that Hamish had spent most of his life at sea and that these objects – which included compasses, spyglasses and pieces of rigging – were, therefore, all real and authentic. They were not the dowdy replicas that could be picked up in curiosity shops.

"You have a wonderful collection," Alex observed.

"Thank you."

The innkeeper smiled and went back to his sweeping, whistling and humming as he worked and occasionally throwing in a few impromptu dance steps in time to the tune.

Alex' gaze followed the line of little triangular flags that stretched from behind the bar, to the ceiling. Obviously, these had once flown above the deck of a ship. Unusually, he noted, the ceiling was composed of a series of varnished wooden panels, set in a frame of thin wooden beams. This form of decoration was a little ostentatious for such a venue, he thought.

Although Hamish did not pause in his sweeping, Alex could feel his attention on him and sensed that he was being watched from the corner of an eye. Alex returned his gaze to ground level and, almost imperceptibly, Hamish appeared to relax.

If the ceiling panels had been subjected to closer scrutiny – at arm's length by a customs officer, for instance – then one or two of them would appear slightly worn along their edges. From the outside of the inn there was nothing unusual about its construction, but – if the heights of the two interior floors were to be carefully measured with a pole – some vertical distance would be found to be missing. This little deception was accounted for by the crawl space hidden between the two floors.

Hamish Pottle was, in all general respects, a wholly law-abiding citizen. He was, however, usually in possession of a few casks of spirits (in his "unofficial loft") that didn't have the red crown of the king's mark burned into their lids. This mark was proof that customs duty had been paid on the contents. His continued connections with seafarers, from his past, meant that he still had acquaintance with a few smugglers. From time to time, the temptation that this presented, had proven irresistible.

Alex bade farewell to Hamish, who continued his diligent sweeping, and walked across the corridor into the kitchen. As he opened the door, the steam and heat hit him. It was like a wall of sweltering dampness.

Caitlan, the innkeeper's wife, turned to greet him, wiping her hands on her apron.

"A bonnie morn to you," she enthused, "I hope you slept well, Sir?"

She felt a stab of guilt, as it flew into her mind that he suffered from nightmares.

"I slept wonderfully," he lied.

"I'm glad to hear it," she replied, indulging him in his deception.

"The feather mattress on my bed makes it feel as if I am sleeping on a cloud!"

Caitlan smiled and gave a little chuckle.

"Well, your silver bought you one of our best rooms with the best beds. Don't go spreading word about your mattress, though. Most folk are faced with sleeping atop bags of straw!"

She laughed at her own humour and Alex politely laughed, too.

"I have to say," Caitlan declared, nodding towards the back door, "That it's been a long while since we've had so many logs split and stacked. Your skill with an axe is impressive! So is the enthusiasm you apply to using it!"

"I... I... I have things..." Alex stumbled and hesitated, awkwardly before shrugging his shoulders in exasperation, "I have events in my life that I would rather not remember. Things from my time abroad. They are quickest forgotten if I put my back into something to distract myself."

Caitlan nodded, her expression sympathetic and concerned, and decided that saying nothing further was the best way she could help.

Submerging her ladle into the bubbling porridge, she scooped up a generous portion and delivered it into a bowl held in her other hand. Alex Brennan accepted the bowl from her and then gladly received a generous pool of milk to cool it down. She dipped a spoon into a jug of honey and held the two items up as an invitation.

"You would only need to go a few miles down the road, South towards Perth, and they would be putting salt onto your porridge. Unlike them, with their warmer weather," she winked, conspiratorially, "We know what cool Summers and cold Winters are all about!"

They both laughed and Alex welcomed a large spoonful of the golden liquid on top of his porridge.

"On that basis, then," Alex retorted, mentally estimating Perth to be less than a two hour ride away, "You'll be regarding London as sharing the same weather as Africa?"

"Well," Caitlan replied, "I am told they have streets paved with gold, down there in London, so I am presuming they have golden weather to match."

There was more laughter and a couple of maids, washing pans at the sink, joined in.

"There's no sense in our Good King James squandering his time up here, in Scotland, in the wind and rain, when he can soak up all that glorious sunshine in London and can sprawl out on a lawn, trimmed neat and short by servants with scissors," Caitlan announced, making little snipping actions in the air.

They both laughed, again, heartily. Caitlan Pottle turned, as she heard – from the public bar – her husband's booming laugh boosting the volume of their own.

"I fear that Good King James has taken a fearful liking to London," Hamish Pottle declared, appearing in the doorway, "I hear tell that his face is as long as a Summer's day in Orkney when he has to consider travelling back up to Scotland!"

"We may not see him again in my lifetime!" Caitlan quipped.

"We may all be strumming a harp in the clouds," Hamish chuckled, with exaggerated gestures of harp playing, "Before he returns to this ice shed we call Scotland!"

Smiling broadly, Alex pressed a forefinger to his lips and cast his eyes skyward, as if seeking divine inspiration, and said:

"I believe that, in the Colonies, they refer to it as *'Going native'*...."

This remark seemed to tickle their sense of humour and left the husband-and-wife proprietors of the inn unable to stand straight. They laughed so hard that they staggered and leaned against the furniture for support. Alex found himself degenerating into a similar helplessness, unsure if he were laughing at their merry behaviour or at his own words. He ended up laughing so much that his sides ached.

The two maids looked bewildered and seemed eager to be away, as if fearing that the lunacy they were witnessing might be infectious.

"I'll set about the laundry," said one, as she quickly left the room.

"And I will lend a hand," said the other, hurriedly making for the door.

Alex, Hamish and Caitlan found the fleeing maids hysterical. With tears streaming down their cheeks, they held their sides from the ache of laughing. Each time they were almost back under self-control, one of them would spot the face of another and this would set them off, again.

Eventually, Hamish marched his wife into one corner of the kitchen and his guest into the other. He then returned to each to press their head to rest against the wall. Hamish retired to a seat against the fireplace, across the other side of the room. Thus isolated, the three eventually regained their serenity. This was not, however, without several relapses along the way.

"I have not laughed so much in a long time!" confessed Alex, accidentally bursting out laughing, again.

The sheer joy at the inn, Alex detected, was all pervading. It was the most overwhelmingly happy place he had ever been.

After a while, the three of them slumped in a line along the bench at the big, heavy table. They shook their heads, cleared their throats, wiped their eyes and each, eventually, recovered themselves.

Alex studiously occupied himself chasing the remnants of his porridge onto his spoon. Suppressing the odd smirk of recollection, he managed to remain restrained. The two maids poked their heads around the door and, after some consideration, judged it safe to return. Looking a little apprehensive, they crept back in to set pans on the stove in preparation for Lunch.

Hamish Pottle hugged his wife and slapped her bottom, then hugged Alex and slapped him between his shoulder blades. It was clear he'd taken a liking to him. They exchanged glances, beaming at each other, but – by unspoken agreement – ventured no words, for fear of subsiding into uncontrollable laughter, again.

Once he was sure of himself, Alex spoke.

"I stood shoulder to shoulder, in Austria," he began, intentionally injecting solemnity, "With Englishmen and with fellow Scots, holding the line against the enemy. Each of us was glad for King James' resolve to support our allies and keep their countries and ours, free."

There was silence and, so as not to intrude on it, the two maids paused in their stirring of the pots. Only the hissing and bubbling of the cooking rose above the quiet.

Both Hamish and Caitlan began to feel a little puzzled by Alex launching into his patriotic speech and they looked at him, blankly. It was then that they noticed the direction of his gaze. He was looking towards the door.

An unseen stranger had come and stood quietly in the doorway behind them. He had arrived without announcing himself or drawing attention to his presence. Within a few seconds of him appearing, however, Alex had become eerily aware of him. With the attention of all three of them now upon him, the intruder graciously inclined his head and his upper body in a bow.

This newcomer was tall and well-muscled. His cloak was drawn back over his shoulders revealing a broad chest and strong arms. His powerful physique was only thinly disguised by his tunic. He wore trousers rather than a kilt, which was uncommon in these parts. The trousers disappeared into a pair of high, black, well-crafted riding boots. It was clear that he was neither local nor even from the surrounding area. His eyes twinkled as the hint of a smile played on his lips. It was obvious that he had heard their raucous merriment.

A long silence hung like a ponderous weight, awkward and uncomfortable. It was Caitlan who found her voice first.

"A fine day to you, Sir," she said.

The stranger nodded and smiled. His lips were bordered by his well-kept beard, which was flecked with early signs of grey, matching his grey eyes.

"How can we be of service to you?" Hamish managed to say, rising from his seat.

"I am on my way to Inverness and wish to break my journey for the day," he replied, amiably.

"On some kind of business?" ventured Hamish.

"Yes," replied the stranger. Then, after a pause, he added: "The king's business."

Hamish fought to keep the shock he felt from reaching his face, but failed.

"What kind of business would that be, if I may be so bold as to ask?" the innkeeper enquired, recovering himself.

"I am a constable," the other announced.

Hamish knew that the stranger was studying his face and did his best to show no further surprise or alarm, hastily putting thoughts of his contraband whisky, brandy and rum as far from his mind as possible.

Hamish knew that there was a constable in Edinburgh, one in Glasgow and one each in Stirling, Perth and Dunfermline. Constables were always well-connected people from privileged backgrounds and high social standing. As the position was mostly unpaid, they had to possess a good income of their own. His mind, whirling and tumbling, could make no sense of why one of them would be straying this far to the North.

Caitlan shrugged and looked puzzled, "In these parts, law and order is usually attended to by the Rangers and by the laird."

The constable crinkled his forehead questioningly, "How do you get along with the Rangers?"

Hamish snorted at the question.

"They are not usually my most favourite of visitors to these premises," he said, contorting his face in disgust, "And I tend to rarely look back on, or forward to, their coming with any degree of joy."

The constable seemed to weigh up this reply in his mind, before nodding slowly.

"The Rangers, or 'The Watch', as they call them, further up," Caitlan said, gesturing to the hills up the rise, "Can be a blessing, under the right circumstances. Often so, in fact. Especially if they are on your side!"

She frowned.

"But....?" the constable asked, responding to the hanging question.

"But," Caitlan continued, "While they are good at tracking down cattle, horse and sheep thieves, they are not above taking the odd animal for themselves! While they do deter burglars and they do catch pickpockets at the fairs and markets, they lack the discipline of soldiers and they don't have a soldier's honour."

The constable nodded, thoughtfully.

"Only a few weeks ago," Caitlan complained, "Two young girls were raped on the road to Perth and people who are well informed and who know what goes on – people whose word is held in high esteem – are convinced that the Rangers were the ones who did it."

The constable looked to Hamish and raised his brow in query.

"Their idea of justice," Hamish took up, "Can be affected by what they see as being good for them. A bit of generosity, by one person or another, tends to alter their idea of what is fair or unfair."

The constable shook his head, sadly, and Hamish continued.

"The laird allows them to draw a tariff from the people they serve, but they tend to want more than is reasonable. Especially if they sense that somebody is weak or they have something to hide."

Their visitor pursed his lips in a tight smile.

"You are an innkeeper. You sell alcohol," he replied, "I have no interest in where you obtain it."

Hamish blinked at the other's bluntness and his mouth dropped open for a second. Quickly closing it, he opened it again, in an attempt to speak, but his shock at the man's remarkable directness rendered him dumb. The constable raised a hand, wagging it in the air in dismissal, then shook his head in reproach of any need for a response.

The constable then cocked his head, enquiringly, "The Rangers are a little expensive to maintain?"

Hamish smiled, ironically.

"Yes," he replied, and then added: "The Rangers in these parts tend to be from the McCarthys."

Hamish left the implication of this observation to speak for itself. The constable didn't seem to miss it and smiled ruefully. Attempting to dispel the awkwardness, Hamish decided to change the subject and pointed to the man's boots.

"The lad is attending to your horse, I take it?"

"*Horses,*" the man corrected, "And, aye, he is."

It was Hamish's turn to raise an eyebrow.

"One is to ride," the constable advised, "And one is to carry."

Hamish nodded, not quite sure if it would be tactful to pry into such an arrangement, but – after a few moments of heavy silence – he decided there was nothing to be lost.

"You have a cargo?"

"Yes. I have a cargo," replied the law man, "In the form of a McCarthy."

Neither Hamish nor Caitlan could disguise their shock and exchanged worried glances.

Recovering himself, Hamish found his voice.

"I have a fine room for you, Sir, and I have a bunk room off the stable for your...," he hesitated, searching for the words, "For your fellow traveller. Though it might be cold, tonight."

His new guest looked straight at him and the merest hint of a smile danced in his eyes and on his lips.

"You don't need to bother yourself about such things," he explained, "This particular McCarthy won't ever be feeling the cold again."

CHAPTER 7

For the second time that morning, Annis regarded herself in a mirror. This time, she was suited in her armour. Its beautiful white lustre never failed to thrill her. From the day her mother had presented it to her, on her twelfth birthday, she had fallen in love with it. It had taken another six years until she was grown enough that it had started to fit her properly. Now, at the age of nineteen, its fit was absolutely perfect.

Annis nimbly descended from her wagon, stepping on only the middle of its three steps and, begrudgingly, allowed herself to be helped up onto her horse. This was a feat that she could accomplish alone, but not with the dignity and poise required of such an occasion as today.

"Thank you," she said, with convincing sincerity.

Annis' honour Guard set off at a steady, solemn pace, giving time for the stragglers to draw together, move out behind them, and catch up. There were three members of her Honour Guard riding ahead of her and four behind. They all sat tall in their saddles and could not fail to impress in their gleaming armour. Annis smiled in amusement as her eyes found the tails of the horses in front of her. Her Honour Guard had actually gone to the lengths of platting and braiding each of their horses' tails with ribbons.

Suddenly, for no reason that she could explain, a conversation she had overheard, earlier that morning, sprang into her head.

"No! You cannot lead the queen's horse!" The cook had been yelling at her young assistant, "Stir that damned pot and stop dreaming of working with horses or I will slap the back of your head so hard that you'll drown in that cauldron!"

Annis could recall having had fanciful dreams when she was that age and felt a pang of sorrow for the young boy. Before she knew it, she was holding up a hand with two fingers extended. Promptly, the sound of a horse's hooves, scrabbling to accelerate, could be heard behind her, then a servant appeared by her side.

"Send me my groom," Annis demanded.

The man looked puzzled, for he knew as well as the queen did, that she had no groom and that her horse was cared for by several different people whom he personally organised at his whim.

"Send me Bobbins," she said, "I would have him lead my horse."

The man's look of puzzlement did not subside, but he went off, obediently, to find the cook's lad.

In less than three minutes, an eager, gleeful and extremely animated Bobbins arrived, running to her as if the Devil, himself, were on his heels.

"Your Majesty! Your Majesty! Your Majesty!" he cried, repeating himself for the sheer exhilaration of addressing her.

Annis nodded to him and he hurled himself, face down, onto the ground.

Aware that every step of her steed drew her further away from the boy, Annis held up her hand and the entire column came to a halt.

"Get up!" she shouted, and Bobbins sprang to his feet and ran to her.

Her voice, she realised, had been sharper than she had meant it to be, for the boy's face was now contorted in grief at the thought of displeasing his queen and he was on the very edge of tears.

"My fine boy," she said, giving him a radiant smile, "You are good with horses?"

His fear vanished, immediately, but his face froze at her question, having had nothing to do with horses, but adoring them, nonetheless, since he could stand. He thought for a moment and then said the best thing he could bring to mind.

"I love horses, Your Majesty!" he declared.

"I believe it might be more impressive, on an occasion such as this," Annis explained, "If I rode with my hands resting on my lap rather than holding my reins."

The boy looked vacant.

"So, because of that, I am in need of somebody to lead my mare," she explained.

The boy looked completely ecstatic and, this time, definitely did burst into tears. Annis motioned to the cavalry officer next to her and used a finger to draw a tear on her own face. The officer looked down at the boy, then back to the queen. He had disgust written on his face. Annis gave him a cold, steely glare and, in a second, his attitude changed. He hurriedly drew a kerchief from the saddle roll behind him and handed it to the boy. After a little coaxing the boy used it, but was obviously overwhelmed at holding such a fine thing in his hands.

"Use it good and hard," Annis instructed.

The boy obeyed. From the corner of her eye, Annis stole a glance at its owner and noted the pain on his face.

"Be aware," said Annis, "That you should not hand it back, for the man who gave it to you has no more need of it."

The man in question breathed an audible sigh of relief. Annis chuckled.

"Now, if you are ready, young Bobbins?" Annis coaxed, allowing him a few moments to collect himself.

Her young helper took hold of the reins she offered, but then stood in a motionless quandary. His mastery of horses, evidently, did not match his love of them.

Leaning down closer to him, the queen whispered some advice.

"You will find that the horse knows absolutely everything there is to know about being a horse. Her name is Bliss. You will find that she is almost like a person. If you are kind to her and show her respect, she will treat you the same way."

As if to confirm this, Bliss turned and gave Bobbins a gentle nudge with her nose and made a friendly chuntering noise.

"She knows about stopping and starting," Annis continued, "And she knows about how fast or slow to walk. I may just give her a little nudge with my knee or the odd word until you are used to her."

The boy's relief was palpable and he looked up at her with complete adoration.

Once he had settled on a likely word, Bobbins gave his command: "Walk."

Annis made ready to give her steed the tiniest hint of a nudge with her knee but Bliss, having decided that she liked the boy, had already set off. The cavalry riders around them, also having heard his command, moved away as well. The rest of the column followed. Bobbins looked around and, realising that it had been he who had set them all in motion, seemed to visibly grow in height.

"Why do they call you 'Bobbins'?" asked Annis.

"Because I'm small. The cook says that I'm no taller than two cotton bobbins, one atop the other, Your Majesty."

"Does the name offend you?"

"I don't really have any say in it, but no, Your Majesty, it doesn't."

"I'm glad."

"If I were a soldier as fine as these, riding a horse as fine as those," bobbins confided, motioning a hand towards her Honour Guard, "Then I would be happy to be called even the worst name in the whole world."

Annis nodded, sympathetically, but – for her – their pomp and finery, while impressive, brought with it a sadness for her.

"My mother, who was Queen of the West before me, was killed by her Honour Guard."

Bobbins' head spun around and he looked at her with shock and horror.

"But they swore an oath!" he protested, before looking suspiciously at the men in gleaming, bronzed helmets around him.

"Those men and these are nothing like the same," Annis assured him, "My mother lost her life when – after tens of years of disagreement and bitter dispute – the Clan Campbell returned to their seat at the Queen's Table."

Annis recalled that the Honour Guard who had betrayed her mother had been tall, athletic men in breastplates and full helms, mounted on fine horses that were adorned with banners and streamers. They had looked like characters from a magical tale in her story books. Despite feeling hatred and contempt for those men of Clan Campbell, she could never relinquish the fact that she had been in awe of their splendour, that day.

"When I was a little girl," Annis told Bobbins, "I loved to read books about knights in shining armour on milk white horses who rode to the rescue of princesses in distress."

Bobbins smiled politely – for, as a boy, such stories were a little too prissy for him – but he listened respectfully, nonetheless.

"I dreamed of castles with towers that touched the sky and of elves that granted wishes. I fantasised about lavish tournaments where knights would compete to win my hand. I imagined them charging at each other with lances and shields, one sending the other crashing to the ground from their saddle."

Annis found her mind swimming with these recollections. She often savoured the way that things had once been. The happiness. The youthful joy of life. The delight and thrill of new discoveries and experiences. She recalled presuming, so innocently, that it could all go on forever. Then came the grief. The loss. The tragedy. The days and weeks and months of numbness and despair.

"If my mother's Honour Guard had been made up of brave and loyal McRory men, such as these," Annis told Bobbins, "Then she would be alive, today."

On hearing her words, the McRory cavalrymen managed to sit even more impressively upright on their horses, though she would have sworn it to have been impossible.

The MacDonald had sent the McRorys because they were his finest mounted fighting force. They were, themselves, members of the MacDonald greater cavalry. Cavalry were a rare thing, indeed, in the Scottish Highlands. The tradition of these lands was of fighting on foot. An attack was usually delivered, not by troops on horseback, but by a mass of bare chested, painted men, charging in screaming hoards, blistering the air with blood curdling war cries. It would be a brave person, indeed, who could stand their ground and not flee when faced with such a wave of undiluted fury.

"Do you know who the Picts were, Bobbins?"

"No, Your Majesty, I have not had much cause for learning things, apart from how to peel vegetables, skin animals, stir a pot and turn a spit."

"If you do those things well, then you have learned well."

"Thank you, Your Majesty, but I wish I had learned bigger things."

"Most of learning is just remembering what you have been told."

"Then would you tell me about the Picts, Your Majesty?"

"Yes, I will. History is one of the things most worth learning. The Picts ruled most of the North of Scotland for a long time, far back in the past. The Picts taught the Scots something and the Scots learned it well. They taught them a lesson in mounted warfare," she said, then added: "That's fighting on horses."

Bobbins nodded eagerly at the mention of horses.

"The Scots had good cause to remember their early clashes with the Picts. The results were repeated, humiliating defeats."

"Humiliating?"

"That's when somebody makes you look really bad."

"I see."

"When the Vikings came to Scotland, to invade and take over, they came across a big battle between the Scots and the Picts. The Vikings waited to see who would win. It was the Picts who won, so they attacked the Picts."

Bobbins opened his mouth to say something, but could not marshal the words. Annis smiled and replied to the question he had not asked.

"It doesn't sound fair, does it?"

"No, Your Majesty."

"Nothing is fair in war. War is a foul and wretched thing."

Bobbins nodded, certain that she was right.

"Did the Picts win or lose the battle with the Vikings, Your Majesty?"

"They lost, but they put up a very brave fight. The troops they had left took on the Vikings without any rest, straight after the battle they had fought with the

Scots. The Vikings were shocked at how well they did. Scholars say that if the Picts had brought just a few more warriors with them, they would have won."

"They must have been good fighters."

"The Vikings regarded the Picts as some of the fiercest people they had ever met."

"Are there still Picts alive, today?"

"No, they were a people who were different to other people for hundreds of years, but – for no reason that has ever been found – they simply disappeared."

"They ran away?"

"No, they didn't go anywhere, they stayed, but as time went on – or so we are told – they stopped being different to the people around them. They stopped having their own ways of being and behaving."

"They just became like everyone else?"

"Yes, that is a very good way of putting it."

"It's good that we still remember them."

"They were very brave warriors and they taught their children to ride horses when they were very, very young."

Annis smiled as she recollected something her mother often told her.

"My mother, Queen Cydara, used to tell me – when I was little – that I could ride a horse before I could walk."

Even now, she was not entirely sure whether it could have been a fact or if it were just a joke.

"Was that true?" asked Bobbins, as if he could hear her thoughts.

"If it were to be true," Annis laughed, "Then it would make me Queen Kiffan!"

Bobbins was just about to ask who Queen Kiffan might be, when there was a sudden noise in the trees, just ahead of them. It was the piercing sound of a bird's alarm call, warning its neighbours of their approach. Two of the cavalrymen knotted their brows and exchanged uncertain glances, neither entirely convinced as to whether the call had genuinely been a bird or if it had been a person. One of them gestured to Bobbins, urging him to lead the queen's horse from ahead of her rather than beside her. Bobbins obeyed, with a leap almost as athletic and graceful as a young deer. Bliss gave a little snort, sounding very much like she, too, were amused.

Their procession came to a halt. The two lead riders, after listening keenly, had motioned back that everything seemed safe, but then held up an arm for the attention of their commander, Balgair McRory.

Balgair was not far away. He was never far away. He and his Second-in-Command, Sachairi McRory, constantly rode back and forth, from the front of their company to the rear, checking on their men and on the safety of the queen's people.

The elite Honour Guard, Annis noted, appeared unconcerned by the presence of either of their officers, but the other thirty cavalrymen visibly stiffened whenever Balgair or Sachairi were near. The remaining two hundred and fifty MacDonald foot soldiers were similarly vigilant of their presence and eager to impress.

Whatever was happening appeared to require a good deal of discussion and a fair amount of gesticulation. Bobbins, unable to contain his energy, obtained permission to run and climb a tree as a lookout.

Now alone, Annis looked back to where her maid, Morag, rode. This was just behind the four riders who trailed her own horse. Annis gave her a smile. Morag smiled back. Annis signalled for her to come forward. With precise and elegant horse control, she came to her side.

"My Queen now has a squire," said Morag.

"Yes, she does," Annis grinned.

"He is keen and eager."

"Yes, he is."

"He brims with enthusiasm."

"Yes, he does."

Annis and her maid beamed at each other, their casual and easy friendship evident and impossible to feign.

"He reminds me of somebody in particular at around that age, Your Highness," said Morag.

It took Annis a lot of effort not to shriek with laughter.

"Yes, I thought so, myself," she agreed, her face illuminated by her smile.

"You turned out well."

Since the age of twelve, when Annis had lost her mother, she had found comfort in Morag's tireless kindness and support. Morag had been widowed because of Annis. She had lost her husband, Leslie, when he had saved Annis' life. After killing Queen Cydara, the Campbell traitors had searched for Annis, as her heir, and had found her hiding place. Leslie had died protecting her. Despite this, Morag had never blamed Annis. She had never displayed one jot of resentment and had never held back any of her love.

"How I turned out, Morag, is – in great part – due to you."

"You do me too great an honour, Your Majesty!" cried her maid, lowering her head, "Your mother is the one who deserves all credit for who you are, today."

"Mostly, perhaps, if you insist upon it, but by no means all."

"I was a poor substitute, Your Majesty, and I…"

"You were magnificent and you very much remain so and I am Queen of the West and my word is the law," warned Annis with mock seriousness, "So I caution you not to argue with me if you wish to keep your head on your shoulders and not find it rolling around on the ground beneath your horse's hooves."

"I quake at your wrath, Your Majesty," replied Morag, suppressing a laugh.

"Well, do not quake any further or the soldier, back there – who seems to have most definitely enjoyed your company and your conversation – may think that you are in some kind of trouble."

Morag had, indeed, been talking to one of the McRory cavalrymen. She had evidently been enjoying the man's attention. Annis had heard her laughter from time to time and, when the man had leaned across from his saddle to speak to her more confidentially, she had seen her maid's uncharacteristically shy look.

"That man has a pleasant face, a warm manner and very kind eyes," Annis told her in a lowered voice, "I waited, earlier, to catch his eye and, when I did, I nodded to him – slowly and with great purpose – to make him aware of my approval."

"You are very kind, Your Majesty, and – if I may say – I approve of your own admirer."

Annis was startled. Surely, she had no admirer? In that respect, she kept herself very much to herself. Why would Morag think such a thing? Then, she saw the direction of Morag's gaze. She was looking towards Balgair McRory, the captain of the cavalry, who was fast approaching them.

Balgair seldom spoke to Annis, making only formal pleasantries when good manners required it, but he didn't seem at all unfriendly. His smile, on the rare occasions she witnessed it, always appeared genuine and not forced. She had, now she thought about it, observed him looking her way quite often. It was usually, she recalled, when he thought she wouldn't see. Annis prided herself on her peripheral gaze being unusually acute.

"Your Highness," he said, touching the rim of his helmet in salute, "We have doubled the number of our troops who have gone ahead of us to assure your safety."

"Very well," said Annis, presuming that this was not all he had to tell her.

"We expected the first scouting party to have returned by now."

"And they have not?"

"No, Your Highness, so far they have not."

There was a sharp whistle from around the bend ahead of them and Balgair looked relieved.

"We will continue, for just this moment, our lost riders have been sighted."

Balgair saluted, again, and began to ride away, but then stopped as if something had just occurred to him. He turned his horse around and rode half a length back to her. She turned to him and Balgair, with extravagant emphasis, reached down and began straightening and smoothing his kilt. She looked down, her curiosity stirred, and her eyes sprang wide in surprise. Balgair grinned at her and, raising the leg closest to her for show, ostentatiously pretended to brush some non-existent fluff from the material.

"The MacDonald Tartan," Balgair declared, "Which I am wearing, Your Highness, for the benefit of Clan Grant, who are at the far side of the river!"

He looked mischievous and she laughed, unable to suppress a huge smile. She gave him silent applause, her hands describing enthusiastic clapping in the air.

Balgair beamed at her, delighted to have been the cause of her amusement.

He was young for a captain, she observed. Perhaps he was recklessly brave? Perhaps he was a hero of some battle? Absent-mindedly, she leaned across and patted his arm, still smiling. Although her head was already turning back to look to her front, she was sure that, from the corner of her eye, she saw his smile falter and his cheeks briefly flush with a hint of pink.

Annis made a mental note that this man seemed to have limited experience of women and, likely, had no sister as a child.

"I need a word with my men, Your Highness," said a now flustered Balgair, tapping the rim of his helmet, again.

"Very well," she said.

As he moved off, he glanced at her, nervously, and she gave him her sweetest, most dazzling smile. This time, he fully blushed.

The captain spoke to the three lead riders and, in response, they urged their horses into a trot and disappeared up the road to confer with their scouts, who – in the distance – had just broken cover from the edge of the forest. The two groups of riders had a brief but animated discussion. Then, the riders Balgair had dispatched, abruptly wheeled their horses around and headed back towards the main convoy at a gallop. Annis waited, anxiously, for them to return.

The leader brought his horse to a stop as he reached their party, its hooves ploughing into the ground and throwing up soil. Steadying his horse, the man brought his mount up alongside them and touched a hand over his heart in salute to the queen.

"According to the scouts, there are plenty of hoof marks on the opposite bank of the Spey," he announced, "They say that the marks look to be fresh. There are broken twigs and branches and disturbed undergrowth leading up into the woods. Our scouting party didn't stay to search around, in case it might look provocative, but they could smell campfires, close by."

Balgair turned to Annis to speak, but she put her hand up to stop him.

"I am a nineteen-year-old girl," she said, "And surely no overwhelming threat to a group of soldiers overlooking our territory from their own."

This was a statement and not a question.

"What my presence – as Queen of the West – represents, however, is a tradition from the old days that doesn't sit well with some people."

The riders exchanged glances, but none of them spoke. They seemed willing to wait to hear where she was heading with her words.

"The Highlands are steeped in tradition. The people who live here are, themselves, a living tradition.

Across the river, those people are not Lowlanders, but nor are they typical Highlanders."

Everybody nodded in agreement.

"They see themselves as different from us and different from the Lowlanders. Some call them Eastlanders. They may not be as fiercely wed to heritage and to the past as we are, but they are not as happy to change their way of life as most of the people who live North of the River Forth and River Clyde."

There were nods of approval and agreement amongst the men and some raised their eyebrows, expressing surprise at the wisdom of one so young and one who was, after all, a mere woman. Any significantly negative thoughts they may have had were carefully guarded and kept in their heads. They were worldly-wise enough to take care what dissent they ventured to express on their faces. She was a queen, and this had to be taken into consideration. Their lives could be abruptly and savagely ended at her whim.

Balgair looked at them and then at Annis. His demeanour displayed the vaguest hint of pride in her. The men, interpreting their commander's expression, quickly looked even more appreciative of Annis' words and began to mumble and grunt their accord.

Coming towards them, following Balgair's returning riders – but at an unhurried, almost leisurely pace – came Gavin Crombie. This man, her senior adviser, had been her personal guard until the arrival of the McRorys. His responsibilities had now become more general, and, that morning, he had ridden off with the

McRory scouts to check their intended route for possible danger. Annis had become aware of a certain tension between Gavin and Balgair, but this seemed significantly more subdued, this morning.

Gavin pulled up his horse and bowed to Annis.

"The Grants have been at the river. They're not there now. They're not far away," Gavin announced, succinctly, glancing between the assembled riders.

Queen Annis nodded her acknowledgement and Gavin added his conclusion.

"They have a point to make," he declared, "So they'll be back, for sure."

"I have a point to make myself," Annis announced, gesturing up the road, "The banks of the Spey are separated by a distance of a hundred and fifty strides but, more importantly, in terms of trust, they are separated by over eight hundred years."

Everybody nodded sagely and seemed pleased with her.

Annis pointed first to Balgair, then to Gavin and then pointed up the road, before encouraging her mare forward a little way. Balgair and Gavin, in response, obligingly followed her.

Annis stopped and, now a group of only three, she spoke frankly.

"What has come about that the two of you are no longer stern and distant in each other's company?"

"I think we are a little more appreciative of each other's situation," Balgair announced.

"Aye, it is so," confirmed Gavin, begrudgingly.

Queen Annis remained pointedly silent and looked at each of them with eyebrows raised in question.

"He," said Balgair, pointing at Gavin, "Is here because he wishes to be. He left his stronghouse and gave up his lairdship to follow you. He did so because he believes in your cause and because he believes in you, Your Highness."

The two men shared a glance of solidarity.

"He," said Gavin, pointing at Balgair, "Is here because he was sent. That is not to say that he would not have volunteered. He and I are both committed to your cause. He, however, is a McRory. He is a long way from home. This makes him, by far, the braver man."

Balgair looked at Gavin appreciatively, and then — injecting modesty — shrugged his shoulders in self-deprecation. As the queen's brows knotted in puzzlement, Gavin paused and bowed respectfully to Balgair.

"If we are defeated in battle and I survive," Gavin explained, "I can rely upon clans loyal to us to protect and shield me on my way home. Balgair, on the other hand, would have to cross Campbell land to reach home. The Campbells would likely be waiting to ambush any McRory survivors, especially him. So, getting home after a defeat, for him, is a probable death sentence."

Queen Annis tried to stifle her shock but was aware that it was with little success. Balgair look slightly bashful. Annis bowed to him, too, and he looked both slightly surprised and slightly embarrassed. She looked across to Gavin and was grateful that he had, tactfully, turned away.

The riders in the main column were getting restless and so, in response, were their horses. They were close to their objective, now, and their mounts could sense the general air of anxiety.

Annis waved for the cluster of riders they had left to their rear to join them and they trotted up dutifully.

"Your Highness," Gavin began, once their column was reassembled, "You could, if you chose, go across the Spey with just your own personal troops."

He looked purposefully across to Balgair.

"That would be unthreatening," Balgair agreed, "But could be risky if there were any problems with Clan Grant."

Balgair met Gavin's eyes and the other made no effort to disagree.

"There are several things you could do," Gavin responded, "You could go just with your own riders. You could go with your McRory riders. You could go with any number of riders, in a combination of both. The more riders you take, however, the stronger you appear. The stronger you appear, the more likely you are to give the impression to Clan Grant that you do not have peaceful intentions."

Gavin and Balgair exchanged satisfied glances, obviously still in agreement. Gavin motioned to Balgair, who promptly accepted the invitation to take over talking.

"You could," Balgair began, "Take only your Honour Guard with you, but parading an Honour Guard, especially one dressed in polished armour and plumes, might be mistaken as a challenge."

Annis looked from one to the other and held both her palms upwards, encouraging them to continue.

"The other option," Balgair offered, "Would be to simply set caution and calculation aside and take your entire force, but..."

"That," interrupted Annis, "Would give them the impression that I am coming to start a battle!"

"Or," Gavin retorted, "That you are wanting to face them down with superior numbers in order to shame them."

Balgair was quick to respond.

"And," he added, "That could store up significant problems for later!"

"And we cannot be sure," Annis rejoined, "Just how many men they have brought with them! The force we know about is unlikely to be the full force they can call upon."

Gavin and Balgair both nodded, exchanging glances and making faces that distinctly indicated their happiness with her grasp of things.

"Whatever you decide to do," Balgair warned, "We risk Clan Grant misunderstanding or misinterpreting our intentions."

Annis looked at them, clearly puzzled, and – opening her mouth – drew breath to speak.

"Your Majesty," Balgair interjected, "We cannot simply go and talk to them."

"Can we not?" Annis challenged and set a hard, thin smile on her face.

Gavin and Balgair looked troubled by this reply. Their faces told her that it was a fanciful idea.

Annis sighed and rubbed her hands together, slowly and thoughtfully, while looking up into the sky in distant contemplation. As one, they all waited – in respectful silence – for her attention to return.

Annis clapped her hands, in apparent triumph, and glanced around her audience. They looked expectantly at her. She gestured for them to come closer and the group of riders coaxed their steeds into a huddle.

"I believe I have a solution," the queen proclaimed.

She leaned forward in her saddle, conspiratorially, and the assembled group responded by leaning still further forward, pressing their horses to bunch together even tighter.

"This," Annis began, "Is what we need to do....."

CHAPTER 8

Janine, having accepted the priest's hand to help her into the coach, lowered herself into the middle of the vacant seats across from the other occupant. The priest began to climb in behind her, but then stopped and called up to the driver.

"Try not to lose the boy off the top of the coach," he urged, "I'm not sure how well he would bounce, especially if he lands on his head."

The driver gave a laugh. Janine smiled to herself. She liked that such a refined and well-spoken man possessed such a good nature that he was on joking terms with his staff.

Reaching for the door, he pulled it closed and sank into the seat next to the other man. Janine cast a brief glance at the two of them, sat side by side, but then stopped and began to stare, open mouthed. Her eyes furiously flitted between them, her face a perfect picture of confusion. They both laughed, good humouredly, revelling in her consternation.

"I am Brian," said the priest.

"I am Bruce," said the other.

"We are identical twins," Brian announced, helpfully.

"But," Bruce chirped, "Only one of us is a priest."

"As far as we know!" Brian chortled.

This seemed to thoroughly amuse them both and they subsided into gales of laughter. Janine found herself laughing, too, and this only seemed to encourage their mirth!

"Of course," the priest, declared, "It could be **he** who is really the priest and **I** just put on the wrong clothes this morning!"

This was a cue for more laughter and Janine could not stop herself from joining in.

"He, of course, is the thin one!" the priest offered.

"And he, as you can see, is the fat one!" his brother retorted.

The two men, being of identical girth and stature, both adopted pretend frowns and scratched their chins, simultaneously, in feigned concentration.

"Of course," the priest admitted, "It **could** be the other way around and I am simply confused!"

The two brothers chuckled at each other's wit and looked down, shaking their heads in a parody of exasperation. Janine was shocked at how their mannerisms were every bit as identical as their appearances. She found this both fascinating and, at the same time, somewhat eerie and disturbing!

"This," Bruce declared, "Is us imitating Romulus and Remus."

Janine stared at them blankly.

"The famous identical twins from Roman mythology?" he suggested.

"Oh!" Janine replied, none the wiser.

"You pompous dolt!" Brian scolded his brother, "Not everybody spends their childhood locking themselves in their parent's library and reading from morning till night."

Bruce looked crestfallen.

"Still," Brian consoled, "Neither of us deliberately set out to become over-educated prigs!"

Brian gave his brother a withering look, but quickly returned to smiling at their passenger, again. Janine was even more confused.

Bruce leaned forward to her, as if for secrecy, and then – gesturing towards his brother – spoke in a whisper loud enough to be overheard at ten paces.

"I am sick and weary of the number of times, while we were growing up, that a female guest or acquaintance would march up to me and, completely unexpectedly, cuff me on the back of my head or slap my face. This would be related to nothing I had done, but to something crude or over affectionate on my brother's part, the aggressor clearly thinking that **I** were **he**!"

"That surely stopped when I became a priest," Brian protested, looking angelic.

His brother gave him a reproachful look.

"Or did it not?" Brian added, in wounded tones.

This provoked another mutual bout of sniggering and chuckling.

"The servants were continually getting our names the wrong way around," Bruce told her, "Until I came up with a solution!"

At this, Brian looked scathingly at his twin.

"Brian was somewhat godlier than I and, straight from the cradle, was a lot more religiously inclined," Bruce explained, prompting more chortles, "So I told everyone to remember that, in constantly checking that we were all being good, Brian was "spy'en" for the Lord!"

Not satisfied that Janine was sufficiently amused by his brilliant wit, Bruce decided to labour the point.

"Do you get it?" he asked, encouragingly, "Brian? Spy'en? You've got to say the two words so it sounds like they rhyme."

Janine made an effort to smile and to laugh a little more convincingly. Her dubious acting skills appeared to tickle their sense of humour, causing great hilarity. After the joviality had subsided, Brian slid forward on his seat and spoke in hushed, secretive tones.

"I am the fortunate one," he told her, giving Bruce a look of mournful pity, "For I managed to hold on to my sanity and a full grip on my mind."

So saying, he contorted his lips in an anguished smile, glanced for a moment towards his brother, then tapped the side of his temple with a finger.

"Our poor mother was grief struck and broken hearted over my brother's tragic mental condition," he confided.

Brian now sighed deeply and gulped in apparent sorrow at his unburdening of himself. He gave her a pathetic sniffle. Janine was immediately gripped by embarrassment. Her discomfort was plain. She turned to the window, composing herself, before turning back to express her heartfelt sympathy.

"I am deeply sorry..." she began, but was interrupted by a sudden shriek of laughter from his brother, Bruce.

With his head thrown back, Bruce guffawed loudly and repeatedly slapped his knee in delight. Brian, meanwhile, snorted, clapped his hands together and began gleefully drumming his fists on his knees.

It took only a second more before Janine realised that they had, again, been teasing her. She began to giggle. Before long, this degenerated into uncontrollable laughter. The two brothers were now sprawled half on and half off their seats, flailing their legs and holding their sides. They chortled and snickered until tears streamed down their faces.

After a good while, all three of them were able to settle themselves.

"This reminds me," Brian announced, straightening his clerical collar, "Of when we were children and our disgraced uncle would visit and have us kicking and screaming on the floor with laughter at his stories!"

Bruce nodded, enthusiastically, with a huge smile on his face.

"Your **disgraced** uncle?" Janine asked.

The two brothers straightened in exaggerated solemnity and Bruce put his finger to his lips, imploring her to secrecy.

"He ran away to sea!" he confided.

Brian shuddered and looked utterly appalled at his brother's words.

"The shame of it!"

The two laughed and Janine was extremely relieved that, this time, it was not the kind of laughter that totally incapacitated them! Brian put a hand on his brother's elbow to urge his silence, cleared his throat, and launched into what Janine took to be a ludicrous mimicry of their mother's voice.

"You are a bad influence on your nephews! You are a disgusting, disgraceful and vulgar man!"

Bruce could not resist joining in, employing similar whining tones.

"You are a blot on your family's character!" he squawked.

Janine giggled, covering her mouth with her hand.

The three of them laughed until they were utterly spent from the effort and relaxed into a comfortable and easy silence. The coach swayed and bumped over several uneven sections of road, at times rocking its passengers violently. Eventually, the brothers decided that it was time to talk, again.

"Where are you bound?" the priest asked, pausing to twirl an index finger in the air, to indicate that he didn't know her name.

"Janine," she offered, obligingly.

"Where are you bound, Janine?" he asked, appending her name to his question.

"I.... I...," she stammered, "I need to get away. I don't care where I go."

"You are on the run!" gasped Bruce in theatrical astonishment.

"No!" Janine objected, alarmed by his accusation, "I wouldn't say that. Well, not exactly...."

The two brothers, almost completely synchronised in their movements, grabbed their chins, craned forward and looked at her with expressions of complete captivation. They gazed, wide eyed, giving the appearance of a pair of dullards.

"Do go on!" implored Brian, in a tone of incredulity.

"Do accept my apologies for my brother's intrusiveness!" gasped Bruce, pretending to be mortified that a priest should be so nosey.

Brian kept his eyes fixed on Janine, while he flapped his hand in the air towards Bruce. With a farcical pretence at absent mindedness, he tapped and flicked at the other's face, as if he were a busy and impatient parent warding off an over enthusiastic child.

Janine could not suppress her amusement at these antics and was completely enthralled by the buffoonery of the two men!

"You have us," began Brian, "In the palm of your hand!"

Bruce scoffed at him in derision.

"**You** have my **face** in the palm of **your** hand!" he protested.

Brian pulled back his hand – as if he'd accidentally placed it on a pile of horse manure – and made play of wiping it on his cloak. They both chortled, loudly.

Janine, feeling inexplicably relaxed and at ease in the company of the two brothers, thrust her hands indignantly onto her hips, huffed imperiously, and made a displeased face at the pair.

They froze dramatically, feigning discomfort, before looking down and sticking out their bottom lips in a sulk.

"I was at Dunkeld Manor," Janine began, "I was a maid to the lady of the house, there."

"You have a fine and noble face for a maid," Bruce interjected.

"Thank you," she replied. Then, after a pause, she added: "It was the way that God made me."

"Just so!" exclaimed the priest, reprimanding his brother with a stern look.

Bruce took a turn at fluttering a hand and tapped Brian on the nose with it, dismissively.

"Go on, Janine," he urged.

"The laird and lady were kind to me and treated me well," Janine attested, "But the laird's Chief of Arms started to cause me problems by paying me attention that was neither fitting nor proper."

Janine blushed, a little, and bit her lip. In response, Brian inclined his head and arched an eyebrow, encouraging her to continue.

"I made it clear to him that his advances were unwelcome," Janine advised, "But he became more and more insistent."

The two brothers nodded, sympathetically.

"I told him that he had to stop and that, if he did not, I would be forced to tell Her Ladyship about what he was doing. He tried to touch me..." said Janine, grimacing in disgust, "In private places, through my clothes."

Suddenly Bruce gasped and threw his hands to his head. Reaching out, he shook his brother's shoulder to draw his attention.

"Dunkeld Manor!" he cried, "Was that not where a man was murdered?"

Janine looked immediately sheepish and lowered her eyes. Her face had gone extremely pale. Her look of guilt prompted the two men to exchange agitated glances.

"Yes," she replied, dully.

The brothers shivered in response.

"The Chief of Arms flew into a rage and he attacked me," she wailed, "He grabbed me by the throat and pushed me against the wall, striking my head against it, and pulled out a knife!"

Tears flooded, unbidden, to her eyes as she spoke.

"He said he was going to kill me! He said that he would dump my body in the woods and make it look like I had been robbed."

Janine began to tremble and could not stop herself from sobbing.

"You are safe, now," the priest assured her.

The coach suddenly slowed. The priest knew that this action would soon be followed by a lurch as the vehicle negotiated a particularly bad pot hole. Timing his move, he stood, turned about face and allowed himself to fall backwards into the seat beside her. It was clear that he had performed this manoeuvre many times.

"You are safe, now," he repeated, taking both of her hands into his own.

"He told me to get my cloak, then started dragging me to the door!" Janine said, putting her head on his shoulder and burying her face in his scarf, "He said that he was going to do terrible things to me, then make it seem like an intruder had attacked me and raped me!"

Janine's chest heaved as she wept. She gasped and choked on her words as she tried to speak. The priest made soft 'hushing' noises and, patting her on her back, whispered words of consolation in her ear.

At least three minutes passed before anybody spoke, then Bruce, who was sat across from them, ventured a question in hushed tones.

"How did you escape?"

"I don't know," she replied, becoming nervous and distracted, "He took me down the back steps. He was pulling and pushing me all the way. We passed the first floor that leads into the rooms behind the kitchen. We continued down and passed the floor for the storerooms, then he kicked me down the short run of steps to the cellars. I was lucky not to break any bones."

She paused to sob and swallowed hard, before continuing.

"He raced after me and stepped over me. He grabbed me by my hair and dragged me into the smaller of the cellars. He threw me on top of some sacks, then turned me over onto my back. He pulled my cloak away and lifted my dress."

She sobbed, again, her face contorted in anguish at the memory.

"He said that if I screamed he would kill me slowly and painfully and that he would make sure that I suffered. He said if I were quiet, he would make it a quick and easy death for me. I told him that I wouldn't say anything if he let me go. I promised I wouldn't say a word to anybody, but he said he could not trust me and that it had to be this way."

Brian hugged her and rocked her gently until she was sufficiently recovered to speak.

"He took out a knife and he put it to my throat. He pulled up my underclothes."

She flinched at the memory.

"He told me to keep quiet. Then..."

She fell silent, a look of confusion overtaking her. She screwed up her face, straining to recall the events. She looked troubled, then – after a few moments – she shrugged her shoulders.

"I don't know what happened," she continued, "I must have fainted. That's what it must be. I came around slumped against the wall. My clothes were all straightened out."

She hesitated and furrowed her brow, absorbed in her thoughts.

"He must have been interrupted. He had not touched me. He had not done anything..... anything shameful to me. I was still..." she blushed crimson, "I was still as I was."

Bruce leaned over and patted her hand, gently, while Brian made soothing noises. She choked back a sob. Then, with a sniff, she resumed her story.

"He was not there. He had gone. I looked around, but I was frightened and I didn't dare stay down there for long. So, I went back upstairs. I took off my cloak and washed my face. I laid down on my bed. A little while later, there were shouts and I could hear the sound of footsteps, people running, and a lot of activity. I heard some men speaking, as they were passing my door, and one told the other that the Chief of Arms had been found dead, in the cellar. They said he had been stabbed, with his own knife."

Janine sniffled and whimpered, then drew in a deep breath. Brian, manoeuvring her slightly to one side, reached into his pocket. A moment later, he produced a handkerchief, which he handed to her. Janine wiped her eyes and her cheeks but then stopped, holding the handkerchief in front of her, looking at it uncertainly. Brian gave the tiniest, good-natured snort and smiled. He nodded to her, encouragingly, but she still looked hesitant. Brian brought his hands up to his face, cupping his nose between them, then inclined his head in a gesture of blowing his nose. Janine looked wistfully at the handkerchief – it was a beautiful piece of material – then she raised it to her face and blew her nose, looking at Brian apologetically.

"Your gracious manners are at odds with your humble status," observed Bruce, from the seat opposite.

Janine looked at him guardedly and then shook her head. There was deep sadness in her eyes. She looked out of the window, her gaze distant and meditative, as if she were no longer aware of them. She sighed a deep, long sigh. The brothers traded glances. There was a sudden air of gloom about this girl. They sat still and waited patiently. A full minute passed. Janine continued to stare out of the window.

Brian noticed that the expression on his brother's face had changed. His look of sympathy had slowly become one of fascination. The fascination had, then, gradually transformed into disbelief. His look was intense. He was completely spellbound.

"What is it?" Brian whispered.

Bruce ignored him.

"What is it?" Brian whispered, louder and more insistently.

Bruce still ignored him. Brian turned to the girl beside him and then back to his brother. As he did so, he jolted in surprise. There, for a split second, was a flash of yellow and orange in the corner of his vision. He swivelled his head back and forth between the two of them, several times. Each time, he saw the same thing, for a brief instant before it was gone.

A moment later, the coach slowed for another substantial pot hole. Brian took advantage of it to reverse his previous accomplishment by gently lifting himself from his seat, turning around and depositing himself next to his twin. The girl's gaze never shifted from out of the window. From his new vantage point, Brian could see what was absorbing his brother.

"That's not possible," he declared, with far less certainty than his words conveyed.

Dappling and rippling across the wall of the coach behind Janine was the reflection of flames. They lit her face, too, with a whirlpool of colours.

"Not possible," his brother agreed, "And yet, plain to see."

The effect clearly emanated from something substantial that was alight, outside the coach window. That, they told themselves, was absurd. The pattern was constant, so they were not passing the source of the conflagration. Rather, it appeared to be keeping pace with them!

"It's as if there is a fire..." Brian began.

"Right there, outside the window," Bruce finished.

They both looked through the window and were astonished to see that there was nothing there that could possibly account for what they were seeing.

"There's nothing but the greenery of the forest out there," Brian observed.

"Just trees, bushes and shrubs," his brother confirmed, "And none of them alight."

They both looked back at the girl. The flames were still there. Turning their heads back and forth, Bruce and Brian looked, alternately, through the window and at the girl. The source of the flames was invisible, but their effect was distinct and unmistakable, as their yellows, oranges and reds glimmered and wavered.

"Impossible," they declared, together.

The same thought struck them both at the same moment.

"There is nothing evil about what we are witnessing, is there?" asked Bruce.

"No. These are good flames," came Brian's reply.

The flames did not inspire a feeling of panic, but of reassurance.

"They are something altogether wonderful," Brian said as he extended his arm and, with great care, gently placed a hand on the girl's arm.

She turned towards him, but her eyes didn't so much as waver. Her countenance did not change. She looked straight through both of them, as if she were in a trance.

Bruce and Brian held their breaths, both taken aback and completely dumbfounded. The coach lurched, abruptly, far more heavily than before. In response, she suddenly sprang back to life. At that precise moment, the flames stopped. She looked at the brothers, quickly from one to the other, in a state of anxiety.

"I'm sorry!" she said, "I don't know what happened. I just...."

"It's okay," replied Bruce, "That's not a problem. You....."

Bruce faltered and felt his brother urgently squeeze his leg, asking him to take care with his words.

"That's not a problem, you were just deep in thought for a moment, that's all."

They both smiled, reassuringly, and – after a moment of indecision – Janine smiled back, a look of relief flooding across her face.

CHAPTER 9

Hamish Pottle's mind lurched as he imagined Duncan McCarthy – the rough, abrasive, foul-tempered leader of the local Rangers – slung, lifelessly, over the back of the constable's horse. He felt a twinge of guilt on realising that the image gave him considerable pleasure. The guilt quickly faded, however, when he considered the McCarthy's most recent victims. The families of the two young Rafferty girls from nearby Killiecrankie, would have every right to be overjoyed at the sight of the corpse. This was the man who had very likely led and participated in their rape and savage beating.

Hamish cleared his throat and swallowed.

"You've encountered the McCarthy's on your travels, Sir?" he asked the constable.

"I have," replied the constable, glumly, "Which accounts for me having a dead one on my horse."

The corners of their visitor's mouth twitched and the twinkle was back in his eyes.

"Yes. I see," Hamish said, somewhat distractedly, "You met more than the one of them?"

"I have only brought the one with me," replied the constable, an almost imperceptible smile appearing on his lips.

Hamish could not suppress a little sigh. The constable stood silently in the doorway, a hint of amusement about him. He clearly understood what the innkeeper wanted to know but seemed determined to extract some effort as the reward for the telling.

"Will I take a seat?" the constable enquired, pointing to a vacant chair, opposite Alex Brennan.

"Oh! Of course! My apologies!" cried Caitlan.

Springing to her feet, as if she had been launched from a catapult, she produced a cotton cover and placed it, deftly, over the seat of the chair.

"Oh!" said the constable, looking at the cover, "You have me wrong. I am as modest as the sky is blue. There is no need."

The constable picked up his bag from the ground, which he had positioned out of sight beyond the door, and strode to the chair. Nodding to his hosts, he sat down, and placed the bag beside the chair. As the canvas of the bag made contact with the stone flags of the floor, there was a dull, but unmistakable, metallic noise.

"Would you like some tea or a wee dram?" asked Hamish.

"A wee splash of whisky, just to wet my tongue, would be most welcome," he responded.

Caitlan poured a little more than the requested amount into a glass and handed it to their new visitor. Holding it up to the light, for inspection, the constable nodded approvingly, flicked up the glass and emptied the contents into his mouth. He made a satisfied noise and dropped the empty receptacle into the palm of Caitlan's upturned hand.

Hamish pursed his lips, ready for another round of probing and interrogation. The constable, noting his expression, gave a short, hollow laugh and held up a finger for him to stop.

"I came across the McCarthy brothers an hour's ride, back down the road," the constable explained, "I had a short discussion with them, during which I made my opinions plain and we appeared to part company on tense but, even still, broadly reasonable terms."

He paused, surveying his listeners, each agog with curiosity.

"I was riding off, to go about my business, when I heard a galloping horse behind me. I spun my own horse around and found their leader approaching me, at speed, with his sword drawn. Having had second thoughts over my parting remark, he had taken delayed offence."

Hamish, Caitlan and Alex sat motionless, captivated by the law man's account. The two kitchen maids, meanwhile, stood like statues, utterly transfixed.

"It was clear that, despite me having furnished my warrant from the king, that he was hostile," the constable continued, "I was compelled to explain to this 'gentleman'..." he said, pronouncing the word with disdain, "The error of his ways!"

His audience were rigid in expectant silence.

"So, I spoke to him!" the constable told them, looking stern, "And he fell from his horse and down onto the ground, dead."

A look of confusion spread across the faces of the people in the room.

"Or rather," explained the story teller, helpfully, "Should I say that I had my companion speak to him on my behalf!"

Again, everybody looked a little confused. At this, the constable picked up his travelling bag, pulled open its covering flap, and revealed the dangerous end of a monstrous pistol.

"**He** is a most persuasive speaker!" the constable declared, tapping the mammoth weapon with his finger.

Alex and Hamish leaned forward, at the same moment, both flabbergasted. Not only was the gauge of this device huge, but where one barrel would normally sit, there were twin barrels, one next to the other. The two men's mouths gaped open in awe.

"This was forged for me in Italy," the constable explained, "And gifted to me by a nobleman of some standing."

"It is a beautiful piece," said Alex.

"A work of art!" agreed Hamish.

"Judging by the size of it," quipped Caitlan, "It fires hens' eggs!"

Everybody laughed.

Hamish's glance fell to the open bag. Below the flap of the pale red satchel were brass letters, riveted through the fabric. They spelled out: "Burberry".

Constable Burberry followed the innkeeper's gaze to the bag but made no comment.

Carefully tucking away his weapon, the constable pulled and looped the cord that held the flap down, ignoring the two heavy straps that were designed to secure it more firmly.

"A moment's delay in reaching a firearm could make all the difference," Burberry explained and, nodding towards Hamish's arms, decorated with a mariner's tattoos, he added: "You'll know so yourself."

"Aye, I do, indeed," Hamish responded and, nodding towards the man's bag, he added: "We carried a line of guns, just like that one, sticking out of the sides of my last ship!"

The two men laughed heartily and Alex and Caitlan accompanied them. Hamish was amazed at how the big man's whole presence changed when he laughed. Gone, in a moment, was the dour and gruff persona, replaced, in its stead, by a cheerful and amiable one. He had a deep, easy laugh that lifted the spirits and a smile that illuminated both his own face and those around him.

Hamish reached for the whisky bottle and inclined its neck towards the constable. Burberry held up his hands in a display of mock horror and raised his eyes to Heaven in a sardonic protest of piety. Hamish smiled, thoroughly amused.

The constable held Hamish's eyes with a steady, unflustered gaze, and the innkeeper could feel the other's guard going back up into place.

"The McCarthys," began Hamish, "Are not forgiving people. They tend to hold a grudge."

The point was not lost on Burberry.

"There are grudges in the Highlands," observed Burberry, jovially, "That have lasted for centuries and ones that will, no doubt, last for a good few centuries more!"

"Aye, true enough," replied Hamish, "But the McCarthys tend to work to more pressing timescales."

Burberry cocked an eyebrow.

"I only have a middle-sized wall above my fireplace, back at home..." Burberry revealed, arching his mouth in a frown.

His audience looked intrigued.

"...And I have, so far, just the one McCarthy," he continued, rocking his head from side to side in contemplation, "But I could, no doubt, go for a brace or – if you would urge the wisdom of it – I could put my mind to having the full set!"

Hamish, Caitlan and Alex looked at the constable as if he had lost his senses.

"Are the three of you implying," began Constable Burberry, in injured tones, "That a constable's Warrant of Office, signed by the king's own hand, is insufficient to guarantee his safety in these parts?"

Hamish, Caitlan and Alex glanced one to the other. They shared a look of awkward discomfort.

"A good job, indeed, in that case," retorted Burberry, "That I can call upon the support – not too far down the road – of thirty brave men of the Lothian Pikes and Muskets, dressed in blue and grey, carrying both guns and swords and displaying the crown of King James on their belt buckles."

The expressions of his audience changed in almost perfect harmony. First, they looked thunderstruck at the offhand disclosure of this information. Then, realising the confidential nature of it, they looked guarded and wary. Then, comprehending the burden placed upon them by being privy to it, their look was one of rebuke.

Constable Burberry held up his arms in self-admonishment.

"**Why** would I tell you something like **that**?" he asked.

Hamish, with clear hostility in his voice, snapped back his response.

"Why, indeed, **would** you tell us something like that?"

The maids, sensing the imperative for discretion, spontaneously lowered their heads and busied themselves, industriously, about their chores. Caitlan turned around to look at them and their stirring and mixing promptly picked up a notch. She cleared her throat and they scurried out of the room.

"Maybe" Burberry replied, posing the supposition like a school teacher addressing his pupils, "Just maybe, I know that I can trust you."

Hamish snorted as if this were preposterous.

"You don't know us!" he exclaimed.

Burberry leaned forward, secretively.

"Maybe I **do** know you," he insisted.

The three of them looked at each other, as if suddenly unsure of who they might be.

"Perhaps I have blackmail in mind?" Burberry asked, puckishly arching an eyebrow at Alex Brennan.

Alex stiffened, taken by surprise, and tried not to look guilty while feverishly racking his brains for anything incriminating. Caitlan and Hamish both looked at him, suspiciously.

The constable shifted his gaze to Hamish, his eyebrow still raised.

Hamish jolted and, while his mind was racing to reassure himself that all the panels in the roof of the bar were firmly in position, he quickly adopted a countenance of pained innocence. Caitlan and Alex both looked at him suspiciously.

The constable slowly moved his scrutiny to Caitlan, who looked nonplussed and slightly offended. After quickly recovering her deportment, she fluffed her skirts in her lap and inclined her head haughtily. Hamish and Alex both looked at her, suspiciously.

"Suspicion lays where it is pointed," the constable said, "For there's not a person who draws breath that doesn't have something to hide."

The constable's demonstration of this wisdom had made the atmosphere in the room tense and uncomfortable, but – in a split second – he dispersed it. His gruffness evaporated in an instant and, with a flash of his charming smile and a twinkle of his merry eyes, the whole room was awash with warmth and good humour.

"I cannot disclose my reasons for having such confidence in you all," the constable declared, "But let me tell you this: We are living in dangerous times."

Hamish and Caitlan both nodded their agreement.

"It is sad to say that a constable cannot rely on a king's warrant alone for his safety. As I travel North I must take care. I may not always be among friends. A careless disclosure, made in haste, might be my last."

Such was the man's aura that none of those gathered in the kitchen were of a mind to challenge him or to delve into his reasoning. The two maids, who were now listening outside the kitchen door, looked at one another and nodded their approval of this bold new guest.

Hamish, Caitlan and Alex, quickly began to relax and, within no time, found themselves beaming at the man as – completely unexpectedly – he began to diverge into a series of amusing anecdotes about his time in the army. Not only did he always include all three of them in the conversation, but he routinely spoke to each of them independently, directing his words first to one, then the next, then the other.

"I am an innkeeper," said Hamish, "And it blesses me with a keen instinct about people. I have an instinct about you. You are welcome here any time of day or night, and any day of the year."

Constable Burberry bowed, solemnly, at his words and – this time – when Caitlan offered him more whisky, he accepted without hesitation. They all drank to each other's health and prospects.

Trading stories of military action, the three men posed this way and that as they demonstrated blows that were delivered, sword thrusts that were made and shots that were fired. Caitlan, for her part, recounted a particularly bloody tale of skewering a rampaging wild boar with a spear from atop the lid of the well.

Burberry took hold of Hamish by the hand and carefully positioned his arm to dramatically re-enact the parrying of a blow. Hamish, catching sight of the jet-black thumbnail on Burberry's right hand, noisily drew in air through pursed lips.

"You look to be sporting the outcome of a more recent battle!" interjected Hamish, pointing to the thumbnail.

"Aye!" replied the constable, "That's the truth of it! I was kicked by my horse. It hurt like the Fires of Hell! I cursed and I swore with every foul word that I had ever known and then invented another six to go along with them!"

They all laughed.

Holding up the thumb for inspection, Burberry made a confession.

"It takes every ounce of restraint I possess to stop myself from picking at it!" he said, "It's a real annoyance. It will fall off, in its own good time when its ready, I expect."

One of the maids returned from making up the constable's room and, peeking round the door, caught Hamish's eye.

"The good gentleman's room is now fully prepared, if it pleases you," she said, motioning towards the constable, "I have furnished the bed with a feather mattress and put on it one of the duck down quilts."

"Wonderful work," Hamish told her, "You can show Constable Burberry to his room and provide him with any amenities he may require."

The maid nodded and held open the door for Burberry to follow her.

"If it's all the same to you," began Burberry, turning to Hamish, "I'll be assured, without inspection, of the fine standards of your hospitality. Instead, if you wouldn't mind, I'll take a walk around outside and maybe limber up with a little exercise before the light fails."

Burberry adopted a stance portraying a physical workout.

"Whatever pleases you, Sir," Hamish replied.

"If you'd like to flex your muscles, Sir," Alex offered, "You can join me at the wood stack. There's a certain satisfaction from splitting logs with an axe that I, myself, find most rewarding."

Burberry nodded his approval and the two made their excuses and went out to the woodshed. Alex selected a sturdy axe apiece and they laid siege to the remaining pile of logs.

The two men laboured, side by side, pouring with sweat, until dusk came, and then beyond. Only when they had reached the very last log and could scarcely see it in the gloom, did they put down their axes.

By the time the last log was broken up into suitable lengths, the sweat had soaked their shirts and was dripping liberally onto the logs and onto the ground. They stood side by side, proudly surveying their work, and then forcefully shook hands, victoriously, and pounded each other on the back.

After panting and gasping to recover their breath, Burberry jerked a thumb towards the stables.

"Would you care to take a look at what a dead McCarthy looks like?" he invited.

Alex Brennan shook his head, eyes cast to the ground, and seemed to disappear into his own thoughts for a moment. Raising his eyes, he locked them with that of the constable.

"If it's all the same to you, Sir, I have seen enough dead men to last me a lifetime."

Burberry nodded solemnly and grimaced.

"Aye. Quite so," he responded.

The two stood a while in a clumsy silence, each searching for a new topic of conversation, before the constable gestured to the line of trees.

"Come with me, if you will, and we'll find a more suitable pastime."

With this, the constable led the way to the edge of the forest and, a few minutes later, they set off back with cupped hands brimming with nuts and berries.

The two set to work laying a little campfire and then, rummaging in the shed, found some long, thin spokes of metal used for holding down straw while thatching roofs. These they pressed into service as spikes to hold their bounty to roast over the fire.

"Let me see if I still have the gift," said Alex kneeling by the kindling and taking out his tinder box.

Extracting the flint and striking rod, he conjured enough sparks to set fire to the dry leaves and grass. The flames quickly took hold and the fire began to crackle and roar.

The noise of the fire was distinct and unmistakable. The crackling and popping gradually grew in ferocity. The two men sat cross legged, both transfixed by the flames.

"There's a beauty in a fire that almost defies words," the constable confided.

"There is, indeed," Alex replied, dreamily.

Alex felt an odd comradery as he marvelled at the flames. Closing his eyes, he listened to the noise of the burning wood and allowed it to fill him with an extraordinary sense of peace and wellbeing. It was a strangely familiar and reassuring sensation that was quite blissful. Alex opened his eyes and, feeling obscurely detached, watched as the other – eyes now closed – smiled serenely, similarly wooed and captivated by the sound of the burning wood.

Absentmindedly, Alex toyed with the tinder box in his palm, turning it this way and that, and caressing it with his fingers.

"A treasured possession?" asked Burberry in a kindly tone.

"Yes. Very much so," Alex admitted.

The two men sat in amiable, contented silence for a minute.

"Do you have any special and significant possessions?" Alex enquired.

The constable looked at Alex long and hard with a steady, thoughtful regard. Alex had the distinct impression that he was being carefully assessed. Oddly, the sensation didn't cause him even the slightest discomfort. After a few moments, his instincts told him that he had passed.

"Yes," replied Burberry, leaning closer to speak into his ear.

As Burberry began to describe his treasured possession, Alex became puzzled, but listened patiently, nonetheless. When he had finished, Alex, was unsure if he had just heard a verse of poetry or, perhaps, a riddle.

Whatever it was, despite its meaning being slightly confusing, there was no doubt that the act of telling had been profound.

CHAPTER 10

The seven riders from Queen Annis' caravan carefully urged their horses forward, down the steep slope to the river, leaning back in their saddles as they went to compensate for the incline. Their horses picked their way gingerly, occasionally sliding a little, but made the descent without incident. Behind them came Bobbins, on foot. As they reached the riverbank, Balgair held up his hand for everyone to stop. Horses and riders came to a halt. Everybody waited, still and silent.

"You know why you are here with us, don't you boy?" Balgair asked Bobbins.

"Here with us and not with the queen," Gavin emphasised.

"Maybe, Sir, because I am known as a fearless warrior?"

Balgair and Gavin were charitable enough to only laugh a little.

"That could be one of the reasons," Balgair confided, kindly, "But it's not the main one."

"Do you not remember?" Asked Gavin.

"It is for the safety of the queen," Bobbins announced, "Because if people see me, there is a good chance that the queen's horse will be nearby and, if the queen's horse is nearby, there is a good chance that the queen will be nearby, too."

"Good lad," said Gavin.

117

"Yes, good lad," Balgair agreed.

"There's another reason, too," Gavin declared.

The boy looked vacant.

"It's because you are able to climb a tree better than a squirrel!"

Bobbins stood proudly and wore a huge smile.

"Would you like me to climb one?"

"Aye, I would," Gavin replied, "I want you to choose the tallest of the ones behind us and get yourself to the top of it. I want to know if you can see any enemy soldiers at the other side of this river."

Bobbins set off, eagerly, but Gavin called him back.

"When you shout to us, I don't want you to do it with your hands like this," cautioned Gavin, cupping his hands to form a bowl and raising them to surround his mouth, "I want you to clench one fist above the other, as if you are holding a two handed sword, then open them up to make a tunnel through the middle of them, and shout down through that."

The boy arranged his hands as instructed, but looked puzzled.

"The first way lets too much of your voice escape to the sides," Gavin pointed out, "The other way makes more of it go straight down."

Bobbins' face lit with comprehension and he bolted off to ascend the tree.

Back on the ground, the horses became slightly restless, longingly eyeing the water ahead of them, eager to drink. Balgair motioned Gavin to come alongside him.

"We may not be able to see our enemy..." said Balgair, quietly.

"But," replied Gavin, finishing the sentence, "They are most certainly able to see us."

The two scanned the opposite bank for signs of activity. After a minute, satisfied that they were no movements for them to see, they agreed that the other riders should dismount. After a few moments they were waved forward to let their horses drink in the river where, lowering their heads, they gratefully sucked in the cold, clear water. Their riders, standing next to them, each cautiously rested a hand on their weapons, which were slung from the saddles to make them available. Meanwhile, Balgair and Gavin, still atop their horses, kept a vigilant watch from the bank.

"There are soldiers," Bobbins' voice announced from above them, "As many as the fingers on both my hands. There could be more. They are hiding in the bushes, across the river. They're just sitting there. They're not moving."

"Good," shouted Gavin, from behind his hand.

"How long shall I stay up here?"

"Keep watch a little while longer."

The riders in the water duly waited until their horses had fully quenched their thirst before leading them back to dry land. Balgair and Gavin now prompted their own horses to move down and into the shallows. Having waited patiently, they drank with relish. The two riders stroked their horses' manes and patted them as they drank. Once their horses had drunk enough, Balgair and Gavin turned them back to the shore and out of the water. There, they joined the other horses in munching grass.

"Taking our time is exhausting," chuckled Gavin.

"It is," Balgair agreed, "I never thought it would take so much effort!"

Presently, Balgair signalled to his Second-in-Command to have the other riders remain where they were.

"Let's go and loiter further upstream, Gavin," he suggested.

The two of them moved the short distance to the fording point that led out across the river. There, the two of them sat, nonchalantly, while their horses feasted on a clump of tall, thin grass shoots which appeared to be very tasty.

There was a rustling in the bushes behind them and their hands flew to their swords. After a moment, a young boy emerged. He was out of breath and panting. The youth spotted Balgair and ran towards him, scrabbling and stumbling as he fought to keep his footing over the mossy stones. The boy reached into a pouch, suspended around his neck, underneath his shabby tunic. From it, he withdrew a piece of paper and, with a trembling hand, reached up and presented it to Balgair.

Balgair read the note and looked surprised. He quickly passed it to Gavin who, on reading it, shook his head, disbelievingly, and passed it back.

"Do you think we should tell the queen?" Balgair asked, wafting the note in the air.

"I think her plan is best executed if as few of us as possible have knowledge of this news," replied Gavin.

Balgair motioned to the boy that he was dismissed. The boy made a hurried attempt at a salute, then padded off back the way he had come.

"We must convince those who are watching us that this message is of no importance," Balgair announced, affecting a yawn and stretching elaborately.

In reply, Gavin rubbed his eyes with the heels of his hands and, then, gaped open his mouth in a mighty yawn that looked like he was trying to swallow the sky.

The two of them sat a while longer, amusing themselves by blowing little clouds of moisture into the air from their breath. Satisfied that they appeared completely unhurried to any onlookers, they finally spurred their horses forward. At a dawdling pace they crossed the shallows of the river out into the middle section where the deeper waters began.

They had, indeed, been watched, for – at the other side of the river – a band of four riders promptly emerged from the undergrowth and began slowly walking their own steeds out into the river. As they came, they talked animatedly and were obviously exchanging jovial banter. They were patently eager to project an air of unconcerned indifference.

"If they are not of Clan Grant," said Balgair, "Then I am a turnip."

"You'd make a fine turnip, but they most certainly are Clan Grant."

The Grants continued their approach to a depth where the water came half way up the legs of their animals. Balgair and Gavin carried on out into the river until their own horses reached the same depth.

The talk amongst the Grants gradually died away and they sat, relaxed in their saddles, exuding an air of detachment. One examined his fingernails, two were stretching as if to loosen tired limbs and the fourth had put his hand to his mouth to cover a yawn. They were all dressed in informal riding clothes, sporting capes, scarves, woollen tunics and had jiggy blankets over their laps, which draped down beyond their kilts to cover their legs against the chill.

Their attire was in stark contrast to that of Balgair and Gavin, who were, despite also being gussied up against the cool breeze, garbed in a noticeably more solemn and elegant manner.

"They've made an effort not to dress nicely for us," whispered Gavin.

The two outer riders, whom Balgair mentally nicknamed, Tim and Jim, had the hoods of their cloaks still raised, leaving their faces mostly in shadow. The two middle riders wore full sized claymores. They also had leather saddle bags, rather than woven ones, and the glint of their cloak pins spoke of polished silver rather than dull metal. Judging from this and from the stance of Tim and Jim as they addressed them, the two with the claymores seemed to be in charge. One was noticeably younger than the two men escorting them and the other noticeably older.

The two parties were around six paces apart, with the Grants stood in the slightly calmer waters. The distance was close enough to permit something approaching normal speech, without effort, for as long as the wind didn't stir too much.

Balgair pulled aside his jiggy, in pretence of scratching his leg, making the move appear as casual and offhand as he could. For added effect, he also reached under his cloak so that it fell far enough open to expose part of the broad band of material that stretched over his shoulder.

On seeing the newly revealed expanses of formal MacDonald tartan, the older of the Grants cupped his jaw in his hand and rubbed his chin thoughtfully.

"You are a long way from home, MacDonald," he declared, "And, if you are wearing your best for the Laird's Ball, you've missed it by over a week and I don't recall you having an invitation."

The other riders around him chuckled politely.

"My Laird MacDonald," replied Balgair, "Would approve of me dressing appropriately, as a mark of respect, in case I might encounter the Laird Grant on my travels."

"Why would you think it likely that you would stumble across His Lairdship? Did you think he might just have been wandering around, scampering and scuttling, like a wee rabbit?"

"The tradition of the Queen of the West reaffirming her boundaries is an ancient one," Gavin offered, "It dates back to Viking times. There are those who honour traditions."

The older Grant looked at Balgair solemnly, as if receiving an unwelcome lecture from a schoolmaster, and made no comment.

"There are those who honour the ways of their grandfathers," Balgair continued, "And of their grandfathers before them. For it is our traditions that define us, along with the heroes of old who made us."

The younger Grant stiffened and spoke curtly with a tone of accusation.

"Do you have any particular hero in mind?" He asked.

The older man stretched out a hand towards him, reproachfully, and gave a little sigh before he replied.

"We live in times of change. We need to do what is right for today."

"When the times demand heroes," Gavin countered, "And if we are judged to be deserving, then fate will provide us with the man..." then, after a well-timed pause, he added: "Or the woman!"

The younger Grant shook his head, clearly annoyed, and made a quiet – but audible – derisory noise, which earned him a sharp glance of castigation from his elder.

"Perhaps we ought to rely more on our own efforts and less on myths and legends," the elder argued.

The younger man, seemingly undeterred by his rebuke, gave them the benefit of his opinion, again.

"We don't need some damned wee lass with a head full of children's bedtime stories!"

The older Grant whirled in his saddle and hissed with venom at the younger man.

"That is his **queen** you talk about and you will give her the respect she deserves!"

The younger Grant blinked in astonishment and, while his mouth moved to muster a reply, he was unable to find his voice.

"If my Laird Grant were here," began the older Grant, "He would wish us to speak of your queen with proper esteem and would require us not to tarnish our clan by showing disrespect."

The junior Grant shot the back of his elder's head a toxic look and sat simmering with wrath and indignation.

Balgair and Gavin met each other's eyes for the briefest instant, but it was long enough to exchange their thoughts. There was something strange about the relationship between these two Grants. The older had authority over the younger, without doubt, but it was plainly not total or undisputed.

The concentration of the two leading Grants suddenly wavered. Balgair and Gavin became aware that their gaze had transferred from themselves to a point in the distance, behind them.

Balgair and Gavin both knew that, by now, the queen would be executing her plan. From that direction, would be approaching the remaining four riders of their advanced party. This addition would increase their number to six. With this in mind, they rode at a calculatedly slow, almost reluctant, pace.

The Grant elder looked to Balgair and, without disengaging his eyes, reached an arm to his rear, where his closed hand briefly sprang open, extending four fingers, then closed again. Dutifully, four horsemen from the Grant party, on the other bank, set off across the river towards them.

"A simple precaution," the elder Grant announced.

Balgair inclined his head in a deep nod to show his acceptance.

"You don't have to look behind you," observed Balgair, "To know that they are coming."

"No," replied the Grant elder, smiling, then adding, with a flicker of a smile, "And nor, of course, do you, yours."

The move was, indeed, pre-planned, but Balgair was caught off guard by the other's unexpected insight, and he snorted with spontaneous and genuine amusement. The senior Grant, without even a second of reluctance, promptly joined in. Balgair's horse, surprised by the sudden noise, snickered and stomped its feet. In doing so, it moved an arm's length closer to the Grants. The younger of the two Grants reached, lightening quick, beneath his cloak and they heard the unmistakable sound of steel emerging from a scabbard. Tim and Jim reached more slowly for their weapons but were content to merely rest their hands on their hilts.

Without looking away and without the smile leaving his face, Grant Senior responded to his companion's motion with three crisp words, each spoken as if an entire sentence.

"Put.... That.... Away...."

Adopting a perfectly synchronised pace, the newly arriving group of Grant horsemen reached the middle of the river at the exact same time as their opposite numbers from the MacDonald / McRory camp. Two of the riders from each rank chose to wear the hoods of their cloaks over their heads. Balgair and Gavin, despite feeling their ears and noses starting to succumb to the cold, left their cloaks down.

"There are different traditions, either side of this river," the older of the Grants began, "And different ways of thinking."

Balgair swayed his head, side to side, in visible consideration of this statement but voiced no opinion.

"Caution is a wise strategy these days," the senior Grant went on, "The king is appointing Bishops to oversee how people conduct themselves in their worship of God. If he takes this much interest in our religious practices, it's hard to gauge just how much concern he might feel obliged to take in a man's other loyalties."

"We both bend our knee to King James," noted Balgair, helpfully.

"You do, MacDonald?" The other asked, pretending to be a little surprised.

Balgair looked thoughtful for a moment before replying.

"I have **two** knees!"

"King James would surely like to claim both of them, MacDonald!"

"I am a loyal subject of King James, as are all of Clan MacDonald, down to the last man," retorted Balgair.

The older Grant pursed his lips and gave Balgair and Gavin a sour look before spreading his arms and holding up his palms in a gesture of exasperation.

"And yet..." The Grant said, allowing the inescapable question to hang in the air.

"And yet," replied Balgair, "I freely honour The Queen of the West as my majesty from a line, unbroken, since the days of the Picts and the Vikings."

"How loyal would I appear to King James if I were to pander to such folklore," protested the Grant elder, "If we were to take part in a symbolic act – her crossing of the Spey – that flies in the face of his rule?"

"You are a loyal subject," replied Balgair, "Of a King of Scotland who chooses to reside in London."

The two Grant leaders shook their heads, sorrowfully, as if they were the disappointed parents of a wayward child.

"Whether he lives in England or in Scotland," the older Grant insisted, "He is our king and we are assured of his loyalty and his protection."

"His protection!" Barked Balgair in sudden outrage.

The abrupt noise startled several horses, on both sides, and their riders had to calm their worried mounts. His outburst appeared to have a similar effect on the two senior Grants!

The older Grant opened his mouth to speak, but Balgair cut him off.

"Our King of Scotland," Balgair sneered, "Is the king whose forefathers – in their day – not only bent their knees to the Viking invaders but threw themselves to the ground on their faces!"

The older Grant looked furious. The younger Grant looked slightly bewildered.

"The Vikings," Balgair goaded, "Must have mistaken them for some kind of floor rugs!"

The two Grants looked flabbergasted at his brazenness.

"Around eight hundred years ago," Balgair continued, "The Vikings swept down the coast and attacked Aberdeen, striking the town both from sea and land. Some of their forces, on their way to Aberdeen, surrounded your stronghouse and you were cut off."

The older of the Grant pair physically flinched.

"It was Kiffan," Balgair scolded, "She whose line would become the Queens of the West, who sent troops to your aid, and **not** one of your proud and noble line of worthy Scottish kings."

The younger Grant, his eyes wide in disbelief, looked to his senior for guidance. The other merely snarled in annoyance and shot his junior a look of contempt.

"It was Kiffan, she who rose from nothing, who came to your aid!" Cried Balgair, spitting out his words with malice, "It was **she** who rode into battle with her army!"

Balgair's raised voice rang out across the river and echoed back from the valley wall, beyond.

"The Queen of the West did not direct her troops from a safe distance but…," Balgair drew breath to hurl the next three words as individual declarations of pride: "in… their…. midst!"

The younger Grant was now staring in open incredulity at his elder, almost beseeching him to refute these words.

"Three hundred Brydda took on eight hundred Vikings," Balgair continued, "They fell on them like howling wolves, screaming down from the hills in a Highland Charge that chilled their quarry's blood."

The senior Grant looked crestfallen as Balgair continued.

"The Vikings, for their part, were so impressed by her valour that they wrote a song about her in their tongue, calling her 'Kiffan the Defiant' in its verses!"

The elder Grant looked mortified and seemed to have lost six inches in height as he sat in his saddle.

"Gordon!" The younger Grant cried to the older, imploring his rebuttal.

Gordon Grant said not one word. He sat, instead, in silent fury, his jaw clenched so tight that Balgair feared his teeth might shatter at any moment.

"The Vikings," Balgair declared, "Were held up for half a day, never managing to truly vanquish the

Brydda. Word eventually came to them, from their leaders, that they were to abandon the battle and march their forces to support the attack on Aberdeen. The Grant stronghouse of Craobhan Àrda *(meaning 'High Trees')* was left standing and the occupants, your ancestors, escaped a massacre."

The younger Grant gave his senior a desperate look, tinged with sullen despair. It was clear, to any bystander, that the younger man had never been educated in this less glamorous history and heritage of his clan.

"The Laird Grant declined to receive Kiffan," Balgair continued, "Instead, he left her camped outside his walls. A vile snub, you might think, for his saviour!"

Everyone in the Grant party remained silent and the gushing and gurgling of the water, as it spilled over the nearby rocks, suddenly sounded intrusively loud.

"The Laird Grant had a son and heir, named Corey," Balgair announced, continuing his history lesson, "Kiffan and he had fought, side by side, against the Viking invaders at the Battle of Clachnaharry. Both had been terribly wounded and were taken to the Monastery of St Maelrubha at Applecross to recover. There, over the months that followed, they grew close. Far too close for his father's liking. His father wanted him to have nothing to do with Kiffan, on account of her Pictish blood. This was despite the fact that she, during the battle, had risked her own life to save his son's."

Gordon Grant turned to the younger, a look of shame on his face.

"The Laird Grant," Balgair went on, "Was spitefully vexed that his son still harboured romantic affection for Kiffan and he blamed her for his son's refusal to marry any of the fine matches who had been presented to him over the years."

Balgair's audience remained in rapt silence.

"The Laird Grant's son had been grievously wounded, again, during the Viking attack," Balgair asserted, "And by the time he had recovered enough to open his eyes, Kiffan and her army were preparing to leave to return to her stronghouse at Fort Augustus. His son insisted on being carried outside to the garden on a stretcher, to pick a violet, and was carried to Kiffan, to give it to her personally. He told her that the violet was to remember him by, for she had grown fond of violets in the gardens of the Monastery of St Maelrubha."

The older Grant shuffled uncomfortably on his horse. The younger Grant sat spellbound, hanging on Balgair's every word.

"The Vikings, on their way back from their defeat at Aberdeen, were – nonetheless – laden with the spoils of war from their other victories on the East Coast," Balgair told them, "After negotiations, they consented to spare Clan Grant and agreed peace terms, which included regular payments of tribute."

Gordon Grant now sat, hunched and despondent, like a man awaiting his own execution. His disposition starkly conveyed that he knew, full well, that there were even worse disclosures to come. The younger

Grant looked at him with his eyes narrowed in an expression of wary suspicion.

"The Vikings knew how to hold a grudge," Gavin announced, taking over the history lesson from Balgair, "They had turned Northwards in the direction of Inverness, but, when they reached the crossroads of the wagon trails – from North to South and East to West – they stopped. The Brydda had set off West the previous evening. Having suffered heavy casualties, Kiffan's warriors were sure to be making slow progress."

Gordon Grant no longer made any pretence at dignity and held his head in his hands. The younger Grant's face crumpled in dismay.

"The Vikings turned West to pursue the Brydda," Gavin declared, ominously, "The Grants, far more familiar with the territory, would have been well acquainted with much quicker routes over and around the hills to reach Kiffan and warn her....."

The younger Grant, picking up inflections in Gavin's tones, now looked anxious, his face drained of colour.

"The Laird Grant was still consumed by ill will towards Kiffan," Gavin told them, "He sent out riders over the hills in the direction of Fort Augustus, for all to see and witness. As you know, they had very particular instructions. They were to ride hard but, once out of sight, they were to stop and make camp. There, they were commanded to stay until the following morning, when they were to turn around and return to Craobhan Àrda."

The younger Grant sat immobile. Numbed by disbelief.

"No warning was ever sent to the Brydda," Gavin declared, "And the Vikings caught them unprepared. They killed most of the surviving Brydda in the ensuing battle. They then proceeded to kill every one of the wounded. They captured Kiffan and took her back to the Viking Chieftain. He accused her of practising Dark Magic and sentenced her to death."

The older Grant looked to the younger with a face harrowed by guilt and self-loathing. The younger shook his head in disgust and turned away.

"Kiffan, Queen of Picts, was presented to King Urokmort to be slain by his own hand. Kiffan's wrists were bound behind her back, then she was forced to the ground and dragged to kneel over the execution stump."

The younger grant looked expectantly at the storyteller, his face filled with concentration.

"Legend has it," Gavin told them, "That King Urokmort asked her if she had any special possession, anything she treasured that she would like buried with her. Her voice steady and without wavering, she replied to him..."

Gavin's listeners waited, in awe, for him to continue, but the voice that came was not his own.

"I have the petal of a violet," queen Annis exclaimed, loudly, while swiftly dropping her hood and urging her horse forward from the backmost line of riders.

The assembled Grants gasped and jolted in surprise at the voice of a woman suddenly ringing out from among the opposite ranks. As she moved, Annis shook free her long blonde hair, which lifted on the breeze and appeared to dance around her head like a golden haze.

"I keep it in a glass thimble!" Said the Queen of the West, clearly and firmly, "I keep the thimble in a pouch. I keep the pouch in a box. It is my most precious thing because it is the symbol of my one true love."

There was absolute silence. Nobody moved. It was as if time had stood still and frozen them in place.

After a long pause, Annis resumed the story.

"King Urokmort told her that it was a tradition that, as a queen, Kiffan could beg of him a kindness before he carried out the sentence of death."

Again, the sound of gurgling water around them seemed to become so loud as to be almost deafening.

"She asked that, from that day forward, no Viking be allowed to enter or to slay any occupant of Craobhan Àrda, the stronghouse of Clan Grant."

The younger Grant gasped in horror.

"It is known!" Cried Tim, the rider at the far end of the Grants, "It is known that they never did!"

That rider moved his horse forward and made his way towards Annis.

"There is no possible way that you could ever have been aware of this fact," he asserted, "Unless you were speaking a true and faithful account of history!"

Slowly and purposefully, Tim pulled down his hood and tucked it behind his neck. The riders to the rear of the Grants immediately dropped their heads in deference. Jim and the two leading Grants also bowed to him. In response, this man, suddenly identifiable as the Laird Grant, inclined his head in acknowledgement.

"Our feud with the Queen of the West is not one in which we can have any pride," the laird confessed, looking contrite, "And the telling of its origins – in the stark and cruel terms you have used – is a sobering admonishment of my ancestors."

The Laird Grant manoeuvred his horse so that he faced Queen Annis and addressed her directly.

"I came here, today, prepared to spill blood," he said, raising a hand to Balgair and Gavin, patently appealing for their restraint before slowly and cautiously taking out his dirk, "But I swear upon this steel, which was my grandmother's," he said, kissing the weapon at its junction between handle and blade, "That we knew not that the safety of Craobhan Àrda, and the sudden disinterest in it by the Vikings, was a gift purchased by the Last Wish of Kiffan the Defiant."

Annis bowed to the laird with a shallow, courteous inclination of her head. The laird, in response, bowed deeply and all the Grants in his party promptly did the same. The laird placed his hand over his heart and then moved his steed closer, still.

"If King James is to be displeased with me and feel that he has basis to question my allegiance," declared the Laird Grant, "Then let him have cause and reason that is bold, brazen and brash and not some weak and limp suspicion that arises from the scampering and scuttling of a wee rabbit!"

Gordon Grant, the laird's closest advisor, bit his lower lip in embarrassment, while everybody else in the Grant ranks laughed. Their laughter, unprompted and unfeigned, was evidently sponsored – in large part – by a feeling of relief. Sensing the collapse in tension, Annis, Balgair, Gavin and the rest of their party laughed, too.

The Laird Grant turned his horse, spurred it to the end of his line and moved part way back across the river before stopping and shouting to his troops in the forest at the edge of the river.

"Soldiers of Clan Grant, escort the Queen of the West across the Spey and guard her, each and every one of you, with your lives!"

CHAPTER 11

The wheels of the coach suddenly clattered loudly as they reached the driveway up to Brech Woorlach and Janine woke with a start. The approach to the Hall was cobbled – or perhaps, more accurately, "tiled" – with tens of thousands of little square stones in every shade of the rainbow.

Janine put her head out of the coach window and gasped at the sight that greeted her.

"This is glorious!" She cried.

Before her, a huge formal residence, built of gleaming white stone, jutted skywards. It was constructed with two main floors with an accompanying basement and attic. It was profound in its tallness and elegance. The clusters of tall chimneys, regularly spaced along the roof, seemed to be reaching for the clouds. Along the bottom of this impressive building was the basement, running its entire length and, across the top, were a multitude of attic rooms, also running from one end to the other.

Her face was creased with concern as she racked her mind to explain why this imposing building was both new to her and, yet, disconcertingly familiar.

Janine withdrew her head and looked to her fellow travellers. They both sat with smiling faces that radiated an aura of pride and self-congratulation. Grateful for her earlier rescue from the roadside, she obligingly took her cue to assume a manner of reverential awe.

"This is like a palace!" Janine gasped, "It is huge!"

This seemed to please the brothers greatly and they beamed with satisfaction.

"This is the home of the Duke and Duchess of Bo'ness," Bruce explained, casting his arm towards the carriage window, "And we are privileged to have grown up, here, in the care of our aunt and uncle."

"Our father," Brian added, "Was taken prisoner by the Spanish, when we were young, and he died in captivity."

"I'm sorry to hear that," Janine told them, sincerely.

The two men nodded solemnly in acknowledgement of her words and seemed to briefly disappear into recollections and nostalgia.

"Our father was an adventurer!" Bruce declared, at last.

"Our father," replied Brian, tersely, "Was a dreamer."

Bruce glanced coldly at his brother.

"Our father," Brian resumed, "Was unable to contain his grand aspirations or keep his big ideas under control."

"Our father," Bruce retorted, proudly, "Was driven and inspired. He had embarked on an expedition to explore new territories, for the crown, when his vessel was taken by a Spanish Man of War. This occurred at an awkward moment in history...."

Bruce looked to his brother for support, but Brian was looking upwards, making a fine pretence of being completely fascinated by the swirling patterns in the stained wooden roof of the carriage. Bruce shrugged and regarded his brother contemptuously.

"Negotiations with the Spanish were extremely protracted," Bruce clarified, "But were...."

"Completely and utterly fruitless!" Brian interrupted.

Bruce clenched both his fists and his teeth in aggravation. Brian smirked, his nose still pointing aloft.

"I am sure that your mother must have been distraught!" Janine told them.

Bruce looked to his twin and spoke pointedly.

"She was beside herself with grief," he disclosed.

Brian tore his attention away from the woodwork and looked genuinely heartbroken. He nodded his agreement.

"She was, indeed," he replied.

The two exchanged a brief, conciliatory look that extinguished their hostility like the pricking of a balloon.

"You must have felt like a pair of princes, growing up here!" Janine exclaimed.

"We were very lucky, indeed!" Bruce agreed.

"Yes, we were extremely fortunate!" Said Brian.

"How were you ever able to explore this huge palace of a house?"

"It was a challenge, for sure," Bruce confessed, "But we had all the time in the world – or so it seemed – with the seasons of the year seeming to go on forever in our little lives, bereft, as they were, of any true responsibility."

"Our mother, our aunt, our uncle and all of the servants were glad for the peace and quiet it afforded them whenever we were wandering and exploring," Brian explained, "We were..." he paused, groping for the right words, "...a handful for all concerned!"

They both laughed.

"Our Governess was exceptional!" Bruce enthused.

On hearing the word *governess*, Janine's eyes popped wider and the two brothers didn't fail to pick up on this tiny prompt. Bruce looked duly embarrassed and Brian made an apologetic little smile as his shoulders slumped ever so slightly.

"We were privileged." Bruce admitted.

"We were." Brian confirmed.

At this moment, the coach pulled to a halt and the two male occupants demurred to Janine to alight first. One of the servants, dressed in stunning red, yellow and gold livery, opened the door for her, placing a set of steps on the ground and bowing deeply and formally.

She had, herself, been a servant.

'No, *not true!'* She told herself, *'You are **still** a servant!'*

From her experience, she knew, immediately, that the servants, here, were something special. These servants were used to excellence. Service, for this class of servant, was an intensely honourable and distinguished calling, worthy of their greatest possible efforts.

Very conscious of her slightly shabby appearance, Janine stepped down, accepting a servant's offer of a white gloved hand to help her maintain her balance. To this man, she knew, her clothing was of no concern and had no relevance. His only focus was on how well his impeccable behaviour would reflect on this household.

Janine gave the servant an almost indiscernible nod. She knew, from experience, that this was the thing to do. This was the most recognition that a lady of breeding would indulge on a servant. As the twins disembarked, she turned to them and spoke in lowered tones.

"I feel woefully under dressed," she said.

"No, my lady," said Brian, courteously, "You look perfectly wonderful. Your clothes inherit your refinement. It is you who refine the clothes. The clothes do not refine you."

Janine felt her cheeks flush a little pink, but suddenly realised that she was standing tall and elegant and was secretly taken aback by such deportment. She was a servant girl. There was nothing about her that contained any style, class or grace. She was, even so, completely unashamed and was oddly disturbed by this unshakable confidence in herself.

"Michael had not even noticed your attire," said Bruce, casting a hand towards the servant who had helped her down.

The servant remained stoically silent.

"Michael?" Bruce invited.

"Her attire? No, Sir, I noticed nothing," confirmed Michael, shaking his head gravely and looking at the ground.

Janine looked at Michael's lowered head and felt overwhelmed with gratitude for his good heart and kindly manner. She was, however – for these purposes – a lady. As a lady, she was meant to take such matters entirely for granted.

"Michael," said a female voice extremely close by.

Janine was a little startled until she realised that it was her own voice and that she had, unintentionally, spoken aloud. Michael looked up, surprised to be addressed directly.

"You," she continued, "Are a servant of the most impeccable character and a most refined individual. You bring great credit to this house."

"Your Ladyship! Thank you!" Replied Michael, nearly bursting with delight.

"Michael," Bruce instructed, "Have Francesca come up to the pale blue guest room and bring Lady Janine some appropriate garments."

"Yes, Sir," replied Michael, "At once, Sir."

Janine felt strange at the use of the title "lady", but conveyed the impression, to everyone, of being completely unruffled.

"And also," Bruce instructed further, "Have a word with O'Keefe and tell him that I speak for the duke when I say that he should give favourable consideration to an increase in your salary."

"Yes, Sir! Thank you, Sir!" The servant gushed, "Thank you, indeed!"

"It would be a dereliction of my duty if I were to fail to take account of the opinion of one so fine as Lady Janine!" Bruce confided to Michael.

Michael, in response, bowed reverently.

Bruce reached out his arm to Janine in an invitation to walk and, as she took it, he drew her a little closer.

"You now have a friend for life," he whispered.

"He is a good man, who has risen in rank without losing his good nature or a genuine sense of humanity," Janine responded.

"You are a good judge of servants," Bruce replied.

"Yes, of course I am, but I would be, would I not? There is a very good reason, which I am sure you realise."

"'We are all servants of God!' as Brian would say!" Bruce quipped.

Behind them, atop the coach, Callum noisily cleared his throat, fearing – correctly – that he had been overlooked. Brian gestured for him to climb down.

"Michael," he called, "Take this young man downstairs and have him put into a tub and cleaned up. His clothes can be discarded. Have him dressed well."

The servant stopped, waited for Callum to run across to him, and then continued to the house, patting the boy on his shoulder as he came level.

Janine smiled and gracefully floated across the paving and up the steps into the hall. She did this without faltering or hesitating once in her instinctively refined demeanour. None of the servants who had witnessed her arrival had the slightest glimmer of doubt that she was, indeed, a lady.

In the grand entrance hall, with its marble columns and gleaming marble floors, Janine was introduced to the Butler and the Matron Housekeeper. It was apparent that they had both been formally summoned to present themselves to her on her arrival. While Janine received their greetings amiably and graciously, she found their reaction, on first sight of her, to be most puzzling. It was as if they had seen a ghost. The butler had stared, open mouthed, for a second, before regaining his decorum. The Matron Housekeeper had gasped and thrown her hand over her mouth to quell herself.

As they walked up the stairs, Bruce waved one of the servants to pass them. The servant carried a small trunk against his chest. Brian, a few steps behind, slowed to fall in beside them and kept pace with their ascent.

"Your pillowcase is in the trunk," Brian explained.

Janine felt instantly grateful for not having to endure the shame of arriving with such a grubby and pitiful thing as a pillowcase on full display. She pounced on this thought and mentally reprimanded herself for such vanity! She was a servant girl who had run away from her employer. She was a lowly individual of no consequence. Yet, here she was, striding around in a huge mansion in the company of two men who were at perfect ease with this lavish and luxurious lifestyle.

She stopped abruptly, mid step, and her two companions came to a rapid halt, one step later. They looked surprised. Janine glanced quickly over her shoulder, checking that nobody was around.

"Do you have a plan or a reason for this deception?" She enquired.

The twins looked hurt and replied, almost perfectly together.

"It's not a deception!"

Bruce leaned close to her, in order to speak discretely.

"Having brought you here," he protested, "We didn't want to announce openly, to one and all, that you are a girl of a humble situation, running from her previous position and fleeing the clutches of thieves and bandits."

"Exactly so!" Brian agreed, "We cannot be sure that your assailants are not still on the lookout for you!"

"We thought," Bruce revealed, "That this would be a safer refuge for you if nobody knew your identity. You could be totally anonymous and still be 'Janine'. If anybody you have previously known were to encounter you, they would not recognise you from your earlier, more humble, position."

Janine looked back and forth between the two of them, her expression sceptical and dubious, before – much to the relief of both – breaking into a smile.

"You were there for me when I was in distress," she told them, "And you are most kind to take me under your wing and give me sanctuary. I scarcely dare think what might have become of me without your intervention."

The two brothers, in perfect harmony, smiled a little smile and flicked a glance between them that said: *'She most certainly does not talk like a lowly servant girl'*

The trio resumed their ascent of the stairs and Janine felt comfortable and at ease with them, again.

They reached the top and began to walk along a corridor. Their new fellowship restored, Bruce and Brian chatted with her, animatedly, as they walked. They told her about childhood memories of the rooms they passed and of the significance of this or that painting, alcove or suit of armour.

Somewhere ahead of them, to the right, a door opened and a servant came out, backwards, alternately bowing and throwing his hands up in consternation. A woman's voice, raised in anger, could be heard. Her words did not reach them clearly enough to make them out.

Suddenly, two small rolls of bread shot out of the doorway, in an arc towards the flustered servant's head. One caught him on the ear, the other straight in the forehead. Janine and her two companions slowed their gait and looked at each other in blank amazement.

"My Lady! My Lady!" Cried the servant, now cowering from what appeared to be the threat of further missiles, "It is the fashion! It is the way in the best social circles of Edinburgh and London!"

The voice from within the room could now be made out and the owner was evidently extremely annoyed!

"Don't serve me stale bread and tell me that it is fashion!" She shouted.

"My Lady!" Implored the servant, "It is not stale. It is hard."

"It is stale! It is hard. They are one and the same thing!" Came the furious reply.

Hearing their approach, the servant turned and, seeing the twin brothers, raised his hands beseechingly. Bruce gestured back with a wave of his own hand. The servant pressed his palms together, as if offering a prayer, to signify his desperate gratitude.

"Aunt Ailsa!" Bruce called, his voice sweet and endearing.

In response, there was a dramatic gasp from within the room. Janine quickly stepped into an alcove, feeling like a trespasser on this private scene. In the reflection of a brightly polished metal plate, hung on the wall beside her, she was able to see back along the hall to the doorway. A woman, dressed in a beautiful peach coloured gown, wafted into view.

Janine's heart missed a beat and she leaned forward to stare more closely into the reflection in the plate. She was unable to contain the bizarre and troubling notion that she **knew** this woman.

Aunt Ailsa stood expectantly, eagerly scanning left and right to locate the speaker of the greeting. Upon finding her nephews stood there, she gave a little shriek of delight and brought her hand to her mouth. The peach fabric swirled as she stepped, quickly and gracefully, to embrace Bruce. Her movements were like that of a dancer.

"My dear boy, you look wonderful," she told him.

Janine's heart lurched, again, at this woman's oddly familiar personal air and bearing. She had a strong urge to bob her head out from her retreat to look closer, but – by sheer act of will – managed to contain it.

Janine could hear their aunt uttering words of endearment and murmuring fondly as she hugged Bruce, closely. Without warning, she dismissively pushed him to the side and pulled Brian into her arms, instead.

"You are such a fine young man," she gushed.

She hugged him close and spoke words of gentle affection in his ear before releasing him, too, in similar fashion.

The two brothers turned to introduce their guest but, on seeing Janine stood discretely aside, quickly changed their minds. After a minute or so of further pleasantries Aunt Ailsa returned to her chambers. The brothers promptly came to collect Janine from her hiding place and ushered her towards her accommodation.

"You should have allowed us to present you," Bruce reprimanded.

"Oh, I could not..." Janine faltered.

"Perhaps she feels things a little too strange, yet, for such things," Brian soothed.

"Yes," agreed Janine, gratefully, "Exactly so."

They twins took her to what they called the 'Pale Blue Rooms' which turned out to be a set of private chambers decorated in colours appropriate to their name. She took stock of her surroundings and, mentally retracing their steps, concluded that they were now at the rear of the building.

Within her assigned chambers, the dressing room window looked out over a long, immaculately kept lawn that rose up a shallow hill to a small thicket of trees. As she stood and looked, her head began to swim and she started to sway. Fearing she was about to lose her balance, she reached out to grip the window ledge. Bruce quickly took her arm and she was glad to be able to lean against him for support.

"I'm sorry," she said, slightly breathless, "I suddenly felt as if I wanted to be sick. I don't understand it. I am normally quite robust!"

The two brothers exchanged a look that had become familiar to her and she knew that they were taking her measure, again. The reason – she decided – was likely their bemusement with her choice of words and the manner of her speaking.

"Do I speak strangely?" She asked.

The two shook their heads a little too eagerly and she felt that they were being more polite than truthful.

Janine had, as a personal maid, attended a lady of noble birth and was conversant with elegant behaviour and mannerisms, but was alarmed to realise that, since arriving at Brech Woorlach, she had subconsciously adopted that exact style of speech and poise. This transition had been accomplished seamlessly, effortlessly and – still more strangely – without so much as a moment's thought.

"If this were a Bible story," Janine announced, "Then it would be the parable about the Good Samaritan, for you have both, most certainly, been that to me!"

"It is our obligation as children of God," Brian replied, "To do what we can to pass on His love."

"Just so," Bruce agreed, making no attempt to hide the grimace he shot his brother for parading religion at her, again.

"Strange, then, is it not," Janine asked, "That I have the absurd feeling that, in actual fact, this is the story of the return of the prodigal son!"

The two brothers peered at her and pondered for what felt, to her, like a very long while. The more they studied her, the more perplexed they appeared to become. They looked at each other in confusion. It was as if she reminded them of somebody that they could not quite place.

"There is something at the back of my mind that escapes me," Bruce told her, "There is a thought that I cannot quite trap."

"I feel the same," Brian agreed, "It is the strangest feeling. I cannot quite describe it. It's almost like I know you, but I don't know you. It's like we have met before, but we have not."

They all agreed that they were feeling some kind of inexplicable déjà vu and that they could not force it to make sense by dwelling on it. With this as their conclusion, the brothers took their leave and Janine found herself alone.

She looked back to the lawn, stretching into the distance. A shiver ran through her and she felt a fleeting moment of panic. Her senses were playing tricks on her! She had experienced an unmistakable wave of nostalgia. An emotion that could not be real! Deny it as she might, she was certain that she had stood at this very window and looked out on this exact same view, before.

CHAPTER 12

The innkeeper, Hamish Pottle, stood behind the bar, casting a leisurely eye around the interior. Try as he might, he could not stop himself from looking up at the door to the inn at least twice every minute. He had been doing this for the past ten minutes and felt slightly worried that the urge to do so was so strong. As a former ocean-going sailor of forty years' experience, however, he knew to never ignore his instincts.

"Is there anything wrong?" Asked Maisie, the inn's serving girl.

"No, there's nothing wrong," replied Hamish, putting on a smile that didn't fool her.

Maisie went off to see to her customers and Hamish went back to trying to occupy his mind.

There was a sudden yelp and Hamish immediately adopted a slight crouch, ready for whatever might be about to happen. Maisie was pulling herself from the grip of an over eager drinker in the corner. After a moment's pause came the sharp thwack of hand meeting flesh as she slapped the man for his transgression.

"Keep your hands off me!" She snapped.

The offender made a feeble attempt to climb to his feet but, being a little too worse for drink, was unable to accomplish it. He dropped back into his seat and cursed her in coarse Gaelic. Maisie gave him a withering look.

Hamish saw the recipient of Maisie's slap screw up his eyes, blink rapidly and shake his head, collecting his sense. Next, his hand disappeared under the table. Hamish, fearing he might be reaching for a weapon, shouted to him in an authoritative tone.

"If you are in a mood for a wench, there are places you can go for that, but don't go delaying my girl," he shouted, "She has other customers, do you ken?"

There was a merry chortle from the dozen or so other customers, sat at the nearby tables. The man growled some offensive remarks, deliberately not loud enough for Hamish to make them out. He, then, spat on the floor and went back to quaffing his ale.

The nagging instinct that had been troubling Hamish had not gone away.

Before long, there was a creaking sound in the doorway of the inn as the floorboards responded to having weight being placed on them. Hamish looked up. Though not visible to him, he knew that somebody was standing at the other side of the door.

"Maisie," said Hamish, sensing rather than seeing her close by him, "Danger."

"I hear you," she whispered.

The door began to move, swinging very slowly ajar. Hamish looked to the shelf by the fireplace, where a strategically placed mirror allowed him to view into the doorway from the bar. There came the noise of what seemed like a second person shuffling behind the first. Hamish felt his heartbeat quicken.

Hamish could see two men, neither of whom he recognised, peering in around the door. The one in front wore a brimmed hat with some heather in its band and had a bag slung over his shoulder. The second, standing immediately behind him, wore a green cap tilted off one side of his head and was craning his neck to look over the other man's shoulder.

Finally, the door swung open and the two men entered. Hamish pretended not to notice them and bent his head to conduct some bogus task under the bar. The first man, in the hat, spoke to Maisie. His voice was raised louder than needed.

"Ale. Good ale. Be quick about it."

As she turned, he caught Maisie by her elbow and leaned close to ask her something. Whatever the question was, Maisie shrugged and shook her head. The man said something else to her and she shook her head again, this time more insistently.

The two men walked to the table by the fireplace, exuding menace, and the two occupants who were already there, looked up uneasily. The newcomers, having come in from the relative chill of the outside, were drawn to the welcoming heat of the peat fire burning in the hearth.

"Move yourselves," the man in the hat said, gruffly, to the occupants of the table, "We will be sitting here."

His tone was distinctly intimidating. The men at the table reluctantly got up and moved elsewhere. The man in the hat placed his bag on the floor and pushed it under the table with his toe.

Maisie arrived with the men's ale and placed it on the table between them. The man in the hat leaned close to her and said something more into her ear. She shook her head. He reached and took hold of her arm and Maisie flinched, looking down at her arm, her face contorting in pain. She tried to pull herself away, but the man's grip was too strong.

"Unhand her!" Shouted Hamish, reaching swiftly to a hidey hole in the wall behind the bar.

"I'll do as I choose!" The man retorted.

Gripping the handle of a razor sharp *sgian-dubh*, Hamish flicked it through the air with a practiced action. The little knife made a dull thud as it embedded itself in the wooden post, a palm's width from the aggressor's head.

The chatter in the bar stopped. Everybody halted and an ominous silence descended.

The man who had been troubling Maisie stopped and turned, with unrestrained animosity blazing in his eyes. Maisie, taking prompt advantage of the distraction, wrenched her arm free and hurried away from him.

"I may have to teach **you** a lesson!" The man snarled at Hamish.

Hamish Pottle instinctively knew the make of these men. He had known it from the very second he had laid eyes on them. Having survived the bloody brutality and barbaric violence of a life at sea, he knew the folly of squaring up to foes such as these using any kind of civilised code. He was certain that no amount of aggressive or threatening posturing would work with these two. There could be no testing and pushing of each other's boundaries, like with any decent people. They wouldn't be simply ramping up the menace until violence became an option. These men loved violence. These men were savages. They thrived on violence.

"Am I frightened of you?" Asked the innkeeper in a measured, even tone, drilling the man with his eyes, "Because if you think I am, then the next mistake you make could be your last."

The man was taken off guard by such a breathtakingly bold challenge and his gaze became furtive, his eyes darting left and right, like a snake, working out his next move. Whatever logic or estimation he used, the man evidently decided that he should not risk trifling with somebody like Hamish.

"We have a simple misunderstanding," the thug cooed, calculatedly reining in his animosity, "We seem to have set off on the wrong foot."

His companion, in the cap, was distinctly unimpressed by this change of heart and was unable to keep it from his face. Even so, he gave a half-hearted shrug to show his acquiescence.

"We are searching for a friend, a former compatriot from our army days," the unpleasant intruder continued, "And the memories of war, recalling those events, have taken their toll on our…. manner."

"Is that so?" Hamish asked, in a flat tone, resoundingly aware that he could not trust a single word that came out of this man's mouth.

Hamish recalled their hesitant entry into the bar and a question flashed into his mind: *Who was it they thought they might find inside? Who was it that would inspire such wariness in two brutes like these?*

The answer came to him swiftly: The constable! He was a hefty, powerful and athletic man who carried a twin artillery piece that masqueraded as a hand weapon! Hamish had to stop himself from smiling.

The constable had left that morning, at first light, proposing to "go about the king's business" but promising, faithfully, to be back in the early evening to enjoy Caitlan's cooking. Hamish imagined that the "business" would include disposing of Duncan McCarthy's corpse, but had little idea what else he might be doing. A thirty strong army, he supposed, gave a man considerable scope for pastimes. These men in the bar were definitely looking for him and, he was pleased to imagine, they would meet their match when they found him!

Hamish felt the tension in the room drain rapidly away and the customers – sensing it, too – resumed their talk, their card games and their boisterous laughter. The scoundrel in the green cap looked at the innkeeper expectantly and Hamish locked his gaze, unblinking.

"Would you have seen a stranger with a costly looking riding coat and high boots?" Asked the man from his seat, "He's a big man. He is broad and tall," so

160

saying, he set his hands in the air, this way and that, to show the size of the person he sought.

Hamish pretended to think for a few moments, looking to the ceiling with his brows knotted in contemplation, before shaking his head and throwing up his palms in apology.

"I'm afraid I cannot help you."

"He was an old army comrade of ours. I would dearly like to find him to talk about old times."

Hamish shrugged, pursed his lips and shook his head.

"Are you **sure**?" The man asked, giving his question a palpable tinge of threat.

The innkeeper looked first at the one, then at the other, and then back again.

"I'm as sure as I need to be for the likes of you," Hamish replied.

The man in the daringly slanted cap stood up from the table, his fists clenched, and turned to his companion. Hamish could not see the look passed between them, but the man seemed to feel encouraged.

There was complete silence as all talk and gaiety stopped around them.

"I don't think I like your tone," the man in the cap said, and then added, scornfully, "My good man."

In his peripheral vision, Hamish noticed the other man, still seated, reach for something out of his bag under the table.

"You are welcome to ignore my tone, if you choose," replied Hamish, "But, for the sake of your health, I strongly encourage you not to press your luck with me."

The expression on both men's faces told Hamish that they weren't used to people defying them. The stance of the man in the cap stiffened and he took a step backwards before violently kicking a chair aside in annoyance. Hamish heard the splintering of the wood but decided to ignore it. As if in preparation for a fight, the man loosened his neckerchief and flexed his muscular shoulders.

"I'd like it better if I didn't hear your voice again, old man!"

Hamish discerned his seated partner move something heavy into his lap. Moments later Hamish heard the faint, but distinctive, metallic click of the sparking drum of a pistol being set. Ignoring the man who had spoken, Hamish locked gaze with the one on the bench. The man's lip curled in a nasty sneer and he made a guttural noise of scorn.

"You'd best settle for hearing from me," Hamish cautioned them, reaching under the bar and picking up a loaded pistol, "Rather than hearing from Ruby..."

Hamish placed the pistol on the counter, then – reaching and retrieving its twin – he added: "Or from Rose."

With this, he deftly arranged the second firearm side by side with the first.

"They make a fearful sound when they're angry," he added.

Both men looked from Hamish down to the pistols. Their eyes flicked expertly from one gun to the other. They noted that both were spark lock pistols that could be fired in a moment. They decided, quite correctly, that the covers over the powder pans would be drawn back and ready. Taking a cotton towel, Hamish draped it over the weapons, leaving only the muzzles showing. This, his adversaries decided, was to prevent any further scrutiny.

The bar remained dramatically silent except for the sound of shuffling as the customers either quickly moved to seat themselves in a safer position or scooted down the benches to the opposite end from the troublemakers.

The seated thug smiled broadly and laughed.

"You'd need to be quick with those things, old man," he said.

The man who was standing lifted both arms, his palms turned up to the ceiling, then let them drop limply back down to slap against his legs. This display of irritation was accompanied by a long, weary sigh. All the while his eyes remained locked on the worn and weathered pair of sailor's hands that Hamish had now folded, one over the other, in front of him on the counter.

"Or," the man added, "You'll not draw another breath."

The man who was seated loudly banged his hand on the table, replicating the other's frustration, and then determinedly and noisily gouged the surface of the table by dragging the ring on his finger across it. Hamish's eyes were drawn to the deep groove in the wood and his lips curled in annoyance.

This deliberate distraction was the fleeting moment the man in the cap needed to make his move. As Hamish's eyes returned to him, he saw his arm coming up from behind his back and the flash of metal as a throwing axe leapt from his hand, spinning in his direction.

Hamish squeezed the trigger of the pistol he had named Ruby. The sparking drum spun, grinding against the abrasion plate and sent a sputter of tiny white-hot metal splinters into the powder pan. The powder ignited in a brief flash and the pistol kicked as the charge in the muzzle propelled a lead ball towards its target.

The expression on the face of the man in the cap changed from triumph to disbelief and then to horror, as he attempted to work out how the pistol had been fired without being touched.

The flight of the axe took less than two seconds, but Hamish saw it coming as it tumbled lazily and unhurriedly through the air as if it were moving through treacle. He had experienced this sensation before. It had happened during pitched battles on the decks of ships, where time suddenly and inexplicably slowed down to a fraction of its normal pace. Hamish recognised it and welcomed it like an old friend, immersing himself in it as he stepped casually aside to dodge the axe. The whirling projectile crashed into the wooden shelves behind the bar sending up a shower of glass and liquor before embedding itself in the wall.

The heavy ball that Hamish had fired hit the man just to the left of his nose, underneath his eye. His head recoiled under the impact as the deadly metal orb narrowly skimmed underneath his eye socket, passed through his brain and exited the back of his skull. Its energy still potent, it came to rest deep in a wooden post behind him.

The man's body flailed, his arms leaping up in a reflex spasm of death. He then he fell to the ground in a heap. Blood was seeping from the acorn sized hole in the front of his skull. Meanwhile, his brains slopped out through the apple sized hole at the back.

Hamish glanced down at the hands before him on the countertop and congratulated himself on how real they looked. Hamish had once accepted these imitation hands and forearms as part payment of a drinking debt from a member of a travelling theatre. He had correctly surmised that, one day, they would come in useful.

By this juncture, the other man, who was seated, had brought his hidden pistol out from under the table and was in the process of raising it to fire. Having dispensed Ruby, Hamish was already squeezing the trigger of Rose. He had the advantage of pre-aiming both guns, with deadly accuracy, while his hands had been covered by the heavy cotton towel he used for wiping the bar. There was a bright flash as the sparking drum threw burning sparks into the powder pan, then a soft *'whoomph'* as the ignition was passed into the pistol's body. The main charge promptly erupted with a cloud of smoke, forcing the lead ball out and sending it towards its target.

The man began to lurch to the side, vainly seeking shelter from the wooden pillar beside him. He had nowhere near the second and a half available to him, that this action demanded. Hamish could see the blurred trail of the ball as it passed through the air and knew, by every instinct he could muster, that observing it like this should really be impossible. Nonetheless, he was able to calmly plot the path of the deadly sphere and predict the point of impact. He could be certain that the shot would hit the man in the heart.

As the villain desperately tried to avoid his fate, the pistol ball struck a billowing fold in his coat, created as the material lagged behind the momentum of his frantic sideways motion. Hamish stared, both fascinated and appalled, as the fabric first compressed against the man's chest, then began to rip and tatter under the impact. At a dawdling pace, a hole began to appear at the centre of several concentric rings of a shockwave that made the air pulse outwards like the ripples on a pond as a stone drops into it. The fabric shredded into pieces as it caved into the wound that was opening in the man's chest.

It seemed just like he had been struck by the tip of an invisible hammer. Blood exploded outwards, spraying in a perfect circle. The centre of the swirl of material hung for a moment, suspended in the air, then retreated into the cavity, as it followed the wake of the ball exiting through the man's back.

His lifeless body tumbled to the ground like a rag doll thrown by a petulant child. It crashed backwards, thudding onto the wooden floorboards with a wet splash as the gaping wound in his back, the size of a man's fist, spilled out his bodily contents. Tattered flesh and heart tissue exited along with white fragments of shattered shoulder blade and ribs. His weapon, which he had not had time to fire, spun on the ground beside him, mocking his demise. His head came to rest in a seeping pool of blood. The staring, lifeless eyes were wide open, still registering the shock of his final moments.

The air was thick with a blueish, acrid cloud of burnt powder from Hamish's, still smoking, pistols. The diligent and scrupulous care that Hamish now applied to cleaning his guns was matched only by the blatant disregard he paid to the two corpses on the floor.

"Now that was a fearful sound!" He declared, as if conversing with the dead men.

The remaining customers in the bar, drank up their ale, paying scant attention to the dead bodies. They exchanged remarks and opinions, in hushed voices, some dismissive, some scornful and others filled with contempt. Then, they all hurried out. If the Rangers attended to enquire about the shooting, none of them wanted to be there.

Hamish called to the serving girl, who was peeping round the edge of the door to the kitchen, and she came back into the room.

"I have a special cleaning job for you!" He told her, "Your admirer and his friend have caused a bit of a mess."

With a graceful flick of his hand, Hamish threw her a coin in a high arc and she caught it, snatching it out of the air. Her look of approval, when she appraised the coin in her hand, confirmed him as a generous employer.

Looking confused, Alex Brennan rushed in, carrying his boots, one in each hand.

"I heard shots," he said, "Is everything okay?"

Alex noticed Hamish looking down at his bare feet.

"In the hurry, I didn't manage to get my boots on!" Alex explained.

Hamish looked at the young man and saw the pistol tucked into the waistband of his britches. He was gratified that his guest was not intending to be just a witness.

"Well, you can take your time, now," Hamish told him.

Alex suddenly noticed the two bodies.

"I'm guessing you won't be sending for The Watch?" He smirked.

Hamish laughed and carried on attending to Ruby and Rose. With loving care, he dabbed a little gun oil into the firing mechanism of one of the pistols. With a delicacy that was at odds with his bulk and size, he loaded the little brush with more oil, dipping it into the pot beside him, and repeated the action with its partner.

Alex, still in bare feet, dragged the two corpses from where they lay and arranged them by the door. Hamish looked up and nodded to confirm that the bodies would be fine left there. Maisie thanked Alex for his exertions and set about cleaning up the blood.

Hamish suddenly froze. The hairs on the back of his neck prickled. There was something wrong. He glanced up and caught his breath. Alex dropped into a 'ready for conflict' stance, his knees very slightly bent, his back upright, and moved his hand to the grip of his pistol.

Within a second, there was a crash and the door to the bar flew open. Somebody had delivered it a hefty kick. The door slammed back to the extreme of its hinges and the frame shook. A man appeared with a pair of pistols drawn and levelled. The man looked to be every bit as vile and nasty as the two brutes who had just been despatched.

Hamish sucked in a breath. The man took a step into the room. His eyes took in the two dead men and then flashed to Maisie, who was scrubbing blood from the floorboards. Hamish watched in fascination as the rapid rhythm of Maisie's to-and-fro brush strokes gave the illusion of becoming slower and slower. All around the bar, time appeared to decelerate to a crawl. The man's gaze passed, with exquisite sluggishness, first to Hamish and then across to Alex.

Alex began to draw his pistol. The man fired at him with the weapon in his left hand. There was a flash, then a loud bang as smoke belched from its muzzle. This was, followed by a finger of flame, as a lead ball sped from it.

There was another loud explosion as Alex fired his own weapon. He had brought it up and into position at blistering speed. From the corner of his eye, Hamish saw the kick as Alex' pistol discharged its round.

With fascinating slowness, Hamish watched the man's eyes as they turned back to him. They were like the dull eyes of a shark. He had seen many sharks, in his time at sea, and they always seemed to have no soul behind their eyes. Hamish heard the loud report of the stranger's other pistol as it was fired at him.

Like raindrops making their way leisurely, down a windowpane, the two spheres of lead, one fired by the imposter and one by Alex, passed each other in the air. Alex turned sideways, minimising himself as a target, as he dropped to the ground. Reaching up, his hand travelling at a dawdling pace, he put his fingers under the edge of the counter and pushed with all his might to accelerate his fall.

Hamish saw the lead sphere jump from the attacker's gun and surge in his direction. Grasping a large knife from under the counter, Hamish had just managed to get it level with the top of it when the man had fired. With huge effort, Hamish hurled the knife, horizontally, his knuckles brushing across the polished wood.

Alex saw the little ball of death approach and was relieved to see that it was about to miss him. The ball grazed the sleeve of his shirt, ruffling the fabric in its passage, and thudded into the wall behind him. He heard Maisie scream. She lifted an arm to shield herself as she crouched down, pressing further to the ground. Her other arm came back, making ready to hurl the brush she was holding.

Hamish grunted as the lead ball that was coming his way hummed through the air. Seeing the object on a line for his head, he swung his head down and to the side and the deadly ball passed within a thumb's breadth of his ear. He heard the clatter and tinkling of glass as more bottles on the shelf behind him dissolved into tiny shards.

The man in the doorway spun sideways, dropping to his knees. Hamish's knife glanced his neck and stuck in the wall behind him. The wound it had inflicted was superficial. With incredible sluggishness, the man released hold of the pistol in his right hand and began to move his hand to reach under his jacket.

Alex' pistol ball was on target to strike the man's temple, but – as fate would have it – he was already lifting his head to dodge the brush that Masie had thrown at him. The shot passed through the tip of his nose, instead. There was a shower of blood and a blurred crimson trail followed the pistol ball as it buried itself into a wooden rail. The assailant's jacket flapped open to reveal a holster over and around his shoulder. His fingers grasped a small pistol and both Hamish and Alex watched in horror as the act of withdrawing it engaged a small catch that slid open the charge pan, making it ready to fire.

The man began to lift the new weapon upwards in Hamish's direction. Hamish was slumping onto the bar as his body followed through from the momentum of throwing the knife. He was horrified to see that he was going to land, sprawled on the counter, exactly where the man was beginning to aim.

Hamish tried to push himself away as he fell, but it was too late. He grappled to obtain some kind of purchase on the edge of the counter but was thwarted by its slippery surface. He mentally cursed his wife for taking such pride in this beautiful slab of wood, which – in its previous life – had been a Captain's table aboard a schooner. His heart fell as he saw the barrel of the little pistol align with his eyes.

Abruptly, the stranger's head shuddered and, for some inexplicable reason, suddenly dipped to the side and slammed into the door frame with a sickening crunch. The pistol dropped from his grasp as a peculiar clang echoed like the striking of some weird kind of bell. Hamish's mind feverishly scrambled to identify the sound, only finding success as he glimpsed the object that had hit the man's skull. It was a spade. The weird sound now made sense!

The spade, having been withdrawn, now descended for a second time, smashing into the man's spine at the back of his neck. There was a brutal snapping sound and the victim's writhing body suddenly lay still. Alex, Hamish and Maisie looked down at the dead body, crumpled against the door, and then up at the person now standing in the doorway behind it.

Caitlan Pottle held the spade aloft in one hand, the way a triumphant gladiator might hold a spear. Nodding scornfully at the corpse, she loudly voiced her fury.

"He didn't wipe his feet on the mat!"

CHAPTER 13

Annis steered her horse off the shoreline of the river and up the bank to higher ground. The edge of the water had become rockier and the margin of sand sufficient for a horse had petered out.

Bobbins, the queen's newly appointed squire, had adorned her mount with a few discreet ribbons and had platted her tail. He now paced around nearby, waiting for his next opportunity to be of use.

The Grant army – for an army it was, and one of over four hundred men – were fanned out along the meadows and woodlands a good way back from the river. The regular soldiers were positioned in the forward ranks, impressive in their better garb, their more prolific armour and much superior weaponry. The smallholders and crofters, who were called to arms, had taken position behind them and were more often carrying pitchforks, clubs and scythes than swords and shields.

The look that Balgair and Gavin had exchanged, on seeing these assembled troops, was unambiguous.

"I am surprised and dismayed," Balgair announced, "That the Clan Grant has brought with them such a large fighting force."

"Aye," Gavin agreed, "They were prepared for serious conflict."

"There is, nonetheless, a feeling of cheerfulness and good will about them."

"I think we all share it. Avoiding a battle and its toll in lives is a powerful reason for happiness."

"It goes beyond that for them," Gavin observed, "A feud that had lasted eight centuries had been resolved."

"And, with it, history's judgement of them as traitors who had betrayed their rescuers."

"The deed that was done still remains, unchanged, but – in fairness to the living – those who did that deed have been dead and buried for a very long time."

"Yes," Balgair conceded, "But the knowledge that it was Kiffan The Defiant who gave them safety from future attacks by the Vikings has humbled them and changed their hearts."

"We had better catch up with her descendant before she thinks that we have abandoned her," said Gavin, much to Balgair's amusement, as he pointed towards Queen Annis up ahead of them.

Annis had ridden a fair way into the fields that bordered the Spey, across a ridge and down to the point where a stream flowed into the river. She pulled up her horse next to the water and turned to Gavin and Balgair, who both promptly rode to her.

"This is far enough," she declared.

Gavin and Balgair both agreed.

From further up the field, The Laird Grant rode down to join them and drew his horse parallel to theirs. He was without his close guards, who had stopped a good distance away from them, and was accompanied by only two of his consorts and they were content to trail a fair way behind him.

"I regret that a long time has passed," the laird remarked, "Since the last time you could ride through here in perfect safety and with no fear of attack."

"This is true," the Queen of the West agreed.

"I know that you have a far greater force in reserve, Your Majesty, than the one you have brought with you, today, and I know that your biggest force, still an hour's march away, includes a substantial number of mounted troops."

The queen remained expressionless, despite her mind being in turmoil. When, exactly, she wondered, had Balgair been planning to tell her that he trailed such a massive deployment of soldiers in his wake? It was a force of far greater size than anything she would have imagined.

"Your apparent display of weakness," The Grant continued, "Is actually a profound demonstration of your true strength."

"I will not insult you," Annis confided, smiling sweetly, "By suggesting that your monitoring of our approach was not a wise precaution on your part."

The laird smiled back.

"I came to cross the river," she confessed, "Believing, beyond any shadow of doubt, that you would rather flee as fast as the wind would carry you, than capture me and hold me prisoner, when – with such a small escort – I was so obviously coming in peace."

"You are right. For I would have loathed to have had further shame to live down!" he observed, bitterly, "But we might have parted you from your closest army, then left you and attacked only them."

Annis sighed. She was simply glad that the confrontation was over.

"As we speak," The Grant said, "Both of our forces are most certainly being watched. I have neighbours along my borders who will be yet unaware of my new status as someone who is now at peace with you."

"It will not please them," said Gavin.

"Please them or displease them," The Grant replied, "I will at least be able to hold my head up."

Annis raised her hand to halt the conversation, uneasy that it might deteriorate. She decided, instead, to strike a more positive note.

"The Vikings had a tradition," she said, "They used to break the head off an axe and burn the handle in a fire to put a conflict behind them. Maybe we should do the same?"

Balgair suddenly sat bolt upright on his horse and turned to them with utter horror written across his face. He stared at the Laird Grant with an expression of shock and alarm.

Annis and The Grant shared a worried look.

"An axe!" Balgair blurted.

With this, he sprang from his saddle and hurled himself to his knees in front of the Laird Grant's horse. Ripping his sword from his belt, he thrust it into the ground, still in its scabbard. The Grant and his consorts jerked in alarm and Annis saw them overcome a forceful urge to draw their weapons.

"The Lady Elise!" Balgair cried, as if this were full explanation.

The Grant cocked his head to the side enquiringly while Annis anxiously looked around, thinking he might, perhaps, be announcing the arrival of a newcomer.

"The Lady Elise Grant was slain by an axe," Balgair said, bowing his head low, his voice trembling, "She was slain most foully by an axe wielded by a McRory, Your Lairdship."

The Grant looked down at him, dumbfounded, as if he had just claimed that flapping his arms could make him fly.

"There was a truce," Balgair went on, "A truce between the Grants and the McRorys, but a McRory party violated it by crossing the river and riding up into the Dappled Woods. It is written and recorded. It is known."

The Grant looked at Balgair incredulously as his confession continued.

"They came across someone on horseback. They took them to be a messenger, for they were dressed in such a manner. To stop that rider getting away and raising the alarm, one of our number threw an axe. It hit the messenger in the neck, at the base of their skull and killed them outright," he made a choking noise of grief, "The rider, it was later learned, was the Lady Elise of Clan Grant."

Annis watched The Grant's face and, instead of anger or outrage, it took on a look of tender indulgence, like a parent hearing a child recount a distressing nightmare.

Balgair reached for his sword, but withdrew only a short measure of it before, inoffensively, grasping the blade between thumb and forefinger to release what remained. Having extracted the whole of it, in that calculatedly unthreatening manner, he stood and offered it to The Grant by its hilt. Balgair then removed his helmet and knelt upright on his knees with his head bowed, deliberately and ceremoniously exposing his neck.

The Grant shook his head and gave a long, anguished sigh.

"This was over fifty years ago," he said.

"We wronged you," Balgair declared, emphatically, "We wronged you most grievously and we did not set ourselves to account. We let **our** misdeed fade, to be forgotten, while – year on year – we rebuked and reviled you for yours!"

"And?" Asked the laird.

"And we must absolve our wrong with blood."

"Your blood?"

"Yes."

All at once, Annis felt sure that she had full stock of this Laird Grant, as she watched the scene unfold.

"Tell me why?" The Grant asked Balgair.

"A rift has been healed, today. The past has been addressed. You stand on the threshold of a new future. My clan has wronged you by murdering one of your high bloods during a truce. By doing so, we have brought shame upon ourselves, upon the queen and upon The MacDonald."

The Laird Grant took the offered sword, held it out at arm's length and let it fall, point first, to skewer itself into the ground. Then he dismounted and, placing his hands under Balgair's arms, lifted him to his feet. The Grant turned to his two companions and – while she could not see his expression – she saw the other two Grants shake their heads solemnly in response.

"It is decided," The Laird Grant told him, "That we do not want your blood to atone for this misdeed, especially not today."

Balgair did not look like a man who had been spared, but a man who had been robbed.

"You, as a McRory, bring your clan great honour and bring great credit to your queen and to the Laird MacDonald by your honesty and integrity," The Grant told him, "To be frank, it refreshes my faith in humankind to see such a noble action, but your people are in no way tarnished by her death for there is something about that day that you could not possibly have known."

Balgair looked plainly puzzled. The Grant took the sword from the ground and raised Balgair's hand to receive it, wrapping the cavalryman's fingers around its handle to make him grip it.

"It cleanses my wounds," The Grant admitted, "And salves my soul to think that anybody else should be so tormented by a wrong committed in the past. Your wrong, however, is but a drop of water compared to the ocean of our own."

"We slew a Grant. There was a truce. It was an act of treachery," Balgair protested.

The Grant stood, for a long moment, looking up into the clouds. It was not clear if he sought inspiration or consolation. Eventually, he abruptly turned back to Balgair with an urgent question.

"The Clan McRory turned up to fight at our side at the Battle of Kirriemuir and then, again, at the Battle of Kingussie. Your soldiers were important in turning things in our favour. That was a strange thing to happen, don't you think?"

The Grant waited for a reply, but Balgair did not answer. Instead, he shrugged his shoulders and then shook his head, apologetically. The Grant's attitude remained sympathetic and conciliatory.

"I'm sure that if somebody cannot admit their wrong to the people they wronged," The Grant declared, "Then making amends in some other way, like that, must go a long way to easing their conscience."

The Grant laid his hand on Balgair's shoulder.

"I regret that, in our case, we Grants chose to be hostile and resentful after our wrongdoing. We nursed a hatred that smouldered in our souls. It was a hatred that proved too much to bear for my grandmother, the Lady Elise."

The Grant wrung his hands.

"Your McRory men mistook my grandmother for a messenger and that is understandable since that is exactly how she was dressed," said The Grant, "But they could not have known what a kindness they did her. Their killing of Lady Elise Grant prevented her from suffering a prolonged and painful death for, unbeknown to them, she had taken a slow and dreadful poison."

Annis, Balgair and Gavin all looked surprised.

"My Grandmother was a deeply religious woman. She carried a messenger's bag and wore a messenger's garb because, in her mind, she was a messenger from our clan to God, on her final journey. She carried a message of shame and regret for our clan's betrayal of Kiffan. It was a shame and regret that eventually destroyed her. She stowed her crucifix, her rosary and her bible in her messenger's satchel, along with consecrated bread and wine from the Holy Communion she had just celebrated, and then drank a draught of poison before setting off for the woods."

The Grant's face looked as if it were carved from stone.

"My father followed her, staying carefully hidden. She had forbidden him from intervening and had made him swear to it on oath. He saw her slain and told me that he wanted to burst from his hiding place and hug the McRory who threw the axe. He would have done so, too, he said, if he had not feared being killed or taken hostage himself."

None of them spoke as The Grant fell silent. Nobody wanted to interrupt his grief. The Grant's lips contorted as he mulled over his dark recollections. His mind, captured by the pull of their morbid spell, blocking out everything around him. At last, he returned to the present, looking up as if waking from a dream.

"My Grandmother wanted to present herself to the Queen of the West and give her life as a penance for our betrayal of Kiffan. My father had become laird, when her husband died, and he – as Head of the Clan – would not allow it. He wouldn't even let her speak of it. He flew into a rage. He regarded the descendants of the Brydda as his enemy. I'm sure that it was a far easier way to deal with the past than by admitting to it."

The Grant filled his lungs and let out the air as a long, weary sigh.

"If my grandmother had known that Queen Kiffan had bestowed protection upon us from the Vikings, I am certain – completely and utterly certain – that she would have gone on her mission, anyway. She would have found the Queen of the West and would have carried out her plan to give her own life."

The Grant shook his head slowly, pressed his lips into a thin line and looked back to the other two closest riders.

"I have struggled, my whole life, with this whole miserable business but I have shielded my son from any part of it," he said, jabbing his thumb over his shoulder towards the younger of the two riders behind them.

Queen Annis and her two consorts shared a glance of dawning comprehension at this unexpected insight.

"Your revelations, Your Majesty," said The Grant, bowing to Annis, "Came as shock enough to me, even with my prior knowledge of our crime, but it has been a potent and devastating blow to my son. He had not even the slightest inkling of these matters."

Annis bit back her urge to apologise, accepting that it would be an inappropriate thing to do.

The Grant turned to his two senior clansmen – these being his son and Gordon, his close advisor – and gestured to them with a flick of the wrist, a twirl of his hand, followed by a flat, forward motion with his palm. A few moments later, an approximation of the signal was passed back to the two soldiers in the near distance. They, likewise, passed it on to the assembled Grant troops in the fields beyond. Before long, a series of short notes were blown, several times over, by a piper. In response, the whole cordon of troops turned, about face, and moved off about twenty paces before coming to a staggered stop, still with their backs turned.

His senior clansmen had remained where they were and the two soldiers, a few paces behind them, had not moved, either. The Grant summoned them to approach.

"Pass word to my army," he told them, "That any man who turns without an order will have their throat cut and their family sold into slavery."

The Grant gestured to the two soldiers, sternly, and they moved off to the end of the field with obvious reluctance. It troubled Annis, greatly, to contemplate what he was about to do that he did not want his people to witness and in which he did not want his troops to intervene.

"Your Majesty," began The Grant, "The blood that ran through the veins of Kiffan the Defiant runs through your veins, just as the blood of all my people before me runs through mine."

With this, he slowly drew his sword and kissed it at its cross-piece.

"I absolve your McRory captain and his clan for the blood on his family's hands, Your Highness, but I cannot absolve myself for the blood on mine. I must stand and give account for our wrong as my grandmother would have done had she known what I know, now."

Annis raised her hand, staying him for a moment.

"We are living in dangerous times, Laird Grant," she said, her voice carrying both authority and compassion, "Times that demand we choose between the grudges of the past and our survival in the future. Your grandmother's generation made their choices. Now we must make ours."

The Laird Grant gestured for Balgair to get back onto his horse. Balgair, bowed deeply and saluted before mounting. The Grant waited until he was back in his saddle before continuing.

"My ancestors lived their lives, if unknowingly, under the protection of your ancestors, who would become the Queens of the West. This being so, we must pay back for that historic betrayal. It happened eight hundred years gone, but it smudges our honour more greatly, today, than ever in the past."

In the same gesture of supplication that Balgair had used to him, The Grant bowed his head and offered his sword to Annis, then fell to his knees, his body upright and neck exposed.

"My Queen," The Grant said, with sombre tone.

Annis stiffened, visibly, for she knew the huge implication of his addressing her by that title. She knew, without a doubt, the consequences that could arise from it. If he were to formally declare her to be his queen and his clan were to recognise her as such, the formal boundary of her sovereignty would extend beyond the traditional five paces from the far bank of the River Spey.

Annis turned to her left, without looking directly at Balgair, and she could feel his sadness and solemnity. She turned to her right, placing Gavin within her peripheral vision, and he, too, exuded a wave of sorrow. She could also sense the tension and anxiety of them both, for they both knew that the two words 'My Queen' carried momentous weight and significance.

The heaviness of the moment hung in the air like an anvil suspended above their heads.

The leader of Clan Grant was offering her his life as her retribution, but, were she to accept it, she would likely put his son on a course of hatred and venom that would match, or even exceed, the woes of the past.

"I want you to live," said Annis, plainly and simply.

The Grant got to his feet and kissed the cross-piece of his sword, again, before turning it sideways and, once more, offering it to her.

Annis felt her heart crumple within her chest. The leader of Clan Grant, his life having been spared, now offered her, as an alternative, not just his allegiance, but his absolute fealty. Annis wanted to groan but did not allow herself. If she were crazed and demented enough to accept the formal obedience of this man, it would likely spark a war with the clans that bordered her lands both to the East and to the South.

She knew this to be an impossible dilemma to which there was no real solution. Whatever she did, she risked sending a wave of disruption and conflict across the Highlands and down into the Lowlands. He offered to die, which would have been disastrous. To be alive as her subject, she realised, could be every bit as disastrous.

Annis watched the Laird Grant as he knelt and she wished, with all her heart, that this moment could pass without her having to make a choice between two versions of potential calamity.

Her blood suddenly chilled. If her frontiers expanded and war ensued, that would not be the end of it! King James would be unable to endure such turmoil and would be compelled to intervene. The troops he would march to quell them, under such a circumstance, would not simply be those from Scotland, but the Red Coats from England!

CHAPTER 14

Janine watched carefully, with a critical eye, as the maid dressed her. She had, herself, dressed the lady of the house at Dunkeld Manor hundreds of times, making her familiarity with the routine absolute. She was pleased that the girl followed a similar methodical process and was impressed by her meticulous care.

"You bring great credit to this house with your skill and abilities," Janine told her, "You have a genuine flair and talent."

The young woman's face lit up and she squirmed with delight, thanking Janine profusely.

The idea of dressing for dinner had always puzzled Janine and struck her as a needless distraction. It was an activity that seemed only to hinder the evening by prolonging and delaying it. Now that she was the one being dressed, however, she began to appreciate the ritual of it and the undeniable pleasure. She made a mental note to mention this observation if she saw Lady Dunkeld, again. Then she smiled to herself at the absurdity of such a thought, having no idea – under the present circumstances – if she would ever see anybody that she knew, again.

"If I may, My Lady, I would like to show you a dress for your consideration," said the maid.

"Yes, of course. Thank you."

The dress that had been conjured up for Janine to wear was a perfect fit. She contemplated whether the dress might have been left behind by a previous visitor. It was either that, she supposed, or she might be the same size as another guest or relative of her hosts. This possibility then led her to imagine the awkwardness and embarrassment that would arise if she were to encounter its owner, in person! She decided to chase this notion to the back of her mind and resolved to rely upon the owner sharing the same all-pervading charm and courtesy that appeared to be common to everyone at Brech Woorlach.

"Oh!" Said Janine, a thought suddenly coming into her head.

"What is it?" Enquired the maid, looking worried.

"The boy who arrived with me – Callum is his name – I was wondering how he fares."

"He will be well treated, I assure you, My Lady."

"Good," Janine replied, sounding distinctly unconvinced.

"I could make enquiries, if you wish."

"Would you mind?"

"It would be no trouble at all, My Lady," cooed the maid, crossing to a tasselled cord by the fireplace and tugging it gently.

Within no time at all, a page boy's head poked around the door. The maid explained his mission to him and he darted off to accomplish it.

"Would it be convenient, My Lady, if I were to attend to your hair?" Asked the maid.

"Yes, of course. I would be extremely grateful."

"It would be my pleasure, My Lady."

The maid quickly set about her task and, before very long, was putting the final touches to Janine's hair, twisting a long, individual strand to hang, at either side of her face, from ear to shoulder. The maid's look of intense concentration was profound and Janine found herself transfixed by it. The girl looked up, shyly, as she caught Janine's gaze. Janine smiled at her, reassuringly, and received a smile in return.

Without having willed herself to speak, Janine heard her own voice ask a question she had not properly considered.

"What is your name?"

The last syllable had scarcely left her tongue before she realised the absurdity of the question. The girl was a nobody, to all intents and purposes. She was a servant. She had a job to do. She did her job. That was it. Her personality, wishes, likes and dislikes were immaterial.

The girl hesitated for a second, palpably refocusing her attention, before giving a reply that conveyed far more confidence that she had expected.

"Francesca," she replied, "I am Francesca, Your Ladyship."

'She must be a very senior maid, to be so self-assured,' Janine thought, *'Perhaps even a personal maid to the Duchess.'*

Janine mentally chastised herself for having such a thought and wondered how it was that she could have slipped into such a frame of mind.

Francesca gave the politest little cough to attract Janine's attention. When she had it, she led Janine across the room to an ornate little table with a marble top and twisted legs and sat her down on a matching chair with a heart shaped back.

"Would you lay your hands flat on the wooden surface, Your Ladyship?"

Janine instantly complied. With quiet efficiency, Francesca withdrew several wide, flat boxes from hidden drawers in the table. The drawers were so perfectly blended into the surface of the table that they appeared not to be there at all, unless a person knew exactly where to press to access them.

Francesca took Janine's left hand and, employing her full range of accessories, she filed and pampered her nails until she had achieved a look of manicured excellence. She then repeated the same process with Janine's right hand. Once both were finished, she retrieved some bottles from another cunningly disguised drawer and proceeded to paint Janine's fingernails.

As she worked, Francesca made no attempt to provoke conversation, content to apply herself to her job wordlessly. Janine said nothing and simply watched. For once, she was a spectator. With fascination, she followed the process that she, herself, had performed for others so many countless times before.

Janine could not fail to notice that Francesca's own nails were completely flawless. She kept them to an immaculate standard that was, in fact, so perfect as to be almost incongruous with her position. After weighing up this observation in her head for a little while, she dismissed it, telling herself that perhaps the girl was simply in a habit of practising on herself in order to hone her skills. If this were the case, she decided, then Francesca had simply forgotten about them and overlooked their strikingly glamorous appearance.

Although neither party spoke, the atmosphere was entirely pleasant, with no sense of unease whatsoever. Janine was so relaxed, in fact, that — had she closed her eyes — she was sure that she would have easily fallen asleep. The company of this girl was inexplicably enjoyable.

Lulled into such a peaceful state, Janine didn't, at first, hear Francesca when she spoke.

"Does my work meet with your approval, Your Ladyship?" She asked, again.

"Yes," Janine replied, "The result is nothing less than beautiful."

Francesca smiled, very happy to receive such generous praise. She regarded her handiwork with pride and satisfaction and then invited Janine to return to the previous chair.

Once she was installed there, Francesca lifted her hand to cover her mouth and made a clicking sound. This was evidently a signal, for there was a soft knock at the door and another maid came in. The new girl was plainly of lower rank and bowed her head to Francesca with deference. Without ceremony or introduction, the new arrival sat herself down on the carpet and took off Janine's slippers. Deftly, gently and with practised skill she set about rubbing lotion from a porcelain flask into Janine's feet.

The feeling of being so pampered was exquisite and the hands working her toes and soles were highly accomplished. Without meaning to do it, Janine arched her back and let out a little sigh. Francesca gave Janine the merest flicker of a confidential smile and then laughed softly as Janine rolled her eyes in mock ecstasy.

Janine's mind spun and whirled as she processed the events since her arrival. She made a careful mental note that the staff at Brech Woorlach were different. It was an inarguable fact that they all had copious volumes of respect, decorum and courtesy. They behaved with impeccable manners at all times. Nonetheless, she was aware of the vaguest hint that the invisible boundary, between master and servant, seemed to be oddly diluted. It was as if that rigid wall, that she had always found to exist, was a little more vague and tenuous, here.

The foot massage continued until Janine felt on the brink of losing consciousness from the pleasure of it. Once it was over, the junior maid opened a little wicker basket and arranged a set of tiny brushes and bottles on a shiny brass platter. She then began to paint Janine's toenails.

Janine watched, mesmerised, as the girl became absorbed in her labours. Gradually, Janine became aware of a slight movement of the girl's lips, from time to time. It was as if she were reciting a list or a set of steps to herself. She seemed totally lost in what she was doing and Janine was utterly captivated to see the tip of the girl's tongue appear, poking out ever so slightly from her mouth, as she concentrated.

The beautiful shades of red and pink that were being applied were stunning in their effect. Janine was enthralled. She decided that watching the girl was like watching a skilled oil or watercolour artist painting at their easel as they created a masterpiece!

There was a tapping sound at the door and Janine felt a spasm of resentment at the intrusion. Francesca wafted across to the door to answer it and, after a brief moment of conversation, she stepped back to allow entry. Janine recognised the first person as one of the senior servants at Brech Woorlach. Behind him came Callum.

"Your Ladyship," said the servant, bowing, "I have had this young man washed, dressed and fed. I have also had his..."

The man's voice died as he decided that his words might cause offence. He gave Francesca a troubled look. Francesca gestured for him to continue, but this only made his dilemma worse.

"Speak openly," Janine demanded, "You need not guard your words."

The man's relief was only slight.

"Your Ladyship, I have had his injuries attended."

"His injuries?" Snapped Janine.

"His bruises," the man explained, visibly quaking as he did so, "and his broken finger."

Callum's face had dread and alarm written all over it. He seemed to be at the point of throwing up whatever food he had consumed. He had realised that the extent of his beatings at the hands of the butcher at Dunkeld Manor were now about to inflict shame on the woman who had delivered him from them. His vivid imagination came to his rescue.

"My kidnappers beat me badly!" He blurted.

By some miracle of self-control, Janine found herself able to quell her astonishment at this "revelation" and managed to keep any reaction away from her face.

"I know that they kept you in shabby conditions, but you did not tell me that they had harmed you."

"I thought you would be angry," he exclaimed, willing her to join him in the deception.

"Angry? I am furious!" Janine growled, clenching her fists, "But it is with them, not with you. I would like to have the ones who did this to you whipped until they are at the very brink of death!"

Callum knew that she meant the butcher.

"I fought back, but..."

"Stop!" Janine urged, holding up a hand to silence him, fearing what kind of fantasy might emerge from his mouth, "You have done nothing wrong. There is no need to explain."

Callum looked disappointed. He was, as she had suspected, about to concoct an epic adventure in which he was the daring, death-defying hero.

"I have had our physician attend him," the servant announced, "And the very finest ointments and lotions have been applied, with no expense spared."

"Thank you. My mind is set at rest."

"If there is anything else that I can do for you, Your Ladyship?"

Janine shook her head and Francesca waved him away with her hand. The servant bowed and Callum, following his example, did the same. As the door gently closed behind the visitors, work promptly resumed on Janine's feet.

The girl who was knelt before her reached into her basket and, with great care, took out a small glass tube with a long, thin brush embedded into the underside of its stopper. Cautiously, the container was opened and the brush rotated in its contents with scrupulous care. Janine was intrigued to see what this substance, so worthy of reverence, might be. To her horror, she realised that it was gold!

Immediately, Janine became conscious of the senior maid studying her face. This, she regretted, clearly illustrated the sudden spasm of panic she had felt. Her expression, without doubt, had just said: *'Surely, it is only prostitutes at high class salons in Paris, Milan or London who had their feet tended quite **this** lavishly!'*

For the briefest moment, she felt Francesca's hand rest on her shoulder and squeeze, reassuringly.

Janine peered, cautiously, down at her feet, looking for all the world like a woman who feared that she had grown flippers! Francesca joined her in the scrutiny of the junior maid's work. Janine's toenails gleamed and glistened richly with sumptuous luxury and – here and there – with tiny, subtle embellishments of gold.

Francesca said a few quiet words to the girl at her feet, using English interspersed with some Gaelic. The softness of her tone was gentle and encouraging and the girl looked up, adoringly, at her. Janine was puzzled. Suddenly, she realised that the girl kneeling at her feet had mental faculties that were far short of her years. She possessed a mind that had failed to grow and mature like most. Janine's heart melted with affection for her.

Francesca did not look away from her junior, but – powerfully and invisibly – Janine could sense that she had detected and approved of "Her Ladyship's" compassion for this young unfortunate.

Janine smiled warmly at the crouching girl and, as she fastened a pair of lovely sandals to her feet, she reached to touch her cheek.

"I'm fit to meet a queen, now!" Janine declared.

The girl looked immediately alarmed, her gaze dropping to the floor as she shifted nervously, no longer willing to meet Janine's eyes.

"What's wrong?" Janine enquired, with genuine concern in her voice.

The girl fidgeted, tugging at her little decorative apron, curling and uncurling the corner of it between her finger and thumb. Francesca motioned for the girl to say nothing, but it was to no avail.

"The duke and duchess are most strict about speaking of the queen. We must guard our tongues," she whispered anxiously, "Many don't believe in her, they say she's just a children's tale, but some wicked people would like to do her harm!"

Despite being stood slightly to Janine's rear, Francesca's excruciating embarrassment was tangible and, evidently feeling perturbed, she hurriedly provided what seemed a patently implausible explanation for the obscure outburst she had just witnessed.

The sweet, charming girl at her feet appeared flustered, too, and Francesca uttered soothing words to comfort her. Finally convinced that there was nothing wrong, the girl was allowed to take her leave, her innocent smile now back on her pretty face.

Janine was thoroughly puzzled. The girl had spoken of a queen. The monarch was a king. He was King James of Scotland and of England. The girl was of simple mind, but surely she would be able to distinguish the difference between a king and a queen? What else had she said? *'Some people think she is a children's tale?'* What a strange thing to say?

Janine pushed the thoughts from her mind and picked up a hand mirror from the decorative table beside her. It was a finely crafted item, decorated with pearls and obviously very expensive. She first used it to assess her hair and makeup, appreciatively, before casually turning it to frame Francesca in its reflection.

Rather than being caught by surprise, Francesca did not flinch. She was, once more, thoroughly composed and merely smiled demurely. Janine could not help but like this young woman and allowed herself to study her with undisguised curiosity. As she met Francesca's eyes, her heart missed a beat. How could a complete stranger feel so very familiar to her?

Janine scrutinised Francesca's brown eyes with their distinct green hue, then her flowing brown hair that shone – almost glowed – with red highlights, then her full lips (rouged with subtle delicacy and great restraint) and, finally, her long, elegant neck. Any man would regard her as extremely beautiful.

Janine was fascinated to note that Francesca stood patiently, in the way that horses tended to stand – tolerantly and indulgently – as they were being combed and groomed. As Janine gazed, with brazen fascination, Francesca slowly turned her head first to the left and then, after a pause, slowly back to the right. Then she raised her chin to look slightly upwards. There was no mistaking that she was actively facilitating Janine's appraisal of her.

A bell rang in the distance. Janine's heart missed a beat for a second time. The sound seemed to come from down the corridor at the head of the stairs. She found its soft, melodic tinkling oddly familiar. It abruptly transported her, for an instant, to a zone of utter peace and calm. Its duration was a mere second, but the feeling of tranquillity it had induced was completely overwhelming.

Inexplicably, Francesca was now in front of her rather than behind her. Janine's mind did a backwards flip! Only a moment had passed, yet Francesca had unquestionably changed positions. Could it be that her fleeting transportation had not been just for a second? Janine closed her eyes and took a deep breath. When she opened them again, much to her relief, Francesca had not moved anywhere else.

Janine was certain that her agitation must be apparent and, this being so, she waited for the inevitable enquiry as to her welfare from the ever attentive Francesca. Much to Janine's surprise, Francesca said nothing. The question never came. It was as if her behaviour had been nothing unusual or out of the ordinary. In fact, ludicrously enough, it was as if it had been predictable.

Janine stood up, drew herself to her full height, and looked Francesca, full in the eyes. Francesca did not waver and looked back calmly and dispassionately.

After a few moments, she addressed Janine with polite civility.

"It is time for Dinner, Your Ladyship."

There was another soft, polite knock at the door. Francesca breezed across and opened it. Bruce and Brian were stood there. Francesca bade them enter and they both bowed to Janine before addressing her.

"May we have the honour of escorting you to Dinner, My Lady?" Brian enquired.

Janine happily accepted the offer, moving to the door, and the two brothers each took one of her elbows in their white gloved hands. With a tall, handsome man on either side of her, she was taken ceremoniously down the sweeping curve of the marble stairs, lavishly decorated with finely carved wooden panels and into the luxurious dining room. As they entered, Brian reluctantly relinquished Janine to his brother, letting go of her arm as if he were giving up the crown jewels.

The room was bright and airy. There were tall windows stretching from floor to ceiling along the length of one wall. Each window had sumptuous crimson curtains hung to the left and right, decorated with golden edging and fat golden tassels. At intervals along the opposite wall there were huge and impressive portraits of noteworthy ancestors of the Duke and Duchess of Bo'Ness, their ornate gold frames glinting in the lamplight.

In the centre of the room stood a long table. The table was utterly spectacular but, at the same time, classically understated. Its surface was of the deepest cherry red and was adorned along its sides with scenes of cherubs and angels embracing, and more of them climbing the stout spiral vines that formed its columned legs.

Servants stood at several points on both sides of the magnificent table, ready to greet arriving guests. It was then that she realised that nobody else was arriving. She glanced around, slightly panicked, and looked questioningly at Bruce, who was surveying her on his arm with blatant pride. He merely smiled at her.

Her heart began to beat fast, with alarm, as it dawned on her that they were proceeding to the head of the table. A place of honour. There was ample room for more than four people, but she noticed that there were only three places set. Bruce steered her to the furthest right of the three positions and drew out the high backed, beautifully carved and upholstered chair. Janine made the slightest hint of movement to sit down and Bruce made a discrete cautionary noise through his teeth. She froze, returning to her fully upright stance. It was plain that the nearest servant must have heard the noise, but he remained resolutely impassive, his eyes fixed straight forward.

Bruce and Brian took up station opposite each other at the top most places of the table. She looked from one to the other, for reassurance – feeling like a fish out of water – and they both gave her a brief smile.

The servants, in their wonderful dark blue livery and glossy, high boots, made no move to seat the brothers and they remained standing. A little over a minute later, just as Janine had begun to feel extremely awkward with the tension, there was a bustle and a stir at the far end of the dining chamber and a man and a woman entered, side by side, holding hands.

The servants attending the table became like statues. The other servants, who were not meant to officially greet the duke and duchess, bowed their heads in respect. The duke was tall and imposing. He had both an air of authority and a distinct personal presence and walked with a lightness of foot. The woman – whom she recognised as Aunt Ailsa – oozed style, charm and femininity and appeared to float, rather than walk, as she moved. Her steps reminded Janine of a ballet dancer.

The two came to the head of the table and the duke pulled out his wife's chair and slid it under her as she sat. Bruce and Brian remained standing, so Janine did, too. A line of guests now entered and quickly stood by their places at the table. The whole table then remained motionless.

Janine looked around, a little ill at ease, and Brian caught her eye. Arching an eyebrow, he flicked his eyes to look meaningfully over her shoulder. Janine became aware that there was an anxious servant to her rear, waiting to manage her chair. Quickly regaining her poise, she turned, very deliberately, to the duke and duchess and bowed to each in turn. They both returned a gracious inclination of their heads and Janine then took her seat. Immediately, the duke, himself, sat. Bruce and Brian sat down, next, followed by the rest of those present.

Brian formed his lips into a tiny, thin-lipped smile. He had obviously been impressed by her deft recovery from the brink of social malfunction. She had managed to make it seem, to all present, as if she had simply been gauging the stillness of the room before showing her esteem to the duke and duchess.

Bruce and Brian exchanged pleasantries with their aunt and uncle while the senior servants busied themselves serving wine to the head of the table. Once this had been accomplished, their juniors performed the same service for the remaining guests.

The twins introduced Janine to the duke and duchess, claiming her to be a lady they had assisted on the road when her horse had gone lame. Janine attracted scant regard as Bruce animatedly explained how Janine's servant had supposedly abandoned her when they had been attacked by thieves and bandits, never returning after having been despatched to summon help.

The Duke leaned forward, his expression grave, "Thieves and bandits, you say? We are living in dangerous times when a lady cannot travel the roads of Scotland without such peril. The two of you did well to bring her safely to us."

The tale dramatically delivered, the duchess turned to acknowledge Janine, a charming smile on her lips. As Janine's head turned and the duchess got her first full look at her, she froze and gasped. Janine was a little startled by this reaction and dropped her gaze to the table. The duchess immediately reached out, grasping Janine by the chin, and raised her head.

The duchess quickly pulled back her hand, as if she had been scalded, abruptly releasing Janine's face. The look of astonishment she directed at Janine was stark and blatant. It was as if she were witnessing an apparition. It was as if a choir of angels had just flown in.

CHAPTER 15

Caitlan Pottle stepped over the body of the man she had just killed and stood in the doorway of the bar.

"You've been busy!" she told Hamish, seeing the other two dead bodies.

Hamish shrugged, "They wouldn't settle their ale account. I asked them twice. I had no option but to make an example of them."

Caitlan gave a disarmingly girlish giggle.

Rigging up a makeshift stretcher out of some heavy canvas and leather reins, Alex and Hamish ferried the three corpses, one at a time, out to the woods. There, a respectable distance from the back of the inn, the two men set to work digging the final resting places of their three unwelcome visitors. The ground was hard and unyielding. The depth of the hole was halfway between their ankles and their knees before it started to become easier and more workable.

"The first snows of autumn are in the air," said Hamish looking up to the darkening clouds with a scowl.

"The wind, when it blows from the mountains, has a cold that works its way to a man's bones," Alex grumbled in reply.

They continued to dig, slamming their spades into the soil and stomping their boots on their top edge to drive them deeper.

"The first two of these thugs were definitely looking for the constable," Hamish announced.

"The third, I'm guessing, was another member of their gang, meant to keep a look out."

"Aye," Hamish replied, "He won't be doing much looking from now on."

"Unless it's for worms!" Alex retorted.

After an hour of excavation, Alex and Hamish finally stopped. Dragging the bodies into the hole and arranging them side by side, they began the task of filling it back up with soil.

After a good, long while of shovelling, the two excavators both gasped loudly and paused for a rest. Sweat was streaming down their faces and necks, darkening their shirts, and making the material stick to their backs. Alex, folding his hands atop the handle of his spade, rested his chin on them and watched Hamish murmuring the words of the traditional prayer for departed souls. Reluctantly, Alex joined in.

"They were big guys," Hamish complained, after a suitable silence, "But it feels like putting the soil back is never going to end!" He paused and then quipped: "You didn't pull one of them out while my back was turned, did you?"

Alex laughed and mopped his brow.

"I still say we should have buried them one on top of the other," Alex complained, "Instead of side by side."

"It's an honour they very likely don't deserve," Hamish declared, "But it feels good to spoil them with kindness, now that they'll be no more trouble to anyone."

Alex panted and caught his breath before replying.

"They are going to be feeding nature and that's probably the best work they have done in a while!"

"Aye, you are right," Hamish agreed, "I cannot imagine that they have earned a living from any honest work for a long, long time!"

"Just so!" Alex agreed, "They are no better than mercenaries. When I was fighting with the Dutch against the Spanish, there were quite a few mercenaries on hand. They were never much welcomed by the regular troops."

With those words, he spat into the grave, contemptuously.

"Having no belief, loyalty or patriotism to motivate them in a flght," Alex observed, "Just a love of money to drive them, the Mercenaries tended to draw a good deal of contempt."

He seemed to weigh up his recollections before continuing.

"I must confess that they were good fighters, though," he conceded, "So, when the battle was raging, people quickly lost interest in their beliefs! Each man had to depend on the other when the shooting started."

"I'm of a belief," Hamish announced, "That mercenaries are mercenaries, the whole world over. Fighting for coin is basically dishonourable."

The two paused, again, and both looked around, checking in all directions to make sure they were alone in the woods and not being observed.

"If it's not the McCarthys behind these three turning up," Alex declared, "Then I would be very much surprised!"

"Aye," Hamish agreed, "They claimed Constable Burberry was a former army comrade of theirs, but I didn't believe that for a moment."

"The question is," Alex suggested, "How long will it take the McCarthys to miss these men?"

"A better question might be," Hamish countered, "Have the McCarthys already met these three ogres and sent them about their task or are they going to miss them because they never arrive?"

"More importantly still," Alex offered, "Is why didn't Constable Burberry return, last night, and did he know about these three men?"

"There is certainly no love lost between the constable and the McCarthys," Hamish mused, "Killing their leader has made certain of that!"

"They are knaves but they will not be fools." Alex asserted, "Their thirst for vengeance will not overwhelm their judgement. They know that if they are responsible for the killing of a constable sent by King James, it will bring the wrath of Hell upon them, if the deed can be laid at their door."

The two men continued shovelling soil for another ten minutes before either one of them spoke again. It was Hamish who broke the silence and he looked troubled.

"Did Burberry say anything to you, last night? Anything about what he might have been intending to do?"

"No," replied Alex, "We just talked about general things. There was nothing in particular that came up in conversation."

Hamish and Alex continued shifting soil. Much to their relief, despite the hole filling annoyingly slowly, the mound was now very much smaller. Both men were visibly anxious to complete the job. Neither wanted to be observed, in the act, by the wrong people.

When, at last, they had finished and were stamping down the soil and strewing it with leaves, twigs and decaying mulch, Hamish pressed his previous question, again.

"Burberry didn't say anything to you at all that might have given a clue as to where he was going?"

"No," Alex replied, shrugging his shoulders, "We just talked about old times and our experiences in the army and about life and fate and things like that."

Hamish looked thoughtful, his brows creased.

"Nothing of any importance?"

"No," Alex repeated.

Alex now recalled the strange little poem or riddle that Burberry had recited, but felt sure that it was of no significance.

"We roasted nuts and berries, ate them and drank too much whisky," he insisted.

"I was a merchant sailor for many a year," Hamish revealed, "New crew were taken on constantly, due to illness, death or people quitting such a hard life at sea. Men would come and go, but there would be that odd time, when new crew were boarding, when you would see somebody and you would immediately know that they would end up being important to you. You'd know it in your guts."

Alex nodded, soberly.

"It was the same in the infantry," he replied.

"This man, Burberry," Hamish remarked, "And – if I may say so – your good self, as well, are two fine examples of that."

Alex inclined his head and lifted his hand to his temple in a brief salute.

"Anyway," Hamish continued, "Forget fate and destiny. Burberry was professing a hearty desire to be tasting my wife's pot roast, yesterday!"

Alex laughed and slapped his thigh.

"Well, **that** would drag a man back from the ends of the Earth!" He laughed.

"It's strange that he sent no word whatsoever of his whereabouts and simply didn't return at all."

Alex, giving a final, conclusive, stamp to flatten the soil, turned back to Hamish and nodded his head in agreement.

"I must confess, it is definitely strange."

"Yet," persisted Hamish, like a dog gnawing at a bone, "He never said anything to you out of the ordinary?"

"No," Alex confirmed, turning back to the grave and loosening the lacing of his britches, "I'm afraid he didn't."

"What are you doing?" Asked Hamish, in puzzlement, hearing the other unbuckle his belt and then seeing him ease down his britches a little way."

"What am I doing?" Alex asked, as way of reply, "I have an obligation to fulfil, here."

"An obligation?"

Hamish first heard the splashing of liquid and then caught a glimpse of a steaming torrent of urine being delivered from Alex' bladder onto the grave.

"On behalf of all the people they wronged," Alex announced, swinging his hips to left and right, propelling the yellow flow in a snaking whiplash, "And all the people they bullied, assaulted or killed. I need to give these men the kind of send-off they deserve!"

Hamish let out a laugh that set a dozen birds to flight from the trees and softly applauded.

"I can only hope that some of that finds its way onto their faces," he sniggered, "Or, better still, into their eyes and mouths!"

The two men, tired and weary, trudged back to the Inn and went around to the horse trough at the front. Here, they took turns at working the handle of the pump while the other washed.

Once they were relatively clean, Hamish called to one of the maids to fetch them both clean shirts and they sat down on the 'gentry steps', outside the entrance to the inn. These were a set of wooden beams stacked to form a short rise of stairs to allow people to board a coach if they were either unable or – for those of a more refined upbringing – unwilling, to clamber up and into coaches by means of its own steps.

When the maid returned with the shirts, she approached them uneasily. Holding out the shirts, her behaviour became hesitant and her face apologetic. Hamish took the first shirt with a grateful nod and then, on seeing the second shirt close up, his face dropped.

The maid looked anguished.

Hamish knew that his wife had sent her with that particular shirt on purpose. He knew that sending that shirt carried a message. The message was one of overwhelming approval of the intended wearer. He agreed with her judgement, but it still broke his heart.

Alex took the shirt, quite innocently and, having put it on, flexed his arms as if performing chest expanding exercises.

"The owner of this one must be a strapping and manly individual!" Alex declared, "Was it left by a guest?"

The expression on Hamish's face was desolate as he replied.

"It was left by my son."

"A fine strong man, to be sure!" Alex declared, cheerfully, attempting to lift the other's mood.

The was a short silence before Hamish spoke,

"My son is dead," he said.

"Oh!" Said Alex, feeling clumsy and stupid, "I'm genuinely deeply sad to hear that."

Hamish didn't reply. He was there in body, but his mind was elsewhere, as was confirmed by his far-off, vacant stare. Alex feared he were reliving some traumatic event from the past but decided not to intrude upon it with any more talk.

After a couple of minutes, Hamish suddenly turned back to him, looking like a man slightly confused by his own actions. Alex put a hand on his shoulder.

"I'll not speak of it further," said Alex.

"It's nothing for you to trouble yourself about."

Alex could not prevent a wounded expression from reaching his face and, seeing it, Hamish relented.

"I take your concern kindly," Hamish assured him, "But his passing has left me numb and empty rather than cross or upset."

Alex paused a moment, to show reverence, then asked a question.

"Was he lost at sea?"

"Aye, he was, but not any sea of salt and water."

Alex looked confused.

"He was lost in a sea of barley," Hamish responded.

The far-off look returned to the innkeeper's eyes. It was a short while before he returned, again.

"My son was a farmer. I persuaded him, after much arguing, not to take to the waves, as I had. He was taken from us by a pistol shot from a Campbell who was disputing a land boundary."

Alex held up his hands in a gesture of helplessness and Hamish, seeing the pained look in his eye, hugged him, then slapped him on his back.

"He would have been about your age, now," Hamish confided, narrowly avoiding a sob in his voice as he choked back emotion.

Hamish turned to Alex but said nothing further.

A tear escaped the brim of the old man's eye and rolled down his cheek. As if in answer, a tear rolled down Alex' own cheek. The old sailor reached out and patted the young man's arm and the two sat quietly, side by side on the wooden slabs.

The silence around them was devoid of any hint of embarrassment or discomfort. It was an easy silence. A silence between friends. It was a silence that shunned anything so basic and primitive as words to share its intimacy.

After a while, a group of birds began singing in the trees. It was almost as if they, too, had held back, out of respect, but now found their song too joyous to restrain. The two men looked up to the trees at the same time. They shared a sad smile.

"It's not so much the things we do that spur regret," Hamish announced, "But the things we hold back from doing. Those are the things that torment us the most."

Alex sat and shared the moment until the other man was ready to talk, again.

"An action can be condemned, in hindsight, and argued – whether wise or foolish – to have been right or wrong," said Hamish, "When we fail to act, however, we expose ourselves to a grief that can consume our very soul. I have a demon to lay to rest. I want no more demons of its kind."

Hamish stood up, quickly and unexpectedly, catching Alex by surprise. Alex stood, too, feeling it the appropriate thing to do.

"He said nothing. Nothing of any significance?" Hamish asked, making it more of an accusation than a question.

Alex looked sheepish. Hamish tilted his head to one side. Alex let out a long sigh of resignation. He knew exactly who 'he' was and didn't need the reference to be explained.

"We talked about possessions, at one point. About things we value," Alex confessed, "I have a tinder box that belonged to my grandfather."

Hamish looked at him eagerly. It was as if he were a cat that had sat by a soundless mousehole, finally hearing movement. Alex looked pained, almost apologetic, as he went on.

"He recited an odd kind of verse or a ditty or something...," said Alex, screwing up his features in contemplation, "It was strange..."

Hamish stood patiently, as if waiting for an over possessive gun dog to give up a pheasant.

"He said: *'I have the petal of a violet. I keep it in a glass thimble. I keep the thimble in....'"* Alex broke off, seeing the shocked expression on Hamish's face.

The innkeeper looked dumbfounded! His eyes were wide and his mouth hung open in disbelief. Alex thought that he could not have looked more astonished if he had just announced himself as the Messiah and that this were the Second Coming.

"Brydda!" Hamish gasped, slapping his hand to his own mouth.

CHAPTER 16

Alex looked puzzled.

"The words of Kiffan," Hamish explained with reverence and awe, "The constable was reciting the words of Kiffan."

Alex' puzzlement turned to bafflement.

"Explanations can wait!" Hamish cried, waving his hands in the air as if he were polishing an invisible mirror.

Alex shrugged his shoulders and got to his feet.

"Horses! We need to get to the horses!" Hamish insisted, setting off for the rear of the inn.

"I'm coming! I'm right behind you!"

"We need to go to Coille Dorcha and take a look around," Hamish shouted, over his shoulder, "The McCarthys! They are The Watch. Coille Dorcha is their base when they can be found."

As Alex would soon discover, Coille Dorcha (or 'Dark Forest') was a forbidding place, no doubt deliberately chosen for its gloomy and inhospitable setting. It was one of Hamish's least favourite places and its inhabitants were, appropriately, his least favourite people.

They hurried round to the stables, taking turns to bellow for the stable lad to saddle up their horses. The stable lad, who looked as if he had just been woken from a nap, sprang into the air like a startled weasel and bounded across to the saddles. Before Alex had his own saddle even half way off the shelf, the boy, his hands a blur of activity, had grabbed a saddle, thrown it up onto the first horse's back and had begun attending to the straps.

In awe of the young lad's dexterity, Alex positioned his saddle and moved to place the first strap underneath the beast. In the blink of an eye, the boy was there, catching both straps and passing them through the buckles at their opposite ends. With the economy of motion of an expert, he hauled the straps tight. At the point they reached perfect tension, the horse promptly looked down, as if to examine his handiwork. The horse seemed pleased.

Alex nodded towards Constable Burberry's second horse.

"If Burberry were not intending to come back, he would have taken his other horse."

"Yes," agreed Hamish, "It's too fine an animal to just abandon."

If either of them had been looking at the stable lad, at this point, they would have seen the guilty look that swept across his face.

As the two riders mounted up, the boy halved an apple and gave a piece to each animal. As they moved off, he inspected his own work with the saddles and, perversely, a momentary frown indicated his satisfaction.

Hamish rode around to the side of the inn and, dismounting, waved Alex to follow him inside. There, he led the way to the cupboards behind the bar. Hamish grimly loaded Ruby and Rose and stowed them into a bag. Next he retrieved Alex' own pistol from a cupboard behind the bar and handed it to him. He then took a knife, ran its tip down the inside corner of the same cupboard and levered out a panel. Hamish eased the panel forward and it swung open to reveal two muskets. Hamish took the muskets out and handed one to Alex.

Alex had not held a musket since he had been in Austria, six weeks earlier, and felt uneasy at handling one again, but he accepted it, all the same. Hamish took out a pair of powder horns and two bags of musket balls.

"Those are lead," Hamish explained, handing Alex the heavier bag, "And these are iron," he said, tossing the remaining bag up and down in his palm a couple of times.

The innkeeper knew that he didn't need to insult Alex by explaining that iron balls, as opposed to lead, flew a greater distance or that, while they delivered less impact, they were less prone to drop short of their target when shot from a long range.

Without a further word, the two men checked and loaded the muskets and made them safe. Hamish went to find his wife, to make his farewells. On returning, he hustled Alex back outside, where they quickly got onto their horses.

"What does 'Brydda' mean?" Alex asked, conversationally.

"The Brydda were a band of warriors from the Highlands who fought the Vikings, almost eight hundred years ago," Hamish replied, "They were stubborn as a tree stump. They fought the Vikings when others had given up. A woman by the name of Kiffan was their leader. They referred to her as their queen. The war she led against the Vikings was said to have been absolutely relentless."

"The Brydda don't exist anymore?"

"Some say they do, but most say that they don't."

"What do you say, Hamish?"

"I say if they do still exist, and most scholars doubt it, then they must be incredibly secretive."

As they moved out onto the road, Hamish put his heels into his horse and set off up the long hill at a pace, putting a stop to any further conversation. Alex prompted his mare to catch up. Hamish didn't slacken off his pace until they reached the summit.

"I have a really bad feeling that the McCarthys have the constable," Hamish announced when Alex reached him.

"You don't think he has gone back to his troops and been delayed for some reason?"

"No, I don't," Hamish confirmed, "Because he would have sent a messenger. I'm sure of it."

"Well, we received no message," Alex agreed.

"We received a message of sorts," Hamish replied, "But it was not via a messenger. He left a message with you. It was both a message and a warning."

Alex made a puzzled face, but Hamish didn't offer any further explanation and they rode on in silence.

CHAPTER 17

It took them a little over an hour to reach the turning leading into the woods that gave Coille Dorcha its name. The two men exchanged looks of unease as they encouraged their mounts down the path. The air in this higher ground was markedly colder and, up ahead of them, they could see snow in the trees.

"This place feels more like a cemetery than a forest," Hamish muttered.

They ventured on for another ten minutes. By this time, the snow was everywhere on the ground, like a fluffy white carpet. In the distance they could see a thin haze where the snow was still steadily descending.

"The snow is still coming down over there, a way ahead, but it's not fallen here for some while," Alex noted, pointing first ahead and then to the ground beside them, "If we are going to be venturing close to these people's hideout, in the snow, then we are going to leave tracks all over the place for them to see!"

Hamish grunted his dismay.

"That's a problem we will have to tackle when we get to it."

Hamish pulled his horse to a stop and raised his hand for Alex to do the same.

"This place," he said, waving an arm towards the partial clearing, a little way in front, "Would be ideal for an ambush!"

The two riders, looking in all directions for any possible trap, coaxed their steeds to walk very slowly, stopping them every few strides to listen. Hamish gestured for Alex to take out his pistol and he did the same. Brandishing their weapons, they dismounted and crept forward, cautiously. The snow made everything ominously quiet, soaking up all noise and delivering a perfect stillness that felt threatening and uncomfortable.

Hamish leaned in close to Alex, bringing his mouth a handspan from the other's ear, in order to whisper.

"Look... signs of a struggle... over there by the bushes."

They edged their way to the spot in question, treading stealthily, their pistols at the ready. The bushes had a couple of broken branches that were stretched back and splintered. Close by, they were accompanied by a cluster of snapped twigs and some fallen leaves. On closer inspection the foliage to the side showed signs of damage, too.

"It looks like somebody has either tripped into these bushes or been thrown into them," Alex remarked.

On the ground, the thin scattering of snow clearly displayed the boot marks of at least three, possibly four, different people.

Suddenly, Hamish grabbed Alex firmly by the arm, preventing him from advancing. His grip was harsh and Alex almost complained. Then, he saw that Hamish was pointing, urgently, to something on the ground.

Hamish dropped to his haunches, staring intently at something, and Alex heard a sharp intake of breath followed by a low Gaelic curse. Alex crouched beside him.

There, on top of the pristine snow, standing out starkly – like a charcoal smudge on a pure white canvas – was a solitary, black thumbnail.

CHAPTER 18

The Laird Grant did not move, except that his outstretched arms, offering his claymore lengthways, wavered slightly under the weight of it. Annis reached out and, grudgingly, took the weapon. Her reluctance was such that it clawed at her soul and made her feel weary.

Fate is cruel, she decided. Fate melts the plans of people like the sun melts ice. This man, she thought, was her enemy less than thirty minutes back and now he would pledge me his loyalty. Why? For the sake of honour! How cheaply men wield their honour, she mused, when the blood of thousands of sons and daughters – born by women – may pour into the soil as a result.

Annis held the mighty sword straight out, her arm rigid, the blade pointing straight up. She revelled in the moment, flaunting her physical strength to the men around her. She held the sword still and true, proudly showing that she could do so without sign of effort or strain. She took her mind inside herself and told her body to obey. It obeyed. A minute passed. The laird remained motionless. Her arm did not so much as sway.

She remembered being a girl and holding her first sword. She had thrown it back at the blacksmith who had forged it. She had cursed him for making it too light. He had made her a new sword. When she held it, she realised that he had been either bold enough or foolish enough to risk her wrath, for a second time!

The blacksmith would have been well aware that she, Princess Annis, had commanded men flogged for holding back when they sparred with her. She required them to give their best. This man had now hammered out a sword that would take substantial strength to hold it and even greater strength to use it. He had either wished to greatly please her or had mustered the courage to shame her.

Annis thrilled at the recollection. She was a woman. She was not a man. That sword had been crafted as the sword of a man. She resolved to make that sword, instead, the sword of a princess. A sword fit, one day, for a queen. She had insisted that her mother give the blacksmith a silver coin.

From that day, she had fanatically exercised morning, noon, afternoon and night. Steadily, she developed the physical power and stamina to master her new blade. She had not used large weights to build up her muscles, but small ones. She shunned weights that would take strength to lift them and, instead, had used weights that were easy to lift, but that required strength to lift them again and again, over and over, on and on. Once she could lift a particular weight a hundred times, easily, she would use a slightly heavier weight. She would then persevere until she could lift that new weight a hundred times with ease. Eventually, after three years, she was lifting hefty weights and lofting them no less than five hundred times.

The men in the royal camp would lift weights several times heavier than she could. They would do so where everybody could see them doing it. She, on the other hand, would lift a quarter of that weight, but she would do so for an hour and always in secret.

Those men, with their huge muscles, the kind that bulged and jutted, loved to show them off. They would swagger and strut with pride like tartan-clad peacocks. She, herself, had developed far less visible muscles. Her muscles were tight and dense. They were rock hard and deceptively potent. She was happy to keep them hidden.

Annis still exercised fiercely and regularly, even now. She continued to use relatively smaller weights with prolonged repetition. She was slim. She was feminine. She was strong. She was powerful.

Her arm was now beginning to complain at her abuse of it, but the sword remained perfectly steady in her grip. As she willed herself to endure and continue, she contemplated the situation that had brought her to be holding the sword. It was a situation where there was no right course of action available to her. Whatever she did, she risked inflicting suffering on one group of people or another.

If she shunned the allegiance offered by The Laird Grant, there was an unlikely – but still dangerous – possibility that he may, in a fit of rage, resume his role as her enemy. She could not easily cope with a resumption of his opposition along this crucial boundary.

If she accepted his fealty, on the other hand, the neighbouring clans in the East would see it as a blatant act of intrusion and would reply with bloodshed. Even more perilous might be the response of the English! They might well see any expansion of her dominion as a deliberate act of provocation. If she appeared to throw down the gauntlet to the English, then the lairds of certain junior clans – who had constant minor and irksome disputes with their neighbours – might take the opportunity to start fighting.

Annis looked wearily across the field and mentally recapped the history of this region. It had evolved through invasion after invasion, repelling armies of every different variety and culture. It seemed as if every military campaign in this part of the globe, at some point, included trying to conquer these Scottish shores.

She imagined hordes of Highlanders screaming and roaring as they charged down these fields. Their cries and shrieks and their bellowing calls chilling the blood of their enemy and turning their guts to water. Then her heart dropped as she imagined a line of a hundred and fifty Red Coat musketeers. Fifty of them laying on their bellies, fifty behind them kneeling up and fifty standing to their rear. Then she imagined them being given the order to fire. In her mind she saw the billowing smoke and smelled the stench of gunpowder from an opening barrage of a hundred and fifty simultaneous shots. She pictured the charging Highland warriors falling to the ground like leaves falling from trees.

Annis remembered the centuries old stories of the Picts fighting the Scots. The Picts had no muskets, but they had fighters mounted on horseback and, wherever the terrain permitted, they used them to spectacular and devastating effect. Annis sobbed, inwardly, and wished – with all her heart – that the Picts on their horses could turn up, now, and charge her enemies for her!

She jerked, with a sudden start, as her mind came hurtling back to the here and now, invigorated by a flash of inspiration.

"Laird Grant," said Annis, Queen of the West, "I have a service to ask of you! This service would make you so valuable to the future of Scotland, that any sacrifice of your life, today, would be an unspeakable blow to it."

The laird looked up and Annis offered him his claymore back. The laird looked at the sword suspiciously, as if it might suddenly leap at him and bite his nose. He began to reach for it, then withdrew his hand.

"I need our shame to end," he said, sullenly, with a look of torment in his eyes.

"I can offer your Clan glory," she replied.

The laird's eyes sprang wide and he reached for his sword with a new eagerness, but then stopped with only one finger resting on its hilt.

"Let me first take an oath, Your Majesty."

Annis eased the laird's armament fully into his grip and gleefully relieved herself of its agonising weight.

"Your deeds, Laird Grant, will testify to your loyalty far better than any words. For I am best served if nobody is aware of your mission."

The Laird Grant thought for a moment.

"You mentioned glory?"

"Yes!" she said, encouragingly, "The kind of glory that singers write songs about."

The Laird Grant's people had not experienced glory for a long, long time and his face came alight as the dull desolation that had dominated it was replaced by hope.

"Horses," Annis said, in firm but confidential tones, "Horses with soldiers astride them. They made the Picts a formidable force, so many hundreds of years ago."

The Laird of the Grants looked at her quizzically, as if trying to discern if she were sincere or if she were mocking him.

"Mounted soldiers," she continued, "They do not perform so well riding up and down steep hillsides. That is the province of foot soldiers. On foot, a soldier can crouch and hide. On foot, they can leap, slide and spring upon their enemies. It is on level ground, across flat meadows and shallow inclines, that mounted soldiers come into their own."

The laird's face became thoughtful.

"You have the Laird MacDonald's cavalry," he said.

"I have them, true, but they are in the West. I need a cavalry in the East. I need them as a shield on my flank, for the future, in case I were to ever clash with the English Red Coats. There are feuds and grudges and skirmishes all around these parts. If I am attacked, I fear that such an intrusion would come here, in the East, and that it would rally people against me. I need The

MacDonalds and The Grants to be like the jaws of giant pincers that would crush an enemy between them and destroy them!"

The Laird Grant stroked his chin, revelling enthusiastically in the idea.

It was good politics, her mother had told her, to bolster a man's feeling of worth by openly reaffirming his value.

"I need a secret force of trusted mounted warriors," she continued, "Warriors who are fierce and loyal. So loyal that I could wager my life upon each and every one of them."

The Laird Grant stood up, his back ramrod straight, filled with a new zeal, his eyes dancing with vitality.

"When the time comes, Your Majesty, and you have need of us, Clan Grant will be this loyal cavalry force. We will answer your call without hesitation."

She breathed in, deeply, and let out a long sigh of relief.

Queen Annis would recall this moment, forever and always. The broken man, bereft of spark and vigour, laid low by his conscience and resigned to ending his life, now appeared to grow in stature before her eyes. His jaw had firmed, his eyes had begun to sparkle, his drooping shoulders had risen and his head was, now, held high.

The man before her swelled to become a giant, flushed with pride and purpose. It was as if a toy puppet in a children's theatre, slumped and dejected with slack strings and drooping limbs, had been suddenly snapped taut and upright.

Annis gradually became aware of the laird staring at his sword. He shrank back from it, slightly, holding it at a distance, as if it were transforming into a monster. She drew in a sharp breath as she saw the flames reflected in his eyes and heard the crackling sound of an inferno. She followed his gaze to his claymore and could see, reflected in its brightly polished surface, a host of yellow, orange and red tongues of fire, dancing and curling.

The laird looked to left and right, seeking the source of the reflection in his sword, but – from his reaction – it was not found. Then he looked, imploringly, at the queen. His wide eyes had a question written large in them.

"Yes," she said, softly, "I can see it."

The laird glanced over his shoulder to his son and his chief advisor.

"They don't see it," she told him, somehow knowing it to be true, "It is only you and I."

It was then that she realised that there was one other person who could see the flames.

Annis turned to see Bobbins. He was staring, open-mouthed, at the laird's sword. He could see it, too. The laird didn't notice, for his attention had already returned to his shimmering, dazzling weapon. He gazed at it in awe and began to twist it, this way and that, to watch the flames swirl and sway. He looked around, again, checking each corner of the meadow, but the source of the image reflected in his blade still defied him.

"Is this devilry?" he asked.

After a moment's pause, he answered his own question.

"No," he declared, "It is something pure and good. There is no hint of evil about this."

He looked around, again, scrutinising the faces of those who were near and appeared satisfied that they could not see this spectacle. He noticed that – if anything – they appeared a little perplexed. Somehow, he did not see Bobbins.

Annis felt herself withdraw into the quietness of some kind of internal space.

'How is the boy able to see this?' She pondered, *'Why can he see what others cannot?'*

The answer came to her instantaneously.

'He is but seven or eight years of age and still in possession of a pure soul. A soul that is unsullied by the ways of this world.'

Annis blinked. The words she heard in her mind were not spoken in the voice of her own thoughts. They were spoken, instead, in the voice of a stranger. The voice she heard was that of a young girl.

Suddenly and without her bidding, Annis found her head turning to the left and, unexpectedly, she found herself looking directly at Bobbins. The boy gave her a reassuring smile. It was the smile of a grown adult. Then he blinked, the same way Annis had done, and she knew with absolute confidence that he had just shared the same kind of strange experience.

Gavin and Balgair sat uneasily on their mounts, conscious that they were excluded from something, but unsure what it might be. The words exchanged by their queen and the Laird Grant made no sense to them. They felt like children listening to parents who were deliberately talking over their heads and beyond their comprehension.

The laird continued to marvel at his sword, completely captivated by its beauty and then, in a tone of wonder, voiced his inner thoughts.

"It's... It's something.... Something sacred."

"It's a sign," Annis declared, "An omen of good fortune."

"Yes. It is."

"It's a blessing. I know it with a certainty that is beyond doubt."

"You have seen this before, Your Majesty?"

"I have never seen it while I am awake. I have seen it, several times before, yes, but only in my dreams."

As though she had experienced a premonition, Annis held up a finger to her lips and raised her face to the clear blue sky. The Laird Grant looked up, too. After a few seconds, there was the sound of rolling thunder. A deep, pulsing rumble that built up, boomed loudly, and then faded.

Gavin and Balgair exchanged confused glances, clearly now even more perplexed and bewildered by the strange behaviour they were witnessing. It was evident to them that something of importance was going on, but that they were not a part of it.

"Come," Annis said, waving Balgair and Gavin to move alongside her.

The two men drew their horses by either flank of her own. Annis reached out her hands to either side and, after a little hesitation, the two soldiers took them. The moment their fingers touched hers, they winced and both made a little noise of alarm.

The Laird Grant did not need to be told that these two men could now see the flames, too. Their expressions spoke for themselves. He was amused to see them mimic his own original reaction, quickly looking around them – here, there and everywhere – like a dog that scents a rabbit but cannot decide its direction. Logic and common sense told them that the flames mirrored in the blade had an origin, but finding it completely defied them.

They all fell silent, enthralled by the mysterious and inexplicable reflection of the cavorting flames.

"You do magic!" Balgair exclaimed.

"No," Annis replied, "I do not. If this is magic, then it is not mine, but the magic of my ancestors."

The calm that had fallen upon the little group was, they would later agree, like the feeling of sitting in a church.

"It is said," Queen Annis began, "That Kiffan the Defiant dreamed of flames many times and that she sometimes saw them when she was awake."

Her listeners looked expectant, but nobody spoke.

"It is said that the Viking Ruler, King Urokmort – on the day that Queen Kiffan was sentenced to die – lifted his sword to behead her and a huge oak tree, around fifty to sixty strides away, burst into flames. The heat should have been overpowering, even in the teeth of Winter, but the Vikings said that it was merely pleasantly warm, like a mild Summer's day. The tree burned for seven days and for seven nights and Urokmort dared not slay her while it burned. Everybody who witnessed this event swore that the tree did not diminish by so much as a single twig in all that time. The flames rolled and boiled and the fire thundered but the tree was not consumed.

The three men listened to Annis in wordless wonder.

"Afterwards, on the morning after the seventh night, the fearsome blaze extinguished itself. The tree was still standing, unblemished and unharmed, exactly as it had before it happened. They say that not one single blade of grass around it was harmed."

The Laird Grant, Balgair and Gavin nodded their heads, wisely, as they weighed up her story.

Annis offered up her palms in a gesture of neutral frankness and felt a twinge of pain from her right arm as it rebuked her for her having held up the Laird Grant's claymore for so long. Gavin saw her wince and gave her the impish smile of a conspirator.

Annis looked into the laird's sword, again. This time, he was holding it perfectly still, almost in adoration. In her mind she pretended that the blade were a glass mirror, the sort she'd used as a child to signal "secret messages" to her friends. She searched her memory and brought back the long-forgotten instincts for bouncing light from the sun and calculating where it would fall. She looked to the sword and then across the field, following the path she had estimated, and her pulse suddenly began to race. Around a hundred paces away, in perfect alignment, was a big oak tree. She stared in fascination at the tree as she felt some benign force, that she could not even describe, begin to emit an intoxicating aura of peace and tranquillity.

Annis could not take her eyes off the tree. It looked so beautiful. As she watched she got the vaguest impression of flickering flames. She told herself that it must be her imagination. She screwed up her eyes and blinked hard, then looked again. It was still there. Annis looked off to the left, away from the tree, and her heart missed a beat. There it was! There were definitely flames! Her gaze shot back to the tree, now clearly on fire, and, in that instant, the flames were gone.

Annis furrowed her brow in thought. This time, she looked off to the right of the tree. The second she did so, the clear and unmistakable vision of flames promptly returned. The moment she looked back at the tree, they were gone.

She was fascinated. The flames were visible in the sword. The flames were visible if she didn't look directly at the oak tree. The flames disappeared when she looked at the tree straight on.

Annis felt a pang of guilt at not drawing this phenomenon to the attention of her companions, but they were – to be fair – still completely absorbed by the flames glimmering in the sword's shining metal.

How was she to explain this strange illusion? She was seeing something that was not there. It was beyond her grasp. She tried to make sense of it but could not. Why was it happening? What was it? What reason could there be for such a thing? Why was this incredible vision at the end of a field, just across the river from her border?

Annis wondered if this might have happened before. Were there stories of this tree? She had heard nothing of them. Should she ask the Laird Grant? She was unsure if she should. When was the last time that somebody had reported such a thing? What was this..... This.... Annis struggled to find the words to define it. What was this.... This fire tree?

CHAPTER 19

Janine was relieved when the duchess eventually seemed to recover her poise. Janine pulled back slightly, eyeing the duchess uncertainly.

The duke, having become aware of some kind of minor disturbance at the dining table, leaned forward to check for its cause and he, too, began to gape in amazement at Janine.

To Janine's dismay, the twins were also, now, studying her with genuine curiosity.

The duke and duchess – Janine decided – were of slightly advancing years, but not truly old. They both had greying hair and a few lines on their faces, but there was still the echo of youth in them.

Looking at the current expression on their faces and in their eyes, Janine decided that the message she was receiving from them was one that had grown all too familiar to her. They were, for some reason, shocked and alarmed by something they saw in Janine.

From the moment she had arrived at Brech Woorlach, Janine had been receiving odd looks from quite a few people. This latest example was even more disturbing, coming – as it did – from the most senior members of the household. Janine found herself self-consciously touching her own face, as if something hidden and elusive could be drawn to the surface and made obvious through physical contact.

The duchess reached out to touch her guest's face and Janine instinctively recoiled.

"Please!" Cried the duchess, plaintively.

Janine detected an overwhelming sadness in this woman and found herself drawn, irresistibly, to comfort her. She took the hand that the duchess had extended and placed it on her own face. The eyes of this woman filled with the most heart-breaking sorrow and she seemed to be on the verge of crying.

Janine looked to the duke and he, too, was visibly upset.

She suddenly realised that the whole room had fallen silent. She looked around, up and down the table, and from face to face of the servants. They all looked at her with an odd, almost exquisite, tenderness. She didn't know these people but, then again, somewhere at the back of her mind, she felt that she did. Annoyed at herself, she dismissed this idea as preposterous.

Janine was now more certain than ever that she was the victim of mistaken identity. In a way, she found this a comfort because, as soon as the error was uncovered – which must, surely, be an inevitability – they could all laugh about it and then put the whole embarrassing business behind them.

Janine looked, again, at the duke and duchess and fixed their appearances and demeanour in her mind. Then she looked at the twins – Brian and Bruce – and did the same. Next, she scanned the faces of the eighteen guests, sat either side of the grand table. Finally, she noted, in detail, the six men and four women who attended them as servants.

Something clicked in her mind, like the elusive final piece of a puzzle falling into place. She realised, conclusively, what it was about the behaviour of them all. They had a peculiar bond that she had previously been unable to define. She now understood that they were – each and every one of them – members of some kind of strange extended family! They were not simply employer and employee in any strict and rigid sense. They were family. She was oddly troubled by her certainty. How could she possibly know this for sure?

Janine felt as if she were waking from a dream. She shook her head, as if the action might somehow dislodge the confusion.

She looked back to the duchess. Her fingers were gently stroking Janine's cheek. Her eyes were misty, brimming with tears, and filled with love and affection. It was as if Janine were a lost child who had returned, finally safe and sound, from years of wandering in a forest.

She looked across to the duke. His gaze was that of a doting parent whose child had just won first prize in a contest at a grand fayre.

She looked over to where Bruce and Brian sat. Their early puzzled incomprehension was now gone – as if a blindfold had been snatched from their eyes – and they, too, looked at her with earnest affection.

"Who am I?" Asked Janine looking into the duchess' eyes.

The duchess breathed in and then let out her breath as a long, long sigh. It was the sigh of somebody who was resigning themselves to the telling of a very long story.

The duke turned to the twins and rebuked them.

"How could you not have seen?" He demanded, "How could you not have recognised her?"

The two shrugged and Bruce apologetically offered his perspective.

"Perhaps we were under some kind of a spell? Perhaps we weren't meant to be able to recognise her."

Janine heard their words at the back of her mind and could make no sense of them.

The duke nodded, slowly and thoughtfully, and pursed his lips, swivelling them left to right, as if weighing up the merits of a reply. He then lifted his shoulders and returned an even bigger shrug. A shrug of resigned acceptance.

"We know you, child," said the duchess, dabbing at her eyes with a handkerchief, "But the shock we feel is at seeing your mother in your face."

The duchess took her hand from Janine's cheek with melancholy reluctance.

"Did your father ever say that you looked like your mother?"

Janine's face illuminated with a huge smile and her eyes began to fill with tears.

"My father used to look at me for a long time, when he thought I was distracted," Janine replied, "I could tell, from the corner of my eye, but I never let him know. I was sure that it was not me he saw, but my mother. He said I was her very image. He would stare at me for ten minutes at a time, if he thought I were unaware."

"Your mother was very fond of reading," said the duchess, "I'm guessing that you had an unusually large number of books available to you as a little girl?"

Janine winced at the sudden realisation that the duchess knew of her humble upbringing. Janine had never thought of it before, not for a second, but now she was faced with it, she realised that a crofter's daughter having dozens and dozens of books to read was almost ludicrous.

"Did you do physically strenuous things with your mother?" Enquired the duchess, "Like hard running, jumping or tumbling?"

"Sometimes we did, now and again, but not so much," Janine recalled, knotting her brow in concentration, "She more often had me go to my quiet place, in my head, and sit and think really deeply."

The duchess gave her a knowing look and nodded with apparent satisfaction.

"When you woke – when you came back from your 'quiet place' – were you tired, aching, sweaty, even sometimes exhausted, maybe?"

Janine's eyes popped wide with astonishment at this strange insight.

"Why, yes! Yes, I did! I always did! I could never make sense of it, but my mother said that if I did energetic things in my mind, then it could make my body think I had done those things for real and it would behave as if it had."

The duchess beamed at her.

"She must have loved you so very, very much!"

Janine burst into tears, sobbing uncontrollably and the duchess gathered her into her arms and hugged her. Everybody in the room – including the twins – politely resumed their business. The guests returned to eating, talking and drinking. The servants returned to waiting at table.

The duchess patted Janine's back, stroked her hair, kissed her head and uttered the gentle, soothing noises a mother might use to settle a distressed child in a crib. All the time she rocked her. Janine drew herself against the duchess, putting her face against her shoulder and abandoned herself completely as she sobbed out the loss, the misery, the hurt, the anger and the pain.

Janine had been strong, for her father, when they had lost her mother. She had quelled her tears so as not to spur his grief. It was not as if her father needed much prompting, in the first year. She had wrapped up her sorrow and buried it. She had locked it away in some vast underground chamber, large enough to swallow a whole town. She had left it to itself. Now, it was as if a dam had burst, unleashing a torrent of emotion that had ached to be free. It washed away her restraint and drowned her pride.

Janine could not recall how long she had cried, but her eyes hurt from it and she felt a dull pain at their inner corners where tears were produced. Presently, she drifted off to sleep and began to dream of her childhood.

The duchess held her, unwilling to relinquish her back to her adult self until she absolutely must. She wanted to revel in the memories of Janine's mother. She wanted to recall being a younger woman, herself, with her life stretching out ahead of her. She wanted to go back to the time, in Brech Woorlach's history, when both it and its occupants were no more than they appeared to be, when keeping secrets had not become second nature for them, and when life had been so much simpler and far less dangerous.

The duchess smiled a bitter little smile to herself. There was a time, before their enlightenment, that they had been the sort of people that she now detested.

She told herself that the past was the past and that the present was the present. She had become the person she had become and her husband had become the person he had become.

She wouldn't, in all honesty, wish to change anything. There was no way that she could ever reconcile herself to their original life. She had no desire to have remained a privileged, conceited, self-congratulating member of the aristocracy with callous disregard for the poor.

CHAPTER 20

Over an hour passed and Janine continued to sleep peacefully in the lap of the duchess, curled up against her chest, looking angelic and vulnerable. By this time, all the guests had made their farewells and left the dining table, leaving just the duke, the duchess, Bruce and Brian.

Their trusty little group had kept watch over Janine and had greatly enjoyed reminiscing about her and her mother and their times at Brech Woorlach. They discussed the decisions that had been taken and the arrangements on which they had embarked in an attempt to protect them both. They talked about Janine's identity and if it were best to continue to hide it from her or to face her with it.

Eventually, with a heavy heart, the duchess sent for a footman and Janine was carried up to her chambers, still sound asleep.

CHAPTER 21

Janine woke in a beautiful bed with silk sheets, sumptuous pillows and translucent curtains around her. High above her, she could see a misty, gauze canopy. The linen smelled of perfume and her nostrils detected the vague aroma of incense. To her side, atop a table, was an oil lamp whose golden glow was calm and reassuring.

She became aware of a hand holding her own. She turned and, through a gap in the drapery around the bed, she saw Francesca, sat in a chair by her bed. Francesca's arm stretched through the space where the curtain was drawn slightly apart. Francesca wore a very expensive night dress with a very expensive dressing gown over it. Glancing in the direction of the windows, Janine could see, from the lack of any brightness, that night had fallen.

Francesca, noticing that her charge had woken, leaned forward and gently stroked Janine's hair away from her eyes. Janine opened her mouth to speak, but then closed it again, knowing that words were wholly superfluous. Francesca's kind eyes met hers and told her, in an instant, all that she needed to know. They told her that all was well, that there was no need to worry and that she would sit guard and keep all harm at bay.

Janine squeezed Francesca's hand and, feeling the squeeze gently returned, fell into a deep, peaceful sleep.

CHAPTER 22

Hamish Pottle's face was as hard as a blacksmith's anvil. His lips were set firm and his eyes shone with a grim determination.

"Constable Burberry," Hamish announced, "Has been in danger from the moment he left Edinburgh and, even more so, since he ventured North of Perth."

"He did come with an armed escort," Alex pointed out.

"He and his escort appear not to have been close travelling companions," retorted Hamish, "**They** will be around a campfire toasting their toes and singing songs about women of easy virtue. While **he** – if he is still alive – will have the prospect of a lead ball through his brain or dangling from the end of a rope..." he paused and grimaced, "And goodness knows what kind of ordeal before that."

Alex nodded in disgruntled agreement but pressed his point.

"It's not as if he has no support to call upon. We cannot say, for sure, that he'd come up around these parts without bringing any troops with him."

"Judging from the marks in the snow," Hamish protested, gesturing at the ground, "The struggle that occurred was one man against two or, maybe, three. I'm pretty sure that an armed escort, had they been around, would have immediately intervened."

Alex nodded, again, reluctantly agreeing with Hamish's interpretation and, surveying the disturbed snow, found no cause to dispute it. Hamish pointed ahead, into the forest, inviting Alex to proceed. Alex gestured his agreement and the two of them began to creep forward.

"It's puzzling," Alex confessed, "Why a man with thirty armed soldiers to protect him, would choose to come and stay at your inn by himself?"

Hamish thought about this for a moment and rubbed the side of his chin with the palm of his hand for inspiration.

"Especially," Alex persisted, "When he had already had an encounter with the McCarthys and ended up killing one of them."

Hamish thought some more and, coming to a halt, shrugged his shoulders as he gave his reply.

"If you are asking me if I know, then the answer is that I don't. If you are asking me if I have any theories, then I'd say – judging from what we know about him, so far – he doesn't seem to be the kind of man to cower away from conflict."

Alex nodded, thoughtfully, and the two men pushed on, ducking branches and skirting around brambles as they continued

"Tell me," Hamish asked, "Was it him you were watching for at the inn?"

This time, it was Alex' turn to bring them to a halt. Alex held the other's gaze for a few moments and then looked away before responding.

"Was it quite so obvious that I was keeping a look out?"

"I have strode ashore from a ship – on more occasions than I'd like to recall – with gold in my purse to buy provisions," Hamish told him, "And stayed unrobbed and alive mainly because I learned to tell who was keeping a watch out."

Alex looked slightly sheepish.

"I was looking for a man by the name of Ramsbrook," he disclosed, "His trade is the same as the two savages we buried this morning. The difference between he and they – besides being alive – is that he is civilised, cultured and, by all outward appearances, a gentleman."

"Do you know who is his target? He isn't after the constable, too, is he?"

"No," Alex replied, "Not as far as I know. Ramsbrook is travelling to Inverness. For what reason, I don't know. My uncle had knowledge of his journey and sent a message to alert me. I want to find this man."

"You are collecting a debt or settling a score?"

"He murdered my sister."

"I'm sorry for your loss," Hamish said, hurriedly, and rested his hand on the young man's arm.

Alex patted the hand in acknowledgement and looked desolate. Hamish remained silent for a minute and, when he spoke again, he had tactfully changed the subject.

"You didn't ask, earlier on, what violets have to do with the Brydda," Hamish admonished, "And I'm pretty sure that you come from the Lowlands."

Alex looked slightly offended.

"I'm from Dunfermline!" He protested.

"Aye? Is that so? Well, it's almost the same, then, isn't it?"

The two men laughed and Hamish was glad that Alex was able to do so. Afraid of the noise they were making, Hamish held his fingers to his lips to caution silence and looked around for danger. Finding no sign of company, he waved Alex to follow him forward to better cover.

"You already knew of Queen Kiffan?" Hamish asked, once they were better hidden.

"Vaguely," Alex admitted.

"She is part of Highland legend."

"My grandfather spoke of her once or twice. I have no great knowledge of her, though," Alex admitted.

Hamish waved Alex to follow him. Together, they trod a wide circuit around the clearing, looking for any signs of a McCarthy presence, but – much to their relief – they found none.

"Queen Kiffan," Hamish said, at length, "Was – as you know – the leader of The Brydda. Her band of fanatical warriors followed her in her struggle against the

Viking invaders. The Vikings eventually managed to capture her and passed a death sentence on her."

Alex murmured his understanding, distractedly, from his position a few steps ahead where he had advanced to survey the terrain, down a slope.

"The words Burberry recited about the petal of a violet were from what Queen Kiffan was said to have told Urokmort, one of the Viking kings. It was part of her answer when he asked her about her most precious possession."

Alex stepped back through a gap in the bushes and came to stand beside Hamish, again.

"Well," replied Alex, "I know that she must have been a hero to lead them. I know that they must have been heroes to follow her. I know that, at least, none of them were bloody mercenaries!"

Hamish was studiously scanning the woodlands for signs of scouts or lookouts, but broke off to grunt his agreement and to give his companion a quick glance and a nod. He turned his head back to his task and stood scratching his head. Suddenly, Hamish snapped his head around, again, his eyes blazing.

"**You** aren't a mercenary, are you?"

"A mercenary?" Alex snapped, clearly offended, "I fight for my conscience not for coin!"

"Horse piss!" Retorted a furious Hamish.

Suddenly, Hamish launched himself at the younger man, striking him a glancing blow on the jaw.

Alex, already moving to dodge the blow, hit him back. Hamish's head jolted with the force of the impact and he staggered, slightly, but managed to recover enough to sweep Alex' leg from under him. He then dropped on top of Alex as he hit the ground. Before the innkeeper's weight could fully apply itself, Alex rolled to the side and struck his attacker with an elbow. Hamish, faster than his years might suggest, grabbed the elbow and, springing to his knees, twisted Alex around and kicked away the foot that was coming up towards him.

Alex rolled into a low crouch and, as Hamish moved forward, he feigned a move to the left, before lurching back to the right. Hamish was not fooled by the manoeuvre and managed to connect his shoulder with Alex' chest. Alex turned to the side to lessen the impact and brought up a hand to strike the older man's jaw.

Alex began to slip his arm over and around his attacker's neck, to take him in a headlock, but the former seafarer predicted the move and ducked, swiftly turning and stepping forwards. Finding Alex momentarily off balance, he lunged sharply, propelling him backwards. Alex brought up his knee as he lost his balance but, instead of Hamish striking it to parry the blow, he grabbed and held it, preventing Alex from falling.

"Stop!" Hamish said in a gruff whisper, "That's enough. I can see that you'll do!"

Alex flexed his leg, to bring himself upright, and Hamish leaned back to take the weight of the motion. Before Alex could voice the obvious question, Hamish saved him the trouble.

"You are strong and you are fast. I'll not worry if I have to rely on you having my back. If you'll forgive me, I'll not walk into a conflict, where I risk my life, without knowing the metal of the man beside me."

Alex' expression went from shock to outrage. Then it went from outrage to contempt. Then, finally, it went from contempt to weary acceptance.

Hamish offered him his hand and, after looking at it scornfully for a few seconds, Alex took it.

"For an old man," Alex said, "You still have a Hell of a lot of young man left in you."

"Aye, it's to be expected," Hamish responded, with a glint in his eye, "For Caitlan has a fearsome grip and the determination of a mule when she has a mind to hang on to that whisky jar!"

They both burst out laughing and both instantly hushed the other, their animosity now swept aside and replaced by mutual respect.

"Should we not alert the constable's soldiers, back at their camp?" Alex asked, dubiously, clearly doubting the wisdom of it, himself.

"The McCarthys will most definitely know about them," Hamish replied, "And if they have so much as a scrap of sense, they'd be sure to have spotters posted to look out for any messenger running orders to them. Anybody carrying word is likely to take a piece of lead put through their skull."

"Can we not go back and send the young stable lad?"

Hamish looked wounded and held up his thumb against the trunk of the tree, beside him.

"I'd rather you nail my thumb to this tree than risk any harm coming to the boy Murdoch," Hamish declared, "And Caitlan would have me sleeping in the stables for the best part of a year if she found out!"

Alex smiled at the image and grunted his acceptance of Hamish's resolve. After they had trudged and barged a little further on, Hamish waved Alex to stop and began circling a yew tree, looking up into its branches.

"What are you looking for?" Alex inquired, looking up into the tree, himself.

"Hunting muskets," replied Hamish in a matter-of-fact tone.

Alex raised his eyebrows and Hamish smirked mischievously in response, pointing up through the snow-laden foliage.

"They grow on trees, don't you know?" Hamish announced, unable to suppress a chuckle, "Or, more accurately, they hang from trees in sacks of sailcloth that have been heavily waxed and oiled."

Alex looked at him blankly.

"Hiding things in plain sight is one of the most trusted methods of smugglers," Hamish announced, "Another is to hide things in the last place that anybody would ever look for them. In this case, that's right under their noses, slap bang in the middle of the McCarthys own back yard!"

"You've actually been to this abominable place before?"

"Yes, I came here with Murdoch a few years back and I sent him up this tree to hang the two sacks in the branches for me. The McCarthys don't strike me as the kind of people to actually look in such a place. If the worst were to happen, and somebody else were to have found them, then they would immediately lay the blame on the McCarthys for them."

Alex looked up into the tree and squinted hard but could see nothing that looked anything like firearms. When he looked back down again, Hamish was bent over, feet astride, with his two hands intertwined in front of him as a human stirrup. Alex accepted the implied offer of a step up, placing a foot into the hands, and Hamish boosted him into the lower branches.

"It's a yew tree," Hamish called up, softly, "And they attract ravens, which are meant to be bad luck. Because of the superstitions, it's an unlikely place to stash guns, which is why it's also a really good place to stash guns!"

Alex could be heard, above, clambering about in the branches.

"If a raven should swoop down and snatch your soul away and drag you across the veil to the dark side, could you remind my Uncle Tain, while you are there, that he still owes me a silver piece?"

Alex snorted and continued rummaging.

"I cannot see anything that could be guns," Alex complained to the accompanying sound of rustling leaves and snapping twigs.

"That's because you are looking too hard!"

"I'm looking at everything that could possibly be what I'm looking to find," Alex objected, giving a muffled cry as he appeared to kneel on something sharp.

"Okay," replied Hamish, "So now look for nothing at all. Just rummage around a wee bit. Pretend that you are hunting for acorns."

"It's a yew tree!"

"Very well," Hamish answered, sarcastically, "Pretend you are looking for acorns in a yew tree, in that case."

"Why would there be acorns in a yew?" Asked Alex, baffled.

"You are saying that muskets are known to favour one tree over another, are you?" Quipped Hamish.

Alex groaned at the jest and could be heard scrabbling around.

"I have found them!" He suddenly announced, with a note of triumph.

After substantial snapping, shuffling and jostling noises, Alex lowered down first one and then the other package into Hamish's waiting hands. This done, he set about descending and, with appropriate cursing and grumbling, he clambered down and dropped to the ground.

"I think nature was set upon claiming them as its own!" Alex declared, brushing off a variety of crawling insects, both dead and alive.

"I swapped these beauties for two kegs of the very best Portuguese brandy," Hamish proclaimed.

Gently, he tugged back the neck of the canvas bag, which, despite years of harsh weather, still remained remarkably supple. After further, more gentle, pulling and coaxing, Hamish revealed the long barrel of a fine Italian hunting musket.

"The owner was being closely pursued by men and hounds of His Majesty's Excise Brigade and didn't fancy his chances of evading them for much longer. He opted to be caught in possession of illicit liquor and to be flogged and survive, rather than be caught with guns and be executed," Hamish confided, grimly, "Being armed with a weapon when you fight with Excise Officers is a capital offence and they will often carry out such a punishment with the very minimum of delay."

Alex managed to release the outer wrapping of the second musket and began the struggle of easing it out from the inner layers.

"This is a mighty fine piece of engineering," Alex said, stroking the barrel and running his fingers over the trigger guard as the final length of wrapping fell away, "And the mechanism is a metal sparker, too!" He cooed, appreciatively, spotting a revolving drum where a holder for a smouldering wick would normally be situated.

"It's been almost five years since I took ownership," Hamish advised, "And the Italians have always been ahead of their competitors when it comes to refining their products. I have only fired them a couple of times, but they are as true as you could wish for in terms of sighting and alignment."

"Have you taken anything down with them? A deer, maybe?" Alex enquired.

"No, but I have done the next best thing."

Alex knotted his brows and puzzled for a few moments before looking blank.

"I have taken down a man **holding** a deer!"

Alex looked a little troubled at this confession.

"Don't worry! It was a MacDonald deer and a Campbell poacher!"

They both laughed, grimly, and Alex had a strange feeling that he was actually serious.

"These," announced Hamish, lovingly caressing the musket he held, "Will take one lead ball or two of iron. It would be comforting to be far enough away to pitch the two at them rather than the one."

"Do you know what is meant by the 'jitters'?" Alex asked.

"Nerves. Worry. Fretting," replied Hamish.

"In Austria, when we were about to go into action against the enemy, almost everyone would get the jitters. I used to think it was the only way that you could ever know, really and truly, that you were still alive."

Hamish took on a wistful look.

"Sailing broadside to an enemy ship," Hamish recounted, "Waiting for them to be in range of your cannon – and hoping that they needed to be closer than you did to fire – was a desperate moment. Seconds seemed to pass like minutes and minutes seemed to pass like hours. If your belly didn't turn to mush and your knees to jelly, then you very likely were **not** still alive!"

The two smiled far off smiles, lost somewhere in the past with their own thoughts.

"Well!" Hamish declared, abruptly, "This won't get the cows milked or the rabbit skinned!"

With that he led the way back to their horses, which were tied up a little distance away. Reaching down, he lifted up his horse's front hoof and crooked it back, then wrapped a leather strap around it to hold it in position. Suddenly, thinking better of it, he withdrew the strap and let the horse's leg relax back down to the ground.

"On second thoughts," Hamish announced, "Maybe we'd best not hobble our horses. I, for one, would not relish the thought of a McCarthy astride my beast if the worst came to the worst and we didn't return."

The horses looked at them, knowingly, for – as intelligent and sensitive creatures – they appeared to sense the dark shadow of imminent danger. Seemingly resigned to fate, the horses went back to contentedly cropping the grass beneath the bushes and blowing billowing clouds of steam from their breath into the cold air. Hamish tied their reins, loosely, to a low-hanging branch.

The two men gathered all of the belongings they would need and stowed them into a pair of canvas satchels. The less glamorous muskets they had brought from the inn were consigned to staying with the horses.

"You didn't think we'd find the Italian muskets?" Alex asked.

"You can never be too sure of anything," replied Hamish.

All done, the two patted and stroked their horses farewell and resumed their trek towards the McCarthy stronghouse. The sun, now directly overhead, was peeking weakly through the brooding clouds.

At first, shunning the main trail had seemed like a good idea. Now, the thick undergrowth and brambles began to snag them at every step and made the going challenging. Eventually, scratched and torn, they made it to within sight of the ridge that led down a shallow hill to the McCarthy's retreat.

Emerging from a thicket, Hamish and Alex froze. Up ahead of them, leaning against the trunk of a tree, stood a McCarthy sentry.

CHAPTER 23

Annis was accustomed to ceremony, protocol and expected behaviour. As a little girl, growing up as a princess, she had witnessed her mother engaging in what seemed like desperately boring and tedious 'good manners', over and over. Back then, these occasions had seemed endless. In retrospect, she now appreciated that they had been far more brief. She did, however, remember wanting to cry with frustration at the time. In fact, more than once, she actually had.

She watched as the Laird Grant, who had retired a distance away to talk with his advisors and his commander, spoke animatedly with them.

"What do you make of him?" She asked Gavin.

"I intended to dislike him, but I have been unable to keep it up," he replied.

Annis turned to Balgair for his opinion.

"I had intended to utterly despise him, but my resolve has weakened."

"When I rode my horse into the river," Annis confessed, "I felt contempt and distaste for him. But I am now unable to suppress a liking for him."

Her interaction with the Laird Grant had turned out to be far more cordial and good natured than it had been solemn or dignified. For one thing, he had shaken her by the hand. She had not been unduly ruffled by this act. It had occurred totally out of the blue, but she had managed not to hesitate or look surprised, which would have made her extremely vexed with herself.

"He shook my hand," she observed.

"That made me very pleased with him," said Balgair.

"I was delighted," Gavin announced.

She knew, full well, that shaking hands was a gesture that men normally restricted for interaction between themselves. For this reason she had felt, in parallel, both oddly peeved and perversely gratified by it. The contradiction of feelings – neither of which she could deny – irritated her intensely. She, nonetheless, appreciated that, under these circumstances, it signified far more than just respect.

"It felt sincere," said Annis, "Not as if he were offering to pretend that I were a man."

"You are the Queen of the West," Gavin protested, "You are worth two men."

"Three," Balgair corrected.

"Exactly so," Gavin agreed, "And he made sure that both his son and his senior aide witnessed the handshake. He was sending a powerful message to them."

"And, not long after," Balgair noted, "He didn't simply place a hand on his heart, he saluted you."

"The more we talk about him, the more I like him," Gavin grinned.

Annis moved her horse forward. Gavin and Balgair remained where they were. The Laird Grant, his attention having been drawn to this, turned his horse around and came back to position himself before her. There was total hush.

Annis looked at the Laird Grant and his eyes were steady, patient, almost indulgent. Annis slowly reached up to the neckline of her fine white cotton tunic. Such flawless, white fabric, pure and stark, was the preserve of the nobility. Wearing white cotton was, in a way, a statement of her rank and elevated status, but it could also be interpreted as a rude flamboyance. She took no joy in wearing such a pristine shade, but accepted that it was expected of her.

Annis gripped the collar of the garment in a fist and then, to improve her hold, she stretched her longest two fingers to gather in the fabric still more. She looked the Laird Grant levelly in the eye. His gaze did not waver. With a sudden downward motion, accompanied by a sudden ripping sound, she tore the front of the tunic down to the waist.

The Laird Grant was startled by what was underneath and his five senior officers goggled in open astonishment. The sun chose that precise moment to burst out from behind the clouds and its dazzling rays bounced off her gleaming steel and white enamel armour to dazzling effect.

The hard steel across her chest spoke loudly, clearly and unambiguously, to address all of the things she felt the need to explain. She had come clad for battle. She had ridden to the Spey, that morning, ready to take up sword against an enemy. She had come to be in the thick of the conflict. To be at the front and in its midst. This was no cowering girl, who planned to stay out of harm's way while the men did her work. This was a true leader.

The five senior Grant officers promptly saluted her, themselves, and the wild cheer that went up from the Grant troops, in response, was completely raucous. They whooped. They yelled. They applauded. They banged their shields, their pikes, their staffs and anything they had to hand.

The queen's own soldiers bristled with delight in the glory of the moment. They sat tall in their saddles as they drank in the fervent adulation. Their appreciation began as spectators, but – before long – they were unable to contain their own enthusiasm and begun to loudly shout their own approval.

Annis had always taken it to be the way of men who were old enough to be her father, that they looked on her with a certain fondness. In this respect, The Grant had been no different. The look he gave her now, however, was one of undiluted pride. He had set his stock and cast in his lot with this young lass from Fort Augustus and he clearly regarded himself as being anything but disappointed.

This man had built her up. He had deliberately offered her absolute reverence. He had gone beyond what was sufficient and had given of himself willingly. This man, whose people had been shunned and looked down upon by the neighbouring clans, had been ungrudging in his acceptance of her and contrite about the shameful misdeeds of a murky past.

The shouting and cheering eventually began to quieten and gave way to the singing of patriotic ballads. This meant that the Laird Grant had no difficulty hearing her when she spoke.

"Thank you," she said.

He smiled and she caught a glimmer of his former youth in his happy expression and could see that he had quite probably once been a handsome man in his prime.

The Grant motioned for his seniors to come forward and the five of them rode to flank him, stopping to either side. The Grant backed his horse out from between them and rode to the top of the line. There he sat, still and composed.

Annis felt her heart leap in her chest. This man would, surely, not dare to pledge his fealty to her. She had forbidden it.

Slowly, the Laird Grant held out his arm, palm downwards and parallel to the ground. Then he waited.

Annis edged her horse to move up in front of the Laird Grant. She held out her own arm, palm face down, and positioned it just below the laird's. The laird removed his hand from above hers, placed it over his heart, then extended his hand, again, placing it below hers.

Annis was relieved. Having been denied a declaration of fealty, he was, instead, insisting on doing the next best thing. He was using the symbolic ritual of the ancients to openly acknowledge her as his leader.

Annis moved her horse along to the side to face the laird's son. With no sign of reluctance, he mimicked the actions of his father.

Annis moved down the line of officers, to the end, and acted out the same routine with each of them.

In a motion, carefully exaggerated so that it was visible from afar, Annis slapped her hand to her chest over her heart. She let it rest there for a few moments and then drew her fingers into a claw. She lifted her hand in front of her, so that the view of it was clear and unmistakable. She paused again and then thrust out her arm, fingers still curved inwards, and waited a moment before releasing it.

If the Grants had cheered before, from joy and from relief, then the almost deafening roar that came, now, was from absolute euphoria. The distant hills echoed to the noise. The forest, far beyond the meadow, resounded with it. The bank across the river shook from it.

From their hiding place, the spy for the Clan Rose turned and scowled, simmering with hate.

Further away, across the glens and mountains to the North and to the South, where the sound did not reach, the clans who had shamed and mistreated the Grants went about their lives utterly oblivious. History would decree that nobody in the Highlands or the Eastlands would remain unaware of the restoration of the Grants, for long.

CHAPTER 24

It seemed that even the weather was happy with Annis. The clouds had cleared rapidly and what had begun as something of a dismal day had become sunny. The cold breeze had relented and had been replaced by the odd gust of pleasantly warm air.

Annis looked across to the line of mountains on the horizon, her eyes irresistibly drawn to them. There were patches of snow at their peaks, trailing down a short way until they petered out. The sun reflecting from them made the white mountain tops look as if they were illuminated from the inside.

As Annis surveyed the mountains, an eagle looked back at her from its lofty perch. It knew that it was her. It knew for certain. It had never been more sure of anything in its life. It had been aware of her presence. It had felt her approach. It had known, since first light, that she was coming.

The eagle shuffled with nervous excitement, moving its weight from one leg to the other and rhythmically flexing and closing its claws around the gnarled branch on which it sat. It made an exultant shriek and flapped its wings for the sheer joy of the moment.

The cluster of knobbly, twisted dwarf trees jutting stubbornly and tenaciously from the rocks on the mountainside had been the nest site where both it and its parents had been hatched and grown. This particular tree had been the nesting place of its grandparents, of its great grandparents and of each successive generation further and further back for hundreds of years. The eagle and its mate had reared their own chicks in this very nest and their offspring had taken up a nest nearby.

The eagle looked down and tapped *'The Precious Thing'* with its beak. The metallic clink was a satisfying sound. It picked up the treasure and shook it, gently, before scooting it, side to side, on its specially composed mattress of soft feathers until it shone. The eagle put its beak close to the treasure and made the soft cooing sound a parent makes to a chick inside an egg.

For century after century, its family and its ancestors had guarded The Precious Thing with their lives and had kept it safe for the day that would come. That wonderous moment had never come for any of them, but they had handed down the sacred duty, kept their watch and kept their faith.

The girl person with the long, flowing golden hair had come! She had come on the back of a horse creature and was wearing a hard, white shell on her upper body and her upper legs. It was all just like the prophecy had said. The shell, he knew instinctively, was made of the same substance as The Precious Thing. The shell gleamed in the sunshine when she moved.

The flames of the sun had, in the middle of the day, come down to roost in the old oak tree. He had seen it! He had seen it with his own sharp eyes! The tree had boiled and seethed with churning red, yellow and orange flames. Its branches had burst alight and the flames had reached skyward. It had looked like hundreds and hundreds of the fire sticks that the human people sometimes carried.

The eagle picked up The Precious Thing, again, and held it in its beak with great tenderness and with an overwhelming sense of pride. He, just like all the ones before him, had taken up his post and kept his seemingly endless vigil, never truly daring to hope that he would be the one.

Today, fate had chosen him, and decided that he **was** the one! The other eagles were stirring and becoming flustered. They sensed his exhilaration. He would tell them, soon, but not yet. He would tell them when the girl person knelt in the river and water was poured on her head. That, the ancients had said, was the moment that had been foretold.

He could see, far below, a little human girl chick threading her way through the crowds, holding the hand of a big, tall human person, and she looked up to where he was perched on the cliff and he think-sent his love down to her. The human girl chick think-sent her love back to him.

"What are you looking at?" Asked the tall soldier, "And why are you smiling like that?"

"Why am I smiling?" She asked, in tones far older than her few years.

"Yes," he replied.

"I have just seen an angel."

"You have?"

"Yes, an angel with claws and a hooked beak."

"Are you sure?" Asked the soldier, "I don't think that is how angels look."

"The world is filled with wonders!" she told him.

"Now you are smiling in a different way," said the soldier, "You are smiling the way someone smiles when they are listening to a storyteller telling a tale and they have just worked out the ending!"

"I have dreamed this story when I am asleep and I have dreamed this story when I am awake," the little girl confided, "And I have heard it from the trees, the grass, the sky and the river."

The soldier creased his eyebrows in thought, but the kindly look in his eyes did not falter and he gently squeezed her hand.

"You need to guard your tongue, little one," he said, "For some would think you a witch if they heard such words and they would not wish you well."

The little girl smiled up at him indulgently and squeezed back with her hand. It was nice that he should worry about her. They both paused, waiting for the priest, who was hurrying a little way behind them. He needed time to catch up.

Father Blair was at an age that he, himself, described as "beyond his best years". Having lost his sandal – yet again – he was hopping and swaying, standing on one leg like a plump brown stork, trying to reunite his foot with his footwear. He was failing woefully. His chubby cheeks were trembling with vexation. The soldier went back to help him, acting as a support post for him to lean against. With this assistance, the flabby man of God was victorious over his sandal.

Queen Annis leaned forward in her saddle, looking into the middle distance. For no reason that she could explain, she could not look away from the little girl who was making her way towards her. She had noticed the girl when she was quite a distance away and could not explain why she was drawn to pay attention. The cluster of people around Annis – Balgair, Gavin, Laird Grant, his son and his senior advisor – picked up on her distraction and, one after the other, they turned to look in the direction of her gaze.

"That's our little Wild Flower," the laird's advisor declared, looking amused, "She likes to sit in the forest and talk to the trees."

"She is also fond of streams, especially with waterfalls, and some say that she is blessed with the gift of the sight," the laird's son added.

"I don't hold with such things, myself," the laird assured Annis, earnestly, "But...."

He left the statement hanging, unfinished.

"But," Annis offered, "The ways of God and His angels are strange and wonderful."

The laird looked relieved and nodded his head, sagely.

As the little group approached, Annis dismounted and the others quickly did likewise. Bobbins, who had been lurking, immediately took charge of Bliss.

When Wild Flower was a few paces away, she began to punctuate her progress with graceful curtsies on alternate steps, each time rising with her head bowed. Balgair and Gavin looked a little ill at ease. The Grants looked slightly disdainful, the laird's senior advisor unable to suppress a sneer. Annis clapped her hands in delight and the gathered men all promptly mended their attitudes and broke into approving nods and smiles.

"I humbly apologise, Your Highness," announced the soldier escorting the girl, simultaneously gesturing towards his charge and bending a knee to the queen, "She said that she must tell you of a matter of great importance. She said you would wish to hear her."

The Grant's smile faltered for a moment and he looked to his senior people with a worried expression, seeking some kind of reassurance. Finding no negative responses, he renewed his smile and made it broader.

"She has a talent for knowing things before they happen," the laird advised, "Which can be quite unsettling at times. She has – I swear it – not one jot of evil or malice in her entire body."

"I can personally testify the same for the Laird Grant," said Wild Flower, smiling the faintest smile.

Annis was astonished to recognise her voice as the one she had heard in her head, not ten minutes earlier. Mistaking her facial expression for one of offence, the laird stiffened, causing his close supporters to become ill at ease. Recovering herself, Annis smiled, broadly. In response, the laird promptly forced a laugh and everyone around him joined in.

"The Laird," Annis announced, "Is a fine man of genuine good character and of a good nature."

Queen Annis, holding the gaze of this very grown-up little girl, allowed the vaguest lifting of her eyebrows.

"Only such a fine man," Annis continued, "Would stand fearless of the words of a seer..."

At this, Wild Flower – her face pointed away from the laird – contorted her features to portray the look like a dimwit.

"...And a jester," Annis quickly added.

The little girl's eyes sparkled with what was absurdly adult merriment and the Laird Grant looked a little disconcerted.

"For such...," began Annis, enjoying their game.

"...Is the way of the great," finished Wild Flower, as if capable of reading her thoughts.

"The very same!" Said Annis, clearly impressed.

The laird tilted his chin a little higher, flattered and charmed by this royal endorsement. Annis allowed her lips to insinuate a smile of commendation for such a flawless and accomplished manipulation of a grown man by such a diminutive child.

Nearby, Bobbins, attempted to conceal the pang of jealousy he felt, but was barely able to do so. Wild Flower, seeing his upset, threw him a wink and a smile that made his heart melt.

"Speaking of the greats," said Wild Flower, addressing the queen, "This site has its own significance, in history, amongst kings and queens."

Annis made no attempt to hide her surprise. The Laird Grant wore a look of wariness tinged with anxiety. It was clear that he knew of what she was speaking.

"Eight centuries ago, here, at this very river and upon this very bank," Wild Flower proclaimed, flourishing her hand in the air, "Queen Kiffan was seized by the Vikings."

Annis snapped her gaze accusingly to the Laird Grant, her eyes challenging him wordlessly for why he had chosen to make no mention of this fact. The Grant looked appropriately bashful.

"This was brought about by a heinous deed," said Annis, firmly, "For which an accommodation has been reached."

Wild Flower bowed her head, graciously, in acknowledgement of the queen's assertion and carried on.

"The Viking chief took a ring from Kiffan's finger. Legend has it that the ring, which she had never taken off since a child, was difficult to remove and, in an outburst of frustration, the Viking cruelly took a knife and cut her knuckle to remove the ring."

Annis looked to The Grant who shrugged his shoulders.

"There is such a legend," he said.

Annis involuntarily looked down at her finger. She touched the scar that ran, in twin arcs, above the first joint of the middle finger on her left hand. It was shaped like Cupid's Bow or, she sometimes thought, like the arcs of two rainbows, side by side.

"Legend also has it," said the little girl, giving Annis a meaningful look, "That the wound never properly healed and left her with a scar in the shape of a number three laid on its side."

"Your mother, Queen Cydara, had the same mark on her finger, too?" Asked Wild Flower, making it far more of a statement than a question.

"Yes," replied Annis, sadly.

"My Laird Grant," said the little girl, bowing deeply to The Grant, "There is a prophecy that has been passed down through the years by the wise ones. It tells of the Queen of the West with her golden hair riding to the Spey in milk white armour."

Annis looked down at the gleaming whitened steel cladding that encased her shoulders, chest, abdomen and thighs. She mentally cursed the enthusiasm of the McRorys who had so vigorously polished it for her, every night since their arrival. The champlevé enamel glistened with a white lustre.

"This armour did not shine, in *this* fashion, until a few days ago," said Annis, fixing Captain Balgair with a reproachful stare, "And I wear it today, not as an ornament, but because I reject and shun the role of the weak and feeble woman who might choose to lead her troops from afar, rather than in the midst of the fray."

The Grant gave the child a warning look, which she promptly disregarded.

"My Queen," said Wild Flower, curtseying magnificently with astonishing style and grace, "It was necessary for your armour to shine, today."

"It was?"

"My Queen, just as the sun sets and then rises, so too the will of God is relentless. What needs to happen, will always happen."

"You speak of *The Quickening*, little girl?"

"Yes, My Queen."

Annis gave the girl a dour look.

'If all this were meant to be,' Annis thought, *'Then why have I felt such terror since becoming queen? How I wish I were as brave as my mother! If this little girl could only guess at the fear and trepidation I hide, even now!'*

"Bravery without fear is no bravery at all," said Wild Flower, as if she could tell what was in her mind, "Just as making the motions of swimming, while on dry land, is not swimming."

If there were such a thing as fate, Annis decided, then it must be devastatingly cruel. It had, back at the age of twelve, thrust her into adulthood by the death of her mother. Not a day had passed, since, when she had not fervently prayed to be worthy of the role, and not a day had passed when she had not tortured herself with the fear that she was not.

Why did her ancestors have to be so conspicuously glorious? Why could the stories about them not be less grand? Why could the mark to which she must measure have been less daunting?

Annis had a dream that often disturbed her sleep. In it, there was a horizontal mark cut across the trunk of a tree and she, on her tiptoes, was hopelessly stretching to reach it. No matter how hard she tried, she could never reach it.

'Of course you cannot reach it!' She told herself, *'For you are the Queen of the West and you would have to reach all the way up into the very branches, themselves, in order to ever be worthy!'*

Annis found her mind reeling. A tree? Yes, a tree! Why did her thoughts have to stray to trees at a time like this? She looked across to the big old tree at the end of the meadow and was shocked to find that – looking directly at it – she could see it completely ablaze. Annis was spellbound! Its previously illusive flames, now proudly blazed without any inhibitions.

'It burns for you, My Queen!' Said the voice of Wild Flower inside her head.

Annis turned to the little girl, who smiled back, sweetly. Annis knotted her brows. Was this real? Was this truly happening? Was she truly hearing the voice of the little girl from inside her own brain?

'*What?*' Annis asked, in her own thoughts.

'*The tree,*' replied the little girl's voice, patiently, inside her head, '*It burns for you.*'

'*You can see it?*' Annis asked, wordlessly.

'*Yes. I can see it.*' Wild Flower's voice assured her, '*It is growing stronger. It is now fully visible to you because the power on which it thrives is growing stronger.*'

'*What is its power?*' Annis asked in her thoughts.

'*Its power is your destiny, Your Highness,*' Wild Flower replied, '*For you are the greatest of your line.*'

'*No! I'm not!*' Annis protested, '*My mother was greater than I and it was Kiffan who was the greatest!*'

'*Kiffan could not be so great unless you were as great!*' Wild Flower replied, speaking the contradiction gently but insistently, into her mind.

'*No! That's not possible!*'

'*It is, My Queen, for her glory shines both in both the past and in the present.*'

'*That cannot be!*' Annis thought, loudly, '*Unless.... Unless I have her soul?*'

Wild Flower gave a little laugh.

'*Your Majesty, if there is a soul shared, then it is* she *who shares your soul!*'

'*No! That is preposterous! I am just a girl!*' Annis objected.

'*The first ever mention of Kiffan, in history, noted that she was nineteen years old. That is exactly the same age that you are, now, My Queen.*'

Annis looked back to the fire tree, feeling forlorn.

'*It burns for you, My Queen!*' Wild Flower thought to her, again, '*The people around you no do not see it, only those chosen to see it.*'

Wild Flower paused and looked over at the mountains.

'*And they see it, too,*' she added.

At that exact moment, in the distance, a group of eagles began to cry. Their voices were clear and melancholy across the landscape. They screeched over and over, their calls rising on the wind, and – as she listened – the sound they made turned from one of heartbreaking sadness to one of overwhelming joy.

CHAPTER 25

Janine woke slowly and with no sense of worry or awkwardness. She found herself quite at ease with being at this luxurious, palatial mansion. She could hear birds singing outside her window. The rays of the sun were dappling the French blinds as they swayed in a gentle breeze.

'All is well in the world.' She thought to herself.

Then, her heart missed a beat as she recalled her escape from Dunkeld Manor, the previous day. She was lucky, she decided. She was very lucky indeed. Things could have gone horribly wrong. Her brow wrinkled as she considered her anonymous protector. Would he follow her here in order to continue watching over her?

'Surely not!' She told herself.

Then, with her mind fluttering around and delivering her absurd conclusions, she pondered whether he might even be under this roof as a guest!

'Absurd!' She scolded herself.

Out of the blue, the thought came to her that he might even be one of the twins, Bruce or Brian! She dismissed this idea, immediately, but it crept back into her mind without her bidding. The brothers had been close at hand when she had been chased, walking the road alone, but – she decided – it could not possibly have been them. Why? Because, if it were, and they were the same person on each occasion, neither of them could have intervened when she was dragged down to the cellars of Dunkeld Manor. That is, unless..... Unless what?

'You are having crazy thoughts!" She told herself, *'You are letting your imagination run wild!'*

In a sudden panic, Janine reached down the front of her nightdress and was hugely relieved to find that her mother's ring was still there. It hung securely in place, suspended on its metal chain. She vaguely remembered attaching it to the chain just before dinner, the previous evening.

Janine cringed at the recollection of dinner. Had it all been just a dream? She feared not! In fact, she knew not, because it was a little **too** clear in her mind.

There was the gentlest of knocks on the door and it opened only a little way as Francesca slipped nimbly in through the crack. She was in her nightgown and padded soundlessly to the large armchair in the corner, which was draped with blankets. It was clear that she had been sleeping there. She looked surprised when she noticed Janine sat up in bed.

"I am sorry to disturb you, My Lady," she said, "I had just gone...," her voice trailed off for a moment, "To make water in the closet."

"You kept me company all night?" Janine asked.

"Yes, My Lady," she replied, "And I am not the only one."

Francesca pointed to another armchair, in the corner, where Callum lay curled up asleep under a blanket.

"He was worried about you. We were **both** worried about you. Last night you were…" she paused to choose the right words, "…Distressed."

Janine looked at her with sadness and despair in her eyes. Francesca quickly got up from the chair and moved to sit on the tall-backed chair by the bed. She gazed at Janine with a long sympathetic look of genuine compassion. The girl's eyes were troubled. Janine had the distinct impression that the girl was suffering some kind of indecision, as if there were something she would like to say but was holding back. Janine decided that she, for her part, could hold back no longer.

"I don't know who I am anymore," Janine blurted, "Yesterday morning I ran away from…," she hesitated, unsure how much to disclose and how it might conflict with what Bruce and Brian might have already said as an official story, "I ran away from somewhere that I was unhappy. The boy was my travelling companion. He was…" she faltered, again, fumbling for the words.

Francesca waited patiently for her to continue.

"He was ill-treated and so was I, though not by beating," Janine revealed, contorting her face to show disgust, "We had travelled only a little way when we were attacked by a group of bandits. I made the boy hide and I ran off. They chased me and I thought that I had escaped them, but one of them found me and…" her mind skittered this way and that, grasping for a plausible version of events that would not lead to too many awkward questions or too many further complications.

"My Lady," implored Francesca, "Do not upset yourself with these recollections. Especially not for any benefit of mine! You are both safe and well, now, and that is all that truly matters."

In the corner, Callum began to stir. He shuffled under the blanker for a moment, before settling again. Janine put a finger to her lips to implore the maid to lower her voice.

"A moment," whispered Francesca as she tiptoed across to the door, "I will have him away to a warm bed where he can sleep as long as he pleases."

So saying, she slowly turned the door handle and opened a gap to peer out. After a short while she made a soft hissing noise through her teeth, obviously seeking to attract someone's attention. Cupping a hand to her mouth to direct her voice, she spoke to someone beyond the door. A moment later, she was opening the door to let them in.

A servant in a smart uniform crossed to the chair where Callum lay and picked him up.

"Hush, wee man," he whispered as Callum whimpered in protest at being moved, "You are safe. I promise you."

The man disappeared out of the doorway, cradling the boy in his arms.

"A child of that age," laughed Francesca, returning to Janine's bedside, "Can sleep in the branches of a tree and feel no ill for it in the morning!"

"I fear he has lived a less than merry life, so far."

"He will find life, here, to his liking. A warm bed, good food, skilled healers and nobody will lay so much as a finger upon him to do him harm."

Janine sighed a long, doleful sigh.

"I am so very grateful for the hospitality everybody has so kindly shown us," Janine told her, "The two gentlemen, Bruce and Brian, took me under their wing. They have adopted me. They have shown the sort of kindness and generosity of spirit that could never be repaid. I fear, however, that my coming here has landed the brothers in some kind of trouble with The Duchess."

Francesca threw back her head and laughed. In a split second she caught herself and her hand shot to her mouth. Her eyes dropped to her lap and she looked embarrassed and remorseful.

"You can speak openly to me, Francesca," Janine told her, encouragingly, "You need not guard your words."

Francesca looked up and met Janine's eyes with a confusing mixture of relief and gleeful amusement.

"I do not think that either Bruce or Brian need fear any displeasure from The Duchess. Nothing of the kind, in fact. She absolutely dotes on them! She is under their spell just as completely as the two of them are under yours."

Janine was astounded by her words, but felt fairly certain that she had kept it from her face. Surely, her assurance of complete discretion could not be the reason for this girl being quite **this** bold and offhand!

"I have a reason – and I mean good reason – to know the job of a lady's maid," Janine told Francesca, "And to know all the things it entails, so it is with some authority that I have to tell you…"

The maid looked shocked and alarmed.

"I hope I have not offended you, My Lady! I hope that I have not spoken too wilfully, if I have…"

Janine held up her hand to silence her. This girl's ability to jump between complete detachment and frantic insecurity was bizarre!

"Francesca, you and I are of an age. I am in my nineteenth year. I am guessing that you are close to the same. Perhaps a year either side."

Francesca nodded, dully. She looked crestfallen. It was as if all the miseries of the world had fallen on her shoulders. Janine could take it no longer. She threw back the covers, leapt to her feet, threw her arms around Francesca's neck and hugged her.

Now it was Francesca who was taken aback.

"Francesca, I have **been** a lady's maid! I have **been** one!" Janine declared, pulling back to look her square in the face.

The maid looked astonished.

"You, Francesca, are a good one. A **fine** one in fact!" Janine assured her.

Francesca's embarrassment evaporated and her expression was now one of calm calculation.

"This is a wonderful place," Janine continued, undeterred, "It is filled with love and warmth. It has an atmosphere of kindness. Everybody is utterly cordial and pleasant, but..."

Francesca gave a little haughty laugh.

"The words you use!" Francesca exclaimed with a grin, "And *you* were a mere maid? Does the way you speak never strike you as unusual?"

Janine was startled. It would appear that, here, being alternately surprised by people and then dismayed at them was an emotion that came and went, flicking to and fro, of its own accord!

"I... I... I must have heard such words," Janine protested, "I must have heard them and simply learned to use them."

"Yes, of course," replied Francesca, with a hint of mockery in her voice.

Janine suddenly felt affronted to be explaining herself to a maid. Not just explaining herself, in fact, but also enduring a hint of derision from her! She caught these thoughts and scolded herself for them! She was acting aloof towards a maid? She, herself, was a maid! Was she not? Surely, she was!

"What do you sense about Brech Woorlach that is odd or strange?" Francesca asked, now a little more appeasing.

"It's just that the relationship between servant and master has, from time to time, an unusually informal feeling to it."

Francesca raised an eyebrow. Janine continued.

"It is nothing blatant. In fact, it is very subtle. There is just that something in the background. They are a little more casual and comfortable with each other than is usual".

Francesca raised her hands and, evidently amused, began clapping politely, if a little condescendingly. Janine was dumbfounded.

"On second thoughts," snapped Janine, "Never mind who *I* am. Who, for the sake of all things holy, are *you*?"

"I am a maid, or rather I am more often a maid than I am not. I greatly favour that role for the humility it gives me," announced Francesca, "I am, however, frequently a lady as well. Now, that is a role I prefer much less, for I have more than enough exposure to that particular persona in my own day to day life."

Francesca grinned impishly at Janine's look of confusion. It was a look that quickly transformed itself into an exquisitely wistful smile of apology.

"I am sorry for the way that I have acted," Francesca continued, "For I am usually an excellent maid.

In fact, if you would forgive me for such a lack of modesty, I am usually completely wonderful in that role. I love it! I lose myself in it!"

Janine gaped with incomprehension.

"When I am my own self and not pretending to be anybody else," Francesca confessed, "I am the daughter of the Duke and Duchess of Bo'Ness."

CHAPTER 26

Janine's jaw dropped open at Francesca's revelation. She closed it, with some effort, and then opened her mouth several times to speak, but could not muster any sound.

She had a hundred questions she wanted to ask. The questions were flying around in her mind like a swarm of insects. Unfortunately, none of them would make it as far as her tongue.

Francesca stood up and walked over to the ornate fireplace where she pulled the tasselled cord that hung there. She then returned to her chair and sat down. A few moments later, a page boy knocked and entered.

"Ma'am?" He said, questioningly.

"Please bring the big chair, in the corner of the room, across to the side of the bed," Francesca directed, pointing to the exact spot on the floor, "I'd like you to put it right there."

"Of course," he replied, crossing to the chair, picking it up with only a little difficulty and then carrying it into position. The task was a menial and trivial one, but the boy did it cheerfully and without question.

"Will that be all, Ma'am?" He asked, politely.

"Yes, thank you," said Francesca giving him a little smile.

The boy went to the door and closed it softly behind him as he exited. Once the boy was gone,

Francesca turned to Janine and motioned to the chair in its new location.

"When you have been both the mover of the chair and the person asking for it to be moved," Francesca told her, "Then you have a meaningful insight into life as it is lived. Life at all levels of high society. Life in a grand town house or in a mansion as imposing as this one. If you know how to give orders and how to take them, no matter how trifling they may be, then you have a better understanding of how the cogs and wheels of running a house operate. It helps us to train better pupils."

"Pupils?" Asked Janine.

"Yes, for we are teachers. We are instructors. We are trainers," Francesca advised, moving to sit down in the big chair.

"What do you teach?"

Francesca held Janine's gaze with a look of earnest contemplation and Janine realised that the answer that was coming was being carefully calculated and assessed.

"We train a special kind of person with a special kind of skill," Francesca said, mysteriously.

She got up and stood behind the chair, her fingers nervously digging into the fabric.

"We train people who can influence the fate of nations. People who can change the direction of history."

Janine looked at her quizzically and climbed back onto the bed.

"Throughout the world, probably since civilisation began, there have been people in power with secrets and people who want that power and who want those secrets."

Janine watched her new friend pace back and forth, her face animated by the passion of belief.

"Sometimes, secrets can be so important that they can cause a war or bring about the end of a war. Sometimes, the secrets are the key to new knowledge. Often, the secrets are about politics, treachery and betrayal."

Francesca returned to the seat and sat down, but it was clear from her posture that she was far too agitated to relax.

"Here, at Brech Woorlach," Francesca declared, solemnly, "We train people to obtain secrets from people who would rather hold on to them. We train people to infiltrate, observe and report."

Janine looked confused.

"We train people to be spies," Francesca announced, "That is our calling and our purpose."

Janine felt that she must have looked slightly perplexed, because Francesca leaned forward and rested her hand on top of Janine's and then gently squeezed it.

Janine took a deep breath.

"I hardly dare ask this question, but…. You are loyal to King James?"

"Yes!" Said Francesca, emphatically.

Janine nodded, thoughtfully, then her face suddenly looked troubled as a flash of inspiration hit her.

"Are you also loyal to another?" Janine asked, not wanting to hear the reply, for she liked these people very much.

"We are loyal first to God," Francesca advised.

Again, the thoughtful expression came to Janine's face, to be replaced, a moment later, by another flash of inspiration.

"And, please tell me," asked Janine, politely, "Do you hold a loyalty that sits anywhere between God and your king?"

Francesca's bright, beautiful eyes fell and she lowered her head to look into her lap. A second passed, then she raised her head again, with what Janine thought was an air of defiance about her.

"Our loyalty is ultimately to God, but it does not in any way conflict with serving King James of Scotland and of England," Francesca announced, "So long as our king is equally loyal to God's will."

Janine's expression became worried.

"You are Roman Catholics?" Asked Janine.

"We are **Anglo** Catholics," Francesca replied, tersely, "But, despite that being the case, I resent you implying that if we **were** Roman Catholics, that it might have been any kind of slur or stain on our reputation! We have no quarrel with them."

"Anglo Catholics? This far North of Hadrian's Wall?" Janine chided, "Now **there** is a novelty!"

Francesca's face became furious and her posture stiffened, then – in an instant – she broke into a huge smile and she laughed a pretty laugh that was genuine and without restraint.

"Hadrian's Wall?" She chortled and lifted her hand to cover her mouth, "Hadrian's Wall, you say?"

Francesca put her head back and, this time, howled with laughter. So infectious and merry was her laugh that Janine found herself laughing, too.

'Hadrian's Wall?', Janine puzzled, trying to work out what was so amusing.

Then, she suddenly realised the absurdity of her reference. Coming from the mouth of a poor crofter's daughter, it was quite some scholarly knowledge. Janine's laughter became as raucous as Francesca's. They laughed until their sides hurt and they both had to wipe tears from their eyes.

"Oh! My lady!" Francesca jested with playfully exaggerated reverence, "You are so very learned for someone who is a mere woman!"

The two descended into uncontrollable laughter, again, and it was several minutes before they had recovered enough to resume their conversation.

In a sudden impulse of affection, Janine swung her legs over the side of the bed and put her hand to Francesca's cheek. She gently stroked it and looked into her eyes, imploringly. Janine silently willed Francesca and her household not to turn out to be bad people. She desperately did not want them to be religious zealots or traitors! As if sensing her dilemma, Francesca hitched her breath and began a reluctant explanation.

"My family are from the North," Francesca revealed, "We originally came from Fort Augustus. My great grandfather was an officer in the West Highland Cannon and Infantry and proudly wore the green and brown."

Janine nodded and mentally noted that she had spoken of her "family" rather than her "clan".

"When he was decommissioned, at the end of his service, my great grandfather was granted a *leaving purse*, courtesy of the Duke of Inverness, which he invested in a venture with a friend."

Janine nodded, again, following her story with rapt attention.

"They bought a sailing ship to import cloth and spices from the East," Francesca continued, "The company made some wise purchases and, whilst many of the ships of other merchants were lost in storms that year, their own ship repeatedly survived to make it home. Their ship was called 'The Good Fortune' and it proved to be just that!"

Janine smiled encouragingly

"Before long," Francesca related with glee, "They had three ships and, in no time, they had made a small fortune. Unfortunately, tragedy struck and my great grandfather caught a fever and died. His widow, my great grandmother, remarried a year later and moved to Inverness. Her new husband had a small fleet of ships of his own and, together, their combined vessels sailed to every corner of the globe, importing silks, spices, liquor and tobacco. After their deaths, at a ripe old age, my grandfather inherited their fortune and he married the Duchess of Bo'Ness. Her family had fallen on hard times when her husband became obsessed with gambling and alcohol. He had squandered every penny they possessed in the gaming houses of London, Paris, Madrid, Rome and Lisbon while drinking himself to death on rum and gin."

Francesca paused, appearing to gather her thoughts and distractedly twirled a strand of her hair between her fingers. Her expression gradually became more remote and she seemed to drift off into some sort of inner depth. Janine waited, patiently. After a minute or so, Francesca resumed her tale as if she had never stopped.

"My grandfather was never a sailor, or so they say, and he stayed well clear of the sea. One day, however, he was invited to enter into a business venture to set up a shipping line in Marseilles in France. He got it into his head that only he could do the deal and refused to send any deputy in his place. He sailed from Glasgow on one of his own ships but was blown off course by a storm and ended up off the coast of Africa. There, they were attacked by pirates and he lost his ship."

Janine opened her mouth in horror.

"My grandfather had thrown his fine clothes overboard and had dressed himself as a sailor, to avoid being held for ransom. He was soon sold by the pirates as a slave. It took him over two years to eventually escape. When he did, he was absolutely penniless and starving. He lived a wretched life, begging and stealing, before he was able to find a Scottish ship and work his passage back home."

Francesca sighed a deep long sigh.

"His bad luck was still not quite over, however. Off the coast of Ireland, my grandfather developed a fever. He had blotches and was vomiting blood, so the ship's healer feared the worst. The captain put him into a rowing boat with some food and water and set him adrift. It seems cruel, but – to be fair – a fever onboard a ship, where the crew eat and sleep shoulder to shoulder in cramped conditions, can be totally devastating."

Francesca began to slip into another faraway, desolate look, but then seemed to catch herself and jerked back to the here-and-now.

"He very nearly died. It's hard to imagine how he managed to endure. He was desperately weak and could not row. He kept slipping in and out of consciousness. He would, a year later, write a detailed account of those times in his journal. I have read it and re-read it, from cover to cover, a hundred times."

Francesca gave a wistful smile and glanced at Janine with momentary embarrassment. There were tears welling in her eyes and Janine felt a physical pain from seeing this girl's grief. On an impulse, Janine grabbed the ornately carved loops that formed the ends of the arms of Francesca's chair and used them to drag it to rest up against her own legs and the bed. The unexpected movement made Francesca wince and recoil. Janine leaned forward and gathered the girl into her arms and drew her into a hug. Francesca allowed herself to relax and Janine felt her shake as she sobbed silently into her shoulder.

"God does not make us to live grandly in the branches of the trees, like gaudy insects with magnificent wings," Francesca wept, "Looking down, with spite and loathing, at the wretched lives of ants and fleas on the forest floor."

"No," Janine agreed, decisively.

Janine reached and took a handkerchief from on top of the cabinet by the bed and gave it to Francesca to dry her tears. Francesca wiped and dabbed her eyes with the handkerchief and stopped, abruptly, looking down at it mistrustfully. She gave a coy glance at Janine.

Janine's mind flashed back to her carriage ride with the two twins, Brian and Bruce. She recalled, with a smile, the magical charm and personal warmth with which the brothers had put her at her ease. Aiming to reproduce the scene, Janine quickly scrunched up her lips and nostrils, nodded encouragingly at the handkerchief and arched her eyebrows.

With evident reluctance, Francesca put the handkerchief to her nose and blew delicately. She then folded the handkerchief and placed it on her lap. Her restraint was unmistakable.

Janine lifted the handkerchief back to Francesca's nose and admonished her with a stern glance. With a little laugh, Francesca steeled herself and, with a shrug of her shoulders, suspended all modesty and blew loudly. Janine applauded, theatrically, and patted her on the head like a Matron commending a small child. They both laughed.

Holding her close, Janine stroked Francesca's back, soothingly, and was gratified when, shortly afterwards, Francesca returned her head to where it had been on Janine's shoulder.

"My grandfather wrote that he reflected long and hard upon his life while bobbing and swaying on those waves. Every day stretched on forever and he had plenty of time to think. He recalled his life of luxury and extravagance. He recalled having lacked nothing and having had his every whim indulged. It compared starkly, he realised, with his more recent experiences. He had lived in grinding poverty and desperation where his major concern had been if he would get to eat that day. It left a mark on him and he vowed to be a better person if only God would allow him to survive and make it back to see his wife, again."

Francesca drew in a long breath and let it out as a prolonged sigh. Janine squeezed her and kissed her hair. The girl made a tiny snorting sound and, despite being unable to see her face, Janine knew for certain that she was smiling at this impromptu demonstration of affection.

"His little rowing boat washed up on the shore along the Westlands on a secluded beach," Francesca continued, "Try as he might, he was unable to climb out. He was too weak and exhausted. He could feel himself sliding back into unconsciousness. He feared, at this point, that he would most surely die. He had come so far and suffered so much, yet..."

This part of the story seemed to tug at Francesca's heart and her eyes filled with tears, once more. She took a deep, shuddering breath, and composed herself before continuing.

"He wrote that, when he woke, he found himself atop a mattress on a wooden pallet inside a tent. When he opened his eyes, he saw a girl with the most beautiful, shining, golden hair looking down at him. Mistaking her for an angel, he genuinely presumed that he had died and gone to Heaven!"

At this point, Francesca smiled and all her sadness dissolved away.

"He wrote a lot in his journal about her. She was very pretty and very kind and extremely gentle. She spoke Gaelic and English and was clearly an educated woman. That was most unusual for the time!"

"Quite a rarity, even now!" Janine chuckled, giving her a wink.

Francesca frowned and lifted her hands in comical pretence of outrage.

"The girl with the golden hair," Francesca resumed, "Had two young female helpers, a senior maid and a manservant. He wrote that it was obvious, from the way they acted around her, that she was a woman of status," Francesca gave a little laugh, "Little did he know quite *what* status!" She added.

Janine's eyebrows shot up, thoroughly intrigued.

"My grandfather was covered in sores and wounds. Some of them were far from pleasant. He said that some of them actually stank. Despite this, the "angel" – for that is what he later took to calling her – performed the majority of the cleaning and dressings of his wounds with her own hands."

Janine's eyebrows arched even higher, in still greater astonishment. Francesca smiled sweetly with an air of jubilation and cleared her throat as if ready to make a formal speech to a crowd.

"She was, indeed, a lady of status, but not any you might usually encounter!" Francesca announced proudly, "She was, in fact, a queen. He had come face to face with the legendary Queen of the West."

www.ingramcontent.com/pod-product-compliance
Lightning Source LLC
Chambersburg PA
CBHW071403300726
48976CB00006B/1967